MAGGIE CHRISTENSEN

Escape to Bellbird Bay

Cover and interior design: J D Smith Design
Editing: John Hudspith Editing Services

Dedication

To my own wonderful soulmate,
the man for whom I followed my heart.

Also by Maggie Christensen

One

Alison Wells gazed blindly out the window at the landscaped grounds of the Western Australian University, unable to believe her ears, a curl of fear snaking through her. She felt sick. Had she heard correctly? Had Richard Ellis, her Head of School, really suggested she take early retirement?

'I'm sorry, Alison,' Richard repeated, avoiding her eyes. 'I know things have been difficult for you lately, but I can't play favourites, and given the situation…' He coughed. 'Also, you may be aware the school has been having budget difficulties.' He paused, picked up a pen and put it down again. 'It's been decided to wind down the Women's Studies program.'

To say things had been difficult was putting it mildly, but what did it have to do with winding down the Department of Women's Studies, the department she had led for the past ten years? And how dare he suggest she take early retirement?

It had all started when Alison found Chelsea Morris, one of her doctoral students, in tears. At first, the girl refused to say what was wrong. But eventually, after several cups of tea in Alison's office, Chelsea revealed she'd been sexually assaulted by another staff member.

Alison was appalled. She'd never had much time for Hugo Martin, who behaved as if he was superior to everyone else on staff. But despite his arrogance and misogyny, she'd never considered he would sexually assault one of the students. She had no doubt Chelsea was telling the truth. Why should she lie? But the boys' club had gone into full force in defending Hugo, suggesting the assault had never happened, and even that Alison had made it all up to discredit Hugo and win the coveted position of Head of School.

As the two most senior members of the School of Business and Women's Studies – a mix which was of expediency rather than the two disciplines having anything in common – Hugo never lost an opportunity to demean Alison at school meetings. And now Richard Ellis was rumoured to be retiring, Alison and Hugo were the two most likely to replace him.

For the past twenty years, Alison had lectured in Women's Studies, helping students examine how sex and gender influenced the way individuals understood the world. But this was her first encounter with it outside of textbooks – and it was a shock. The jokes, innuendo and thinly disguised insults she suffered made her realise what many women experienced on a daily basis. Now in her mid-fifties, she realised what a sheltered life she had led. Although she knew her mother had suffered from domestic violence, and it was what had led her to major in Women's Studies, Alison had never personally experienced this sort of behaviour… till now.

The final straw came when a particularly rude caricature of her was posted on the staff noticeboard. She tore it down, then, incensed, her blood boiling, her face red with humiliation, she headed to Richard Ellis's office, ready to complain about the harassment. But once there, he'd pre-empted her with the mention of early retirement.

For a full minute there was silence in the room, broken only by the hum of his small fridge in the corner and the squawking of a group of cockatoos feeding on the yellow blossom of a banksia outside the window. Then Alison found her voice. 'What about my students?'

'Those close to graduating will be able to finish, or we can manage to accommodate them in other programs if they wish. The graduate students…' He cleared his throat. 'We can arrange for them to continue their studies elsewhere.' He paused. 'Take a break and think it over. I believe you're due some long service leave. A few months away from this place might help you see things differently.'

Alison left his office feeling as if she'd been run over by a truck. What had she been thinking when she imagined he'd understand her position? Of course, he was part of the boys' club, too – and her years of dedication, the awards she'd accumulated, the addresses given to groups and societies, all counted for nothing when they wanted to close ranks against the person they saw as rocking the boat. She should have known.

*

'What are you going to do, Ali?' Sally asked.

The two women were having Saturday morning breakfast in one of their favourite cafés overlooking the Swan River. Alison had just recounted her experience of the day before, still angry with Richard's attitude, and his facile dismissal of Chelsea's situation.

The pair had been friends since high school, and while Alison had gone on to university and to pursue an academic career, Sally had found an internship with a local newspaper and was now women's editor for a prestigious West Australian magazine.

Neither woman had married, each having her own reason for avoiding commitment; Alison because of her mother's experience at the hands of Alison's father, and Sally because of her determination to make a name for herself in journalism. Both had dated over the years, but always steered clear of commitment and enjoyed their single lives.

Alison considered Sally's question before replying. 'The semester's almost over. I have a pile of marking to do before I can do anything.'

'You were planning to visit your brother for Christmas, weren't you?'

'I'm still going.' Alison's face broke into a smile at the thought of seeing Adam. Torn apart as children when she and her mother fled to Western Australia, Ali and her brother had only reunited a year earlier. Now a successful author, Adam lived with his new partner in the small coastal town of Bellbird Bay on Queensland's Sunshine Coast.

Maybe she'd follow Richard's suggestion, take her accumulated leave, and spend the next few months reconnecting with her brother, while she considered her future. An escape to the small coastal town of Bellbird Bay might help provide the answer.

Two

Neil Simpson stared at the photo on the front page of the Brisbane weekend paper and the lurid headline which accompanied it and felt ashamed. While he had no part in the financial skulduggery the chair and several members of the school board had engaged in, as principal, he should have suspected something was amiss. The newspaper certainly held him responsible. There was his photo, taken at a recent sporting event, where he and the chairman of the board were standing side by side with broad smiles on their faces. Who would believe Jake Barton had pulled the wool over *his* eyes as well as over those of the parents, parents who had paid dearly for the privilege of sending their sons to the prestigious school, the school which now looked to be about to close, unless money could be found to replace what had been squandered in gambling.

At least the police believed Neil was innocent. They'd cleared him of all wrongdoing. He wouldn't accompany Jake to court charged with misappropriation of school funds, followed, in all likelihood, by prison time. But mud sticks, and Neil had been advised to take indefinite leave of absence.

So, here he was, planning to avoid any whiff of scandal by escaping to Bellbird Bay, to the town he still called home. It had been a good place to grow up. It was where he'd learnt to swim, to surf, and where he'd developed his love of books and learning, spending hours in his dad's bookshop. Harry Simpson had owned *Bay Books* in Bellbird Bay for what seemed like for ever.

Neil was on his second cup of coffee, standing on the balcony of his Hamilton apartment, staring out at the Brisbane River, grey in the morning light, when his phone rang. He sighed at the sight of his ex-wife's number on the screen. Pippa must have seen the headlines, too.

'Is it true, Neil?' she asked, her private school accent more pronounced than he remembered.

'You've seen the paper?'

'I think all of Brisbane have seen it. Are you going to be charged?'

Was there a gleeful note in her voice, or was she worried about the reaction of her pretentious friends to the news her ex was in trouble, worried she might get caught up in the scandal?

'No, Pippa. I'm completely innocent, though I should have suspected something was going on when…'

'How could you not have known?' she interrupted.

'You and the Courier Mail.'

'Sorry, but…'

Neil imagined her expression. It was one he'd seen only too often.

'What will you do?'

'I'll go up and stay with dad while it blows over. After that, who knows? If the school survives, I might be able to resume my position, if not, I'll look for another.'

There was a pause, then, 'I was wondering… Bronte is at a loose end. She's deferred her studies…'

'Again?' Neil couldn't hide his disapproval. Their twenty-year-old daughter was on her second – or was it third? – different course of study since leaving school. She was a bright girl but didn't seem to be able to make appropriate choices. He was of the opinion her mother was partially to blame but refrained from saying so.

'She just hasn't found the right course,' Pippa said, defensively, 'so I wondered if she could come to stay with you. I know she's not a child, but it's time you shouldered some responsibility for her.'

Neil had no problem with Bronte joining him in Bellbird Bay. He was on good terms with his daughter who often arrived unannounced in his apartment full of complaints about her mother and life in general. It would do her good to spend time away from Pippa. But how would Bronte react to being shunted off to Queensland for the summer? Would she even agree? She was old enough to make up her own mind.

'Have you discussed this with her?'

There was a long pause, then, 'I thought you might...'

'No, Pippa. This is your idea. It's up to you to tell her. She may have other plans for the summer.'

Pippa's sigh of exasperation told Neil it was Pippa who had other plans, but he didn't intend to let her off the hook.

'Tell her Dad and I will be happy to have her join us, if that's what she wants.'

As he ended the call, Neil wondered if Bronte would agree. Spending the summer in the small coastal town with her dad and grandfather probably wasn't at the top of her list of ways to spend the summer. He thought of all the summers he'd spent there as a boy and teenager, even in his holidays from uni. He'd loved the peace of Bellbird Bay, loved spending the hot summer days swimming, surfing and hanging out with his mates. Maybe Bronte would enjoy it, too, though she'd no doubt miss her friends. He suddenly realised that, although he and his daughter regularly spent time together, he really knew very little about her life.

*

Bronte flung herself down on the sofa. She'd arrived at his door without any warning in a foul mood.

'What's the matter, honey? I spoke with Mum. She thinks it would be a good plan for you to come up to Bellbird Bay with me for Christmas.'

'Not just Christmas, for the entire summer. She and her new *friend...*' she rolled her eyes, '...plan to go away for two months and she's renting out the apartment.'

So, Pippa had a new man in her life? It didn't surprise him. 'You could stay here,' Neil said doubtfully. He'd purchased the one-bedroom apartment when his appointment as principal at *Beckwith Boys' College* coincided with his divorce from Pippa. It wasn't designed for a twenty-year-old who would no doubt want to invite her friends to party during the festive season.

'No, it'd be good to get away for a bit. I remember going to Bellbird Bay when I was little... and Grandad's bookshop.'

'I'd love to have you there. I'm sure Grandad would too. But are you sure? What about your friends here in Brisbane?'

She took out her phone and stared at it for a few moments, then slid it back into her pocket. 'Oh, why does life have to suck?'

Neil felt his gut clench. What was wrong with Bronte, what had happened to make her so negative about life? At her age she should be filled with excitement, with anticipation about the future. Instead, she sounded as if she had the cares of the world on her shoulders.

'What's really the matter, bub?' he asked, using his baby name for her, before joining her on the sofa and pulling her into a hug, feeling strands of her blonde hair, so like his own, tickling his cheek.

'Everyone's leaving town,' she said with a sob. 'Mum's off to some retreat, the girls are going to the Gold Coast for six weeks, and...' She sniffed as a tear trickled down her cheek. 'I was planning to go with them, but Mum won't put up the cash, and I don't have a job at the moment. I was supposed to be focussing on my studies, but... I don't suppose you'd... no, I guess not,' she added, seeing his expression. 'Anyway, their arrangements are all finalised.' She sat up and wiped her eyes. 'I guess it's Bellbird Bay, then. Thanks, Dad. I'd better go, or I'll miss the ferry.'

Neil watched her leave, wishing he knew how to help, to transform his lovely daughter into the happy girl who'd been full of plans for how she'd spend her life.

Maybe they'd both find an answer in Bellbird Bay. He certainly hoped so.

Three

Alison nursed her cup of lemon and ginger tea and gazed out at the tiny harbour where the sun was glinting on the water and a few fishing boats were unloading their catch. It was early morning in Bellbird Bay and the scene was a far cry from her home in Perth.

She turned back into the townhouse she'd rented sight unseen when her life in the Western Australian city had fallen apart – when the career she'd worked so hard to establish had threatened to disappear almost overnight. The place was basic, but comfortable, the tiled floor and standard Ikea furniture giving it an impersonal appearance. But she could soon fix that with a few throws and some flowering plants.

She hadn't packed much, locking up the Perth house as soon as she had handed in her students' results, eager to leave the site of her humiliation. She'd worry about the rest of her belongings later. Meanwhile, she intended to use this time, and the peace of Bellbird Bay to plan her next move.

She was glad she'd managed to find this place so quickly. While her brother had offered to have her stay with him and his partner, she didn't want to impinge on their new-found happiness. She loved Adam and had quickly developed a friendship with his new partner, Libby, but she was too old to share a home. She'd only moved back into the family home in Perth when her mother's health started to fail.

Finishing her tea, she showered and changed. She had promised to meet Adam for breakfast at a café on the esplanade. It had been late when she arrived last night and all she wanted was to fall into bed.

She hadn't been prepared to meet the questions she knew her brother would ask.

Last time they'd met, she'd been a successful academic, filled with enthusiasm about educating a new generation in the Women's Studies which was her passion. Now, she had come to Bellbird Bay to escape the humiliation which was the result of her own actions.

Adam had told her *The Bay Café* was a regular haunt of his, where he used to have breakfast every day before he and Libby got together. It was easy to find as Alison walked from her apartment along the concrete path, in which patterns of surfboards and fish were embedded, to where the path met the esplanade with its collection of small shops and cafés.

Alison saw the dog before she saw her brother. Milo, the large, ungainly animal belonging to Libby ran to meet her, wagging his tail and pulling Adam behind him. She couldn't help laughing at the picture they made. 'Libby not joining us?' she asked, when they'd hugged and were seated at one of the outside tables, Milo now calmy lying at Adam's feet, his head on his paws.

'She's working today, so you'll have to make do with me.' Adam grinned.

'No problem.' While Alison would have preferred to have a woman's support in the conversation she knew would ensue, Adam was her brother and, although they'd spent over forty years apart, she had no wish to keep secrets from him.

It wasn't till they'd been served breakfast of eggs benedict accompanied by a large black coffee for Adam and a pot of lemon and ginger tea for Alison, that he asked, 'What's up, Ali? You were coming for Christmas, then suddenly your plans changed. You said you're here for a couple of months at least. What gives?'

'It's complicated.'

'No worries. I can do complicated.'

'I've become persona non grata with my faculty head… with most of the faculty. All because…' Ali gave a sigh and carefully poured herself a cup of tea.

'What happened?'

'It started when one of my students told me she'd been sexually assaulted,' she began, recounting her humiliation and disgust.

'Wow! Our mother…'

'I know, but I was so young at the time, and Mother never talked about it. I know now, I didn't fully realise what it must have been like for her. And I only had to endure verbal abuse. I feel ashamed how familiar I was with the theory, with so little understanding of how the victims must feel. I've led such a sheltered life for over fifty years.'

'But surely that's not what led you to decide to spend time here? Don't get me wrong, Libby and I are delighted we'll have your company for longer, would have been happy for you to stay with us, but I can't believe the sister I know would let a few bad experiences force her to take leave.'

'That's not all.' Regardless of the meal getting cold, Ali continued, 'Richard plans to cut my program and suggested I take early retirement,'

'Early retirement? You're younger than me.'

'Fifty-five.'

'So you decided to come here? I'm glad you did.'

'Thanks, Adam. I had some long service leave due, so Richard suggested I take a break and think it over. He may be right. A few months away from the toxic atmosphere might help me.'

'Well, you've come to the right place. There's something about the air here, some might call it magic.' He rubbed his chin.

'Come on. I don't remember you being so fanciful when we were growing up.'

'I wasn't back then, not for a long time after, either. But ask Libby – or any of our friends. Bellbird Bay has a way of getting under your skin. Once you come here, it's difficult to leave – and good things happen.'

'Not for me,' Ali scoffed. 'I'll stick out my few months' leave, then I'll be going back to face them. There's no way I'll let the bastards win. I mean it,' she said, seeing her brother's disbelieving expression.

'You wouldn't consider a different position… in another university? With your reputation, I'm sure it wouldn't be difficult. You did mention moving to Canberra.'

'That was when I thought you lived there. There'd be no point now you've settled here. My life's in Perth. It's where all my friends are.'

'Hmm. Better eat your breakfast before it's completely cold.'

'Yeah.' Ali began to dig into the food which had almost congealed on the plate, but after a few bites she pushed it away. 'Sorry, Adam. I'm not really hungry. I haven't been since I met with Richard. The hide of the man!' She was still full of suppressed anger at the memory of the meeting with him. 'Sorry, I didn't mean to bore you with my problems. Maybe you can write about it sometime,' she joked.

'I don't think so, and there's nothing to be sorry about. What sort of big brother would I be if I wasn't prepared to listen? You were there for me last year.'

'True.' Ali smiled at the memory of how Adam and Libby's relationship almost fell apart due to a misunderstanding. 'But all's well now?'

'Couldn't be better. All those years I spent afraid of commitment, when I just needed to find the right person. It's not too late for you either, Ali.'

'I hope you're not going to try your hand at matchmaking. You may have found your soulmate but it's definitely too late for me. And I have enough to worry about right now, without complicating my life any further. But, enough about me, what's happening with my famous writer brother? Is the television deal still going ahead?'

The rest of their conversation was taken up with Adam reporting on the progress of the plans to transform one of his novels into a television mini-series, and the new series he was currently writing.

By the time they rose to leave, Ali was in a better frame of mind. Deciding to put the humiliation of the past few weeks behind her for the time being and enjoy what Bellbird Bay had to offer, she agreed to meet Adam and Libby for dinner at the surf club where Adam assured her, 'All the best people in Bellbird Bay eat on a Friday evening'.

Four

'Hey, Dad!' Neil, with Bronte trailing behind him, entered the bookshop, the familiar aroma immediately taking him back to his childhood. He remembered the days when he rushed there after school to lose himself in the latest book from his favourite author. It was here he developed his love of reading, a love which had never left him. While his peers spent their time on the beach, making out and surfing, he was lost in the imaginary worlds of books.

'Neil, good to see you… and Bronte.' Harry Simpson emerged from behind the counter to hug them both.

'Looking good, Dad.' Neil gazed around the shop which was busy with people choosing Christmas gifts. The place was decorated for the season with a large Christmas tree taking pride of place in one corner, while a couple of wooden reindeer stood guard by the counter. A display of Christmas novels completed the festive scene.

'Thanks, son. I try my best, which isn't as easy as it used to be.'

Neil glanced warily at his dad who appeared frailer than he had on his last visit. Was it really six months since he'd been here? He made a vow to come more frequently in future. Harry wasn't getting any younger, but surely, he still had a few good years ahead of him? Neil tried to remember exactly how old his father was. He remembered them celebrating his eightieth birthday and hoping that he'd be as active at his dad's age. How many years ago had it been? The years seemed to fly by so fast, it was difficult to remember exactly.

'Oh, look, Dad!' Bronte had been wandering around the shelves and was holding up a copy of Adam Holland's latest novel. 'Your favourite author,' she said. 'Looks like a new series.'

'It is,' Harry said, taking the book from her, and stroking the cover. 'Adam has become a local, and this new series is set in a town not unlike Bellbird Bay. But he's a bit of a recluse, hates publicity, so you won't see him signing books in here. But you might bump into him in town.'

'Really?' Adam Holland had been one of Neil's go-to authors since his first book was published and, even before then, Neil had followed his political column. 'Is it true there's to be a television series?'

'So I hear, but I understand Adam's a bit reticent about it.'

'I'll take this one, Dad.'

'No charge.'

'No, I insist. You can't make a profit giving away books.'

Grumbling, Harry agreed. As he began to slip the book into a bag and enter the price into the computer, Neil noticed a tremor in his dad's hands. Was this something new?

'Are you okay, Dad?' he asked.

'Why wouldn't I be?' The older man sounded defensive. 'I may be a tad slower than I used to be. You'd be too, if you were my age.'

Neil decided to say no more, but to keep an eye on his dad. Perhaps the old man was failing, perhaps not. Maybe it was time for him to slow down, downsize, even. He was still living in the family home close to the centre of town, just a few streets back from the esplanade where the shop was situated.

'Have you been home yet?' Harry asked, as if reading Neil's mind.

'Not yet. I knew you'd be at the shop, so we came here first. We'll head there now and see you when you get home. Maybe we can go out to dinner if you're not too tired.'

'I may be getting old but I'm not past it yet,' Harry said. 'I'll see you there.'

*

I'd forgotten how laid back it is here,' Bronte said when they left the shop. Across the road from the esplanade was the beach where they could see groups of holidaymakers on the sand, families enjoying cooling off in the sea between the flags, and a few surfers riding the waves. At one end of the beach was a van, outside of which was a large sign indicating it was *Bay Surf School* offering surf lessons and board hire. 'It's a while since I did any surfing. I might take it up again. Did you surf much when you were growing up here, Dad?'

'A bit, but I was never part of the surfing crowd. Guess I was a nerd back then, more interested in books and study than in catching a wave. I remember Will Rankin who won the championship one year, and his mate, Coop, who left to become a photographer, but I was never part of that crowd.'

'Can we have coffee before we go to Grandad's?' Bronte asked, as they passed a café with several sun-bleached wooden tables outside.

Neil checked his watch. It would be some time before the shop closed. 'Sure.'

They were soon seated at one of the tables with a chai latte for Bronte and a macchiato for Neil, along with two slices of banana bread. Sitting here, with the late afternoon sun beating down on them, the scent of the sea in the air and the sound of happy chatter around them, it was almost possible to forget the trauma of the past few weeks. But it hadn't disappeared entirely. The memory of the headlines, the curious glances, the way some of the people he'd considered friends gradually disappeared or found they were too busy to meet, would take more than an afternoon in Bellbird Bay to fade. But being here was a start, and it would be good to spend quality time with Bronte and his dad. Thinking of his dad reminded him of the tremor he'd noticed. He supposed it was just old age.

As if mirroring his thoughts, Bronte asked, 'Is Grandad okay? He looks a lot older than I remember.'

'He's getting older, like all of us. It's some time since you were here. You're always off somewhere with Mum when I come to visit.' Neil looked across at his daughter. She'd grown up, too, but she'd always be his little girl despite her lovely face now sporting a ring in one nostril. And he'd noticed a small tattoo on her wrist.

'He's been on his own a long time, hasn't he?'

'Ten years... since your nan died.' Neil pictured the energetic upright man his dad had been back then. Now, with his mop of white hair and trim beard, he looked more like one of the characters in his books than the man who'd challenged him to read all the novels of Dickens in one year.

'He must get lonely in that big house.'

'Mmm.' It was something Neil had never thought about. One didn't. One's parents were always there… till they weren't. This was the first time he'd noticed a marked change in his dad, and he wondered if things were getting too much for him. Maybe he needed to raise it with him, though he didn't look forward to that conversation.

'Can we go now?' Having finished her coffee and banana bread, Bronte was eager to move on.

With a sigh, Neil agreed. He'd forgotten how lively his daughter could be, and how easily bored. He hoped she'd be able to find enough to keep her occupied during the summer. Otherwise, their time here would be difficult. Before Pippa's call, he'd planned to spend his summer relaxing, catching up with the reading he didn't have time to do during the school year, and updating his CV in case the worst happened and he was in the job market again. Now, it seemed, he'd also have to make time to keep Bronte occupied.

*

Neil and Bronte were unpacked, and Neil was enjoying a beer while Bronte was engrossed in her iPad, when Harry arrived home from the bookshop.

'Home sweet home,' he said, plonking himself down in the well-worn armchair Neil remembered from his childhood.

Some things never changed. The house and all the furnishings were exactly as they had been when Neil lived here and, while they brought back pleasant memories, they could do with an upgrade. The entire house could do with one.

'I got Joan to fill the freezer and fridge so there's plenty of food in the house. But you mentioned going out to dinner?'

'Joan? You mean…?'

'Joan Davidson, my neighbour. She comes in a couple of days a week to keep the place ship-shape. Your mother would never forgive me if I let it go.' He reached for a cigarette, then seemed to change his mind.

Neil had a vague recollection of a grey-haired woman he'd met on one of his previous visits. She and her husband lived next door. It was good to know there was someone looking out for his dad when he couldn't be here, but he felt an unexpected rush of guilt at the knowledge his dad had to get help from a stranger.

'I thought maybe the surf club,' Neil said. 'Show Bronte some of the bright lights of Bellbird Bay.'

'I don't get there much these days, not as often as I used to. It would be good to see the old place. Spent a lot of time there when I was younger, when you were growing up, too. Your mum liked to sit out on the deck of an evening with a glass of something.' He gazed into space, lost in the memory of days gone by.

'Right, then. Are you up for the surf club, Bronte?'

Bronte raised her head from the iPad which had been the focus of her attention. 'Whatever, Dad. When do you want to leave?'

'In an hour or so. Give your grandad time to take a bit of a rest.'

'I don't need a rest, son,' Harry said, but he made no effort to move from the chair. Neil noted it was placed strategically in order to enable his dad to watch television, keep an eye on the road outside and that he had the control close at hand along with a copy of the local paper, a pack of cigarettes and a lighter. He suspected he spent most of his time there when he was home.

It was almost two hours later when the three of them entered the surf club. It was already filled with members eager to celebrate the end of the working week. A trio of musicians were playing in one corner almost drowned out by the combination of chatter and the noise of the poker machines. They wound their way through the crowd to find an empty table close to one window, where they could look out onto the deck. It was too dark to see much beyond the edge of it, though a spotlight did provide some illumination.

'Beer, Dad?' Neil asked. 'Bronte?'

Harry nodded, and Bronte said, 'White wine for me, thanks, Dad.'

When Neil returned with the drinks, Bronte and Harry were already studying copies of the menu.

'I'll have the salmon,' Bronte said,

'You, Dad?'

'Always have the burger and chips. Best I've ever tasted.'

Neil forbore to comment that no doubt the chef had changed since his dad was last here, but decided it wasn't a bad choice.

While they were waiting for their meals to arrive, Neil glanced around. He didn't expect to recognise anyone. It was years since he'd been here and most of the guys he'd known when he was growing up would either have left town or changed beyond recognition.

He was surprised, therefore, to see one face he recognised. The man was sitting at a table on the deck with a woman with ash-blonde hair. Another elegant woman, her hair more white than grey was seated opposite. Even from this distance, he found her intriguing. Neil felt an unexpected jolt of attraction. 'Isn't that...?' he asked his dad.

'Adam Holland. It is. The woman with the ash-blonde hair is his partner, Libby Walker. She's lived here for a few years. Widow. Works in the library. Her daughter and granddaughter moved in with Nick Armstrong who owns a boatyard up the coast. I don't know the other one. She's a stranger.'

'Do you know everyone in Bellbird Bay, Grandad?' Bronte asked.

'No, only those who read,' Harry chuckled.

Neil relaxed. This was more like his dad. Maybe the old man had just been tired before and had lost the sense of humour Neil remembered. Now it was back.

Their meals arrived and were as good as anything Neil had eaten in the city. His dad had been right about the burgers, and Bronte seemed happy with her salmon.

They left just as the music was becoming louder and several of the younger couples began to dance. Bronte looked as if she might have liked to join them as they made their way through the crush, stopping from time to time as Harry was greeted by friends and acquaintances. Neil had forgotten the way people here all tended to know each other, and Harry, being the owner of the town's only bookshop, was a local personality.

As they made their way back to the car, Neil felt relaxed. It had been a good evening. His only regret was that he hadn't managed to speak to the author whose books he enjoyed. But there would be plenty of time and, knowing Bellbird Bay, they'd bump into each other sooner or later. He might even discover the identity of Adam Holland's companion.

Five

Although Ali had already visited Bellbird Bay several times in the past year, it had always been as a visitor when she stayed with Adam, then Adam and Libby, when her brother moved in with his partner. Now, she was seeing it through different eyes.

As she walked along to the esplanade for the second time that day, the sound of the waves in her ears, a flock of rosellas flew overhead almost deafening her with their cries. When she looked up, she could see the bright green and red of their plumage filling the sky. It was so different from the city skyline she was accustomed to that her face broke into a smile.

Adam and Libby were waiting for her outside the surf club. Libby came forward to hug her. 'Welcome back,' she said with a smile. 'We're so glad you're here for longer this time. Adam told me about your challenges. I'm so sorry, Ali.'

'Thanks.' Ali guessed *challenges* was one way to describe what had happened to her. It was a word she'd often used herself to describe the problems of other people. It sounded strange to have what she would call a disaster referred to in such a way.

Once inside the club, Adam went to the bar to order drinks while Ali and Libby made their way out to the deck to secure a table. It was still early, so they were able to find one free and settled down to examine the menus.

'I don't know why I bother,' Libby said. 'I know it by heart.'

'What do you recommend?'

'Adam usually has the burger and chips the club is famous for, but I prefer something lighter. The salmon is always good, or the Thai chicken salad.'

'I think I'll have the salad.' Ali laid down the menu and gazed out at the darkening ocean. There were still a few figures walking along the beach. It suddenly occurred to her that, here, she was free to do that, too. She had no classes to prepare for, no assignments to mark, no deadlines to meet, no parent to worry about. For the first time in twenty years, she was free to spend her time in whatever way she chose. Stifling the little voice that said she was also in danger of having no job, she decided to focus on the present and enjoy her time here.

'Here we are.' Adam appeared, carrying two glasses of white wine and a bottle of beer.

'Thanks,' Ali said, taking a welcome sip of the icy liquid. 'I'd forgotten how lovely it is here.'

'We like it,' Libby said, squeezing Adam's hand.

Ali looked at her two favourite people, the only family she had left. It was difficult to believe that, until a year ago, she and Adam hadn't seen each other for over forty years. Torn apart in their childhood when Ali and her mother fled to escape the violence of her father, the brother and sister had finally found each other.

'What do you plan to do while you're here?' Libby's question interrupted Ali's thoughts.

'Nothing.' Ali laughed. 'Sorry, that came out wrong. I plan to relax, try to forget everything that happened back in Perth, maybe even put together a plan for my future. I don't need to look for work, not immediately. And I do still have a job to go back to. I haven't been sacked – not yet.' She became more serious, remembering her last meeting with Richard Ellis. 'Anyway, I don't need to worry about money. I plan to spend my time lying in the sun, swimming, catching up on my reading, finding my way around Bellbird Bay and the surrounding area… and spending time with you two, of course. I realise I may become bored after a time – I'm not used to being a lady of leisure – but I'll face that when it happens. In the meantime…' she stretched her arms in the air and grinned.

'Maybe you'll meet someone.' Libby smiled at Adam, then looked back at Ali.

'No! Sorry, that came out stronger than I intended. I'm not looking for anyone to share my life, Libby. You've been lucky twice in your life,' she said, referring to the fact Libby was a widow when she and Adam met, 'and Adam was lucky to find you. I know he avoided any hint of commitment for years. I have, too, and it's too late for me.'

'It's never too late,' Libby said gently. 'And maybe, now you've seen how happy Adam and I are…'

'No,' Ali said again. Her mother had brought her up to distrust men, and her recent experience had only reinforced it. While she'd had several flings in her younger days – and a few one-night stands she regretted afterwards – she was past all that. It was liberating to know she had no need to suffer the indignity of rejecting someone whose only crime was to want a relationship with her. 'I'm happy as I am.'

'I thought I was, too, till I met Libby.' Adam joined the conversation.

'It's different for you, you're a man.'

Adam laughed. 'That's for sure, but don't let yourself fall into the trap of thinking all men are like Dad – or those male chauvinists you work with at the university. Some of us are really genuine guys. I want you to be happy.'

'I *am* happy – or I was till all this blew up.' But Ali knew what her brother was trying to tell her. No matter how much she loved her independent life, there were times when it would have been nice to have someone to share things with, someone to chat with at the end of a busy day, to understand what she was going through.

Their meals arrived, and Ali was saved from any further discussion of her single status. The deck filled up with other diners, and the music from the restaurant blasted out each time the door opened to admit more patrons.

They had finished their meals, and Ali was enjoying coffee with a second glass of wine when a couple stopped at their table.

'Ali, how lovely to see you again. Here for Christmas?'

Ali looked up to see a face she recognised from her visit to Bellbird Bay the previous Christmas. She, Adam and Libby had spent Christmas Day at the home of Grace Winter and her partner, Ted Crawford, along with what seemed like half of Bellbird Bay. It had been a fun time and felt like more than a year ago when she and Libby had drunk champagne on the beach watching Adam swim in the surf lifesaving fundraiser. Then on Christmas Day they'd joined Grace's family in a festive feast before a game of cricket on the beach.

Ali smiled and was about to reply when Adam forestalled her. 'A bit longer this time, Grace. Ali's taken some well-earned long service leave and is in Bellbird Bay for the summer.'

'How lovely. We must see more of you while you're here. We're having a barbecue on Sunday. Why don't you all come? You met my daughter last Christmas, didn't you, Ali? She'll be there with her daughter and partner, along with a few other friends. It'll give you the opportunity to meet some of our neighbours.'

'I don't…' Ali began, but Adam spoke before she could complete the sentence.

'We'd love to, thanks, Grace.'

'What can I bring?' Libby asked. 'How about some dessert?'

'Thanks, Libby, that would be good. I expect Bev will bring along one of Ruby's cakes from the café, but you can never have too many desserts.'

Ali felt she was being swept along on a wave of something she didn't understand. She had envisaged spending her days in peaceful contemplation, meeting with Adam and Libby from time to time, not being expected to socialise with Adam and Libby's friends. But it would have been rude to refuse. She smiled weakly.

Six

'What do you want to do today?' Neil asked Bronte as they were having breakfast. He was rested after a good sleep and couldn't wait to reacquaint himself with the town.

'Beach,' Bronte muttered through a mouthful of toast and vegemite. 'It looks amazing. I want to check out the surfboard hire place I saw yesterday. The surf here looked amazing, too.'

'I'm going to wander into town, may give Dad a hand in the shop. Okay with you, Dad?'

'If you can still remember how things operate in a bookshop,' Harry said. But there was a twinkle in his eyes.

'It's not something I could ever forget.' Neil remembered how he'd loved helping his dad when he was still so small he had to stand on a stool to see over the counter, how he'd felt so grown up to be allowed to ring up a sale on the old cash register. 'If you pop in after your surf, maybe we can have lunch together,' he said to Bronte.

'Maybe. I'll text you.' Bronte rose and left the kitchen, to reappear a few minutes later dressed in a pair of shorts and a tee-shirt emblazoned with the slogan *Save the Whales*. Her feet were slipped into a pair of thongs, there was a cap on her head, and a bag from which a towel was protruding, was carelessly thrown over one shoulder. 'See you, Dad, Grandad.'

Neil watched his daughter head off, part of him wishing he was twenty again without a care in the world. But that wasn't completely true. At twenty, he'd been in his final year at uni, unsure where his future lay and in the throes of his first serious romance. It was some years later, and he was firmly entrenched in his teaching career, when he met Pippa and thought he'd found his life partner.

'I'm off, too, son. I'll see you later.' Harry carried his breakfast dishes to the sink.

'Leave them, Dad. I can do them,' Neil said without thinking.

'I'm still able to look after myself, Neil. I've managed it for all these years since your mother passed, and I'll manage it again once you leave.' Harry glared at his son.

'Sorry, Dad.' But Neil could see such a change in the old man, a change that made him want to try to make his life easier in any way he could.

*

Left alone, Neil made himself another cup of coffee and opened the local paper. He knew from experience that *The Bay Bugle* was the place to discover what was happening in the town. He was right. It was an old copy and, as he flicked through the pages, he learned the results of the recent triathlon, read about the wedding of world-renowned photographer and Bellbird Bay local, Martin Cooper, and found a report of the arrest of a local identity called Milton Harris on charges of bribery and corruption. There was also a half-page ad for *Bay Books* with an old photo of his dad which made him smile. He wondered how long Harry would be able to continue running the bookshop and what would happen to it once he was no longer capable.

He took a long drink of coffee and turned the page, scanning the list of properties for sale and jobs vacant. Nothing there to interest him. He closed the paper, seeing the back page held the usual breakdown of local sports teams. As he tossed the paper onto the table, a flier fell out. Picking it up, Neil saw it was advertising an exhibition of paintings and photographs of local buildings at the art gallery in town. Thinking it might be worth a visit, he folded the leaflet and stuck it into his pocket.

The town hadn't changed much since Neil was a teenager. A few buildings had had a makeover, and there were several new shops to cater to the growing tourist trade, but he could still have found his way around blindfolded. Even his old school still looked the same, the students milling around in the playground wearing the same uniform he remembered. He wondered what his life would have been like if he'd chosen to stay in the state system instead of being drawn into the doubtful prestige of teaching in a private boys' college. At least there would have been no school board to misappropriate school funds, no scandal to become embroiled in.

By the time he reached *Bay Books*, Neil felt as if he'd never been away.

The bookshop was busy again today, and there was a queue of people waiting to be served. With a smile and a nod to Harry, Neil joined him behind the counter, quickly falling back into the routine he'd never forgotten.

'Come back to give your dad a hand?'

Neil peered at the old woman. He recognised her face. Ruby Sullivan had seemed old for as long as he could remember. She must be as old as his dad... older, even. When he'd been around seven or eight, he and his friends thought she was a witch. She lived in an old house on the headland at the top of the boardwalk, and when they were kids, he and his mates used to knock on her door, then run away to hide and giggle when she opened the door and peered out.

'I'm back for a few weeks,' he said. 'How can I help you?'

'This one, please.' She handed Neil a copy of Adam Holland's latest book. 'I like to support local talent.'

Neil suppressed a smile. As if the famous author needed her support. He was slipping the book into a bag when she spoke again.

'It'll all work out for you. The road ahead may not be the route you expect, but it will bring you more happiness than you have ever imagined.' She nodded to herself.

Neil stared at her. He'd heard about Ruby and her strange predictions and, like most of his friends, had rubbished them as the weird ramblings of an old woman. But this one, aimed at him, took his breath away. *How could she know he felt he was at a crossroads in his career?* If the charges being levelled at the board members stuck, the school might not survive, and his job would disappear with it.

Deciding to ignore her words, Neil only said, 'I hope you enjoy the book,' as he completed the sale.

But Ruby hadn't finished. As she accepted her change, she leant across the counter and, in a low voice said, 'Take care of your dad. He's not as strong as he used to be. He's going to need your help.'

'What did Ruby have to say to you? I saw your expression when she left,' Harry asked when the rush had subsided.

'Oh, you know Ruby, some rubbish,' Neil said, trying to dismiss the uneasy feeling her final words had stirred up. *What did Ruby know about his dad that he didn't?* The old man had seemed frail yesterday, but today, he appeared to be back to his old form, greeting customers as usual and moving easily around the shop. Perhaps yesterday he'd just been tired, or maybe Neil had been tired himself after the worry of the past few days and weeks. But it might be worth keeping an eye on his dad, all the same.

'She didn't predict you'd find romance here in the Bay?' Harry asked with a chuckle.

'Not a chance, Dad.' But Neil couldn't help thinking of the woman he'd seen in the surf club the previous evening. It was a small town. He'd be sure to see her again, and next time, maybe he could find out who she was.

Seven

Unsure what to wear to the barbecue, Ali pulled on a pair of jeans and a long-sleeved linen shirt, then threw a sweater into her bag. She was just ready when she heard Adam at the door.

'This is a nice place you have here,' he said, walking in and gazing around, 'though I don't know why you couldn't have stayed with Libby and me.'

'Not again, Adam. I told you. Since I plan to be here for a few months, I need my own space, and this suits me fine.' She was happy with the apartment which was already beginning to feel like home. Yesterday, she'd made a visit to a shopping centre on the far side of town and had purchased a couple of multicoloured throws and several cushions. These now adorned the sofa and armchairs. Then, she'd dropped into the local garden centre. She'd been surprised at the size of it and browsed happily for almost an hour before selecting the pot plants which now graced her living room and balcony.

'Okay!' Adam held up both hands defensively. 'Only saying. You'd have been very welcome.'

'I know.' Ali reached up to kiss her brother on the cheek. 'Now, can we go? Libby will be wondering where you've got to. I could have made my own way. Grace's house is just up the boardwalk from yours. It's not far, and I do have transport.' Ali had arranged for her car to be transported from Perth by train and had picked it up in Brisbane.

'I wanted to see where you were living.'

'And does it meet with your approval?' It was strange to Ali, who'd relied on her own judgement for all her adult life, to suddenly have her big brother taking an interest in her.

'Just about.' Adam grinned.

Ali linked her arm in his. 'Let's go,' she said. The sooner they arrived at the barbecue, the sooner she'd be able to leave and return to the haven of her new home.

She'd been right. Grace's yard was filled with a crowd of people, most of whom were strangers to Ali. She recognised Grace's daughter and Ted's son from the previous Christmas, and one of the women looked familiar. When she was introduced as Bev Cooper, Ali realised she'd met her in the garden centre when she was buying plants. It appeared Bev owned the centre and had lived in Bellbird Bay all her life. The others Ali was introduced to were all a blur of names and faces.

She was glad when Adam handed her a glass of wine, and she was able to find a seat in a secluded corner where she could stay out of the crush and observe everyone.

She had only been there a short time when Grace joined her.

'Sorry if you feel you've been thrust into a crowd of strangers,' Grace said, 'but sometimes it's best to meet everyone at once. We're a friendly community in Bellbird Bay, and those of us who live here on the boardwalk have come to know each other very well. We were delighted to welcome your brother into our midst last year.'

'It has been a bit of a shock,' Ali admitted. While she didn't know Grace well, the woman, who must be around ten years older than she was, seemed kind.

'Libby mentioned you had a few challenges back in Perth,' Grace said. When Ali appeared startled, she added, 'She didn't go into details. Libby isn't one to gossip. She just wanted me to understand if you didn't want to mingle. It's never easy coming to a new place, especially when everyone else seems to know each other. I can remember when I arrived in town. My sister lives here and she seemed to think it was her duty to help me make friends – even to matchmake. I actually met Ted at one of her dinner parties, though at that time I wanted nothing to do with him – or any other man. I was still grieving for my husband and trying to cope with two daughters who disapproved of my moving from the family property.'

Ali smiled. She could relate. Back in Perth, she'd become wary every time she was invited to dinner by a married friend or colleague, suspicious there would happen to be a single man there just for her benefit. She'd begun to refuse all such invitations.

'Look,' Grace said, 'I don't mean to be pushy, but sometimes it helps to talk with someone outside the family, someone completely independent. If you ever feel like a chat, give me a call and we can meet for coffee or lunch.'

'Thanks, it's kind of you.'

'Grace!' Ted called, and, with an apologetic smile, Grace disappeared, leaving Ali feeling comforted somehow. Maybe she'd take Grace up on her offer. Adam and Libby were kind and had her best interests at heart, but they were too close and wanted to do something to help. There was nothing anyone else could do, but it might be good to talk through her problems. If Sally was here, she'd be able to provide a sympathetic ear, though even she tended to want to fix things. Ali had the impression Grace would only offer advice if she was asked for it.

When Adam appeared, intent on bringing Ali into a group around Libby, she didn't refuse and found herself caught up in a discussion about Christmas. When Grace joined the group, too, having managed to satisfy whatever Ted needed her for, Libby asked, 'Are you intending to re-enact last year's festivities, Grace?'

Grace smiled. 'Not this year, Libby. We're all going to Sydney to spend Christmas with Lou. My older daughter,' she explained to Ali. 'She lives there and has managed to persuade all of us to join her – even my son, Ben, who can rarely be persuaded away from his archaeological dig in North Queensland. I'm really looking forward to seeing her – and my Sydney granddaughter. Little Gracie will be almost two and she very nearly wasn't born. We're renting a large Airbnb on the Northern Beaches to fit us all in. It'll be our first Christmas together since I left our family home in New South Wales.' A shadow crossed her face, to be quickly replaced by her customary smile. 'So you'll have to do without me this year.'

'I'm sure Libby and Ali can manage between them,' Adam said with a grin, 'though I doubt we'll produce anything like the feast you provided last year.'

Ted called out to let them know the barbecue was ready, and they should grab plates and head over to collect their steaks and sausages.

While they'd all been chatting, Grace's daughter, Mel, had loaded a table with platters of salad, and the dessert Libby had brought – a magnificent strawberry carob cheesecake – was sitting there, too, alongside several other exotic concoctions. Grace had outdone herself again.

To Ali's surprise, she enjoyed the rest of the evening and stayed until everyone began to drift away. When she thanked Grace and Ted for inviting her, Grace whispered in her ear, 'Don't forget what I said.'

After persuading Adam she was quite happy to walk home, Ali set off down the boardwalk. It was a glorious evening, the sound of the waves providing a backdrop to the thoughts milling around in her head. Adam was so settled here, and his friends were all so welcoming. It was difficult to adjust to the friendly atmosphere, making Ali realise how fraught her life had become in the hothouse of the university atmosphere where every remark was analysed for a hidden agenda. *Did she really want to go back to that?*

Eight

Neil was beginning to get used to a life of leisure. Each morning, after his dad had gone to open the bookshop, and Bronte had headed to the beach, he'd saunter over to the esplanade for coffee in *The Bay Café* before going for a swim or surf. At the beach, he was careful to keep out of Bronte's way, having been told in no uncertain terms that she didn't want to be seen with 'an old guy like you, Dad'.

But it wasn't all relaxation. He'd got into the habit of dropping into the bookshop each afternoon, enjoying the familiar aroma and the memories it evoked. After a few such afternoons, Harry had put him to work sorting out deliveries and pricing the new books before adding them to the shelves. It demonstrated to Neil that, if nothing else, the bookshop was still a thriving business.

It was around a week after his arrival in Bellbird Bay when he noticed his dad seemed to be taking longer to process the sales and sometimes faltered when speaking to a customer. He hesitated to mention it, knowing what Harry's response would be, but it worried him sufficiently to make him decide to have a quiet word with the neighbour who helped Harry out at home.

He chose a day when he knew Joan would be arriving to clean and delayed his morning trip to *The Bay Café*.

'Sorry, I didn't know you'd be here,' Joan said, when she opened the back door, her grey hair curling around her cheerful, round face, a container of cleaning products in one hand. 'Would you like me to come back later? I don't want to interrupt you.'

Neil turned from his laptop where he'd been checking the headlines yet again, relieved the story of the school had been relegated to page four and only consisted of a small paragraph. He supposed it would gain prominence again when the court proceedings began but that could be months away. He hoped the fate of the school – and his position as principal – didn't hang in the balance till then. 'Not at all. Actually, I wanted to have a chat.'

'Oh, if you'd rather I didn't come when you and your daughter are here…' Joan's forehead creased, '…I'd understand.'

'No, it's not that. It's Dad.' Neil paused, unsure exactly how to approach this. He cleared his throat. 'Have you noticed anything… has he seemed different recently? It's been some time since I saw him, and he suddenly seems to be much older.'

'We're none of us getting any younger,' Joan said wryly, 'and your dad took the loss of your mum badly. We all did. She was good to me when my Bert had the accident. But your dad rallied, started to live again. It was then I began to pop in. I think the bookshop was what saved him. It gave him a purpose, a reason to get up and out of the house. We all need that,' she said, as if talking to herself.

Neil remembered Joan's husband had suffered from an accident when his fishing boat had been hit by a storm. It was a long time ago now. He'd been in university at the time and recalled his mother saying something about it.

'But recently,' he repeated. 'Has he been different? Frailer?'

'Well, I don't see much of him. I usually come in once he's gone for the day. But I do recall one day when… I don't want to speak out of turn…'

Neil waited patiently.

'He was still here when I arrived and was in a terrible state. He'd had a fall, bruised himself and was having trouble getting himself together. I offered to call an ambulance or the doctor, but he pooh-poohed the idea, said he only needed a bit of time. I made him a cup of tea and, by the time he'd drunk it, he seemed to be back to normal and left for work. It only happened once… as far as I know.' Her brow creased again at the realisation Harry could have experienced this at another time when she wasn't around. 'He won't thank me for telling you this,' she said grimly. 'He doesn't want to be a bother to anyone…

and he'd be lost without the bookshop, but sometimes I wonder if he's fully aware of what's happening around him; it's as if he sometimes forgets where he is. Another morning when I came in, I found he'd let some eggs boil dry. The house stank and he hadn't even noticed.'

'Thanks.' Neil sighed. 'I'll let you get on now. And I won't tell Dad what you've said.' But it confirmed Neil's suspicions that Harry wasn't as well as he liked to pretend. It might even be worse than he'd thought. The challenge was going to be persuading his dad to admit it and seek medical help.

*

Although Neil tried to watch his dad out of the corner of his eye during the afternoon, he saw nothing untoward. Perhaps Harry was moving more slowly than he used to and sometimes appeared to be having trouble with his balance, but wasn't that just a normal sign of his age? He'd also heard him complain about feeling stiff, but Neil knew *he* sometimes felt that way, too, especially if he'd missed his exercise for a few days. Maybe the shuffling gait Harry seemed to have adopted was a result of stiff joints.

'Something the matter, son?' Harry asked during a lull in customers.

'No, Dad,' Neil was quick to assure him. But he was more conscious than ever of time passing. Harry wouldn't be able to keep the bookshop going for ever, and how would he cope without his daily routine?

No more was said as Bronte hurled herself into the shop to lean over the counter, her eyes sparkling and a wide grin splitting her face. 'I've found a job, Dad.'

'I didn't know you were looking for one.' It was refreshing to see Bronte excited. Neil had been worried she'd become bored and regret agreeing to accompany him.

'I wasn't, but I met this guy…'

Neil felt his hackles rise. Who had she become entangled with? What would Pippa say if Bronte became involved with some undesirable type when she was supposed to be in Neil's care? Though at twenty, Bronte was quite able to choose her own friends. He forced himself to remain calm and allow her to continue.

'He's so cool, Dad. He's a local surfing champion and has his own business, designing and making surfboards.'

Neil's heart sank, his worst fears realised.

'I met Owen… that's his name – Owen Rankin – when I was hiring a surfboard. He was looking after the van for his dad and…'

Something clicked into place in Neil's brain. 'Rankin? Is his father Will Rankin?'

'I don't know.' Bronte brushed aside the question. 'Anyway, he suggested I look at buying a board if I'm going to be here all summer. When I came in, he'd handed back over to his dad and took me up to his workshop. Oh, Dad, you should see it, see the boards he's designed – they're amazing. Then…' she took a deep breath, '…he said he was looking for an assistant – for the summer – someone who could help with the designs. I'd told him how I flunked out of uni and really wanted to do design, but Mum thought it a crazy idea, said there was no future in it.'

Neil gazed at his daughter as if he was seeing a stranger. Why had he never heard of this ambition? He remembered how Bronte had always loved drawing, had produced a magnificent design project in her final year of high school, but he hadn't been aware she'd harboured any desire to take her talent further, or that Pippa had prevented her from fulfilling her artistic potential.

'You were always good at art at school,' he said. 'Why did you never speak to me about this before? I thought you'd chosen to drop it when you applied for the degree in… wasn't it business studies you enrolled in first?'

'It was Mum's idea – to get a degree that would lead to a good job. She didn't consider art would lead anywhere. But Owen's workshop, Dad…' She spread her arms.

'He'd be Will Rankin's son,' Harry said. 'He's a fine young fellow, lost his mother and brother, one after the other. Will's done a good job bringing him up alone. Local surfing champion three years running, if I'm not mistaken. Ted Crawford is the only other to do that. Bronte can't go wrong with him.'

'See, Dad. Grandad knows him,' Bronte said, exultantly, as if that made everything okay.

'You'll remember Will Rankin, Neil?' Harry asked.

'I do.' Will was in Neil's year at school, one of the surfing heroes Neil had no desire to emulate. It seemed life hadn't been kind to him. So, it was Will who ran the surf school on the beach. Who'd have thought it?

'He has a good business there,' Harry said. 'Town councillor, too, runs the surf committee and supports a number of local charities. He's quite the local hero, and his son seems to be following in his footsteps.'

'Hmm.' *Nothing wrong with the old man's mind, today*, Neil thought. But at least it appeared Bronte wouldn't come to any harm working for Will's son. 'Sounds as if you've found a way to spend the summer,' he said. But he wondered how Pippa would react. He was sure it wasn't what she had in mind when she suggested Bronte spend the summer with him and his dad in Bellbird Bay.

'Mum doesn't need to know, does she?' Bronte asked, the same thought clearly going through her mind. 'She'd go spare at the idea of me working with a surfer.' She grimaced, as if imagining Pippa's reaction. In Pippa's world, surfers ranked with the worst sort of low life and were definitely classed as undesirable companions for her daughter.

'I guess not.' Why did Neil feel a frisson of delight at collaborating with Bronte in keeping a secret from Pippa? 'You're just going to be working with him... not...?'

'Dad, don't be so dumb.'

She hadn't answered his question, but Neil decided there was no point in pursuing it further. Bronte was an adult. She'd make her own decisions. And he hadn't been too clever at the decisions he'd made at her age, he thought, remembering some disastrous relationships he'd made before he met Pippa. She always joked how she'd saved him from making any more mistakes, but sometimes he wondered if she'd been the biggest mistake of all. Then he'd look at Bronte, and knew he'd never regret the marriage which had resulted in his beautiful daughter.

Nine

Ali felt she was on a perpetual holiday. It was as if she was in a dream from which one day she'd awaken; living in an alternate universe far removed from the reality of her life at university. In the meantime, she spent her days relaxing on the beach or on her small balcony, sunbathing and reading. Her initial plan to write a book on Women's Studies had been shelved for the time being as she enjoyed the slow pace of life in Bellbird Bay.

But she hadn't forgotten the events which precipitated her decision to come here, to join Adam and Libby. Her friend, Sally, kept her informed with news from Perth and she'd kept in touch with Chelsea. The student had chosen not to press charges, deciding she couldn't cope with the publicity which was bound to follow anything beyond the formal complaint she'd made to university authorities, and while Ali understood her reasoning, she wished she'd made a different decision. Hugo Martin had escaped with a warning. He deserved to be punished.

An email from Chelsea telling her how she was coping, reminded Ali of Grace's words at the barbecue. While she hadn't forgotten the other woman's offer, she hadn't done anything about it. Now, she realised she needed to act if she was to meet with Grace before she left town to visit her daughter. It was already part-way through December, and she had no idea when Grace planned to go to Sydney. She picked up her phone.

*

'I'm glad you decided to call,' Grace said.

The two women were seated in the café in the garden centre where Ali had bought her plants. The place was decked out for Christmas, and in the background was the sound of carols reminding Ali it wouldn't be long till the big day.

'It occurred to me you might be leaving for Sydney soon.'

'Not till next week, but we have a lot to do before then. I've barely started Christmas shopping yet.'

'Me neither.' It was something Ali kept meaning to do but had been enjoying her solitude too much to face the shops.

After some inconsequential conversation, and once they'd been served with pots of tea and the brownies which Grace had insisted Ali must sample, Grace asked, 'Now, what's bothering you? I promise not to judge or offer advice but I'm happy to listen. Sometimes talking things through can help. Most of us newcomers to Bellbird Bay have a story about what brought us here.'

Ali took a deep breath. 'It's like this,' she began, before launching into the story of Chelsea, Hugo Martin, her own humiliation, and Richard Harris's ultimatum. When she had finished, it was as if a load had been lifted from her shoulders. 'So here I am,' she said. 'Officially, I'm on long service leave, but it's not clear if I'll have a job to go back to.'

'Oh, my dear, how dreadful. I lived close to a university before I came here, and I heard some stories… but I can't believe what you've been through. Lecturing in Women's Studies, what a worthwhile choice of career. I'm guessing you may not want to go back, even if your job is still there.'

'I… I haven't decided.' Ali had refused to contemplate what she might do when her leave was over, preferring to imagine this was a normal break. She hated the idea of letting her students down but might have no alternative.

There was silence while the two women sipped their coffee, then Grace said, 'What happened to your student happened to a friend of my daughter, Lou. Maryann was only sixteen at the time. The poor girl couldn't cope with the shame of everyone knowing. It was in a small country town. She committed suicide. Things are different now. There are more support services available, but back then...' She shook her head in despair.

'She must have felt so alone,' Ali said, glad she'd put Chelsea in touch with a support group and advised her to arrange counselling. She also intended to keep in touch to make sure she was okay – as okay as she could be. There was no way the girl could continue her studies in the same university, so she had applied to transfer to one closer to her home in Adelaide.

'It's why I support our local women's centre in any way I can.' Grace looked at Ali. 'It may be something you want to consider... volunteering with an organisation such as that. They do a lot of good work.'

'Women's centre?'

'It's a large centre which includes a rape crisis centre and women's refuge. It's run by women for women and operates from a feminist philosophy.'

'There's a need for that in Bellbird Bay?' Somehow Ali had imagined it was a Brigadoon sort of place, insulated from crime and violence.

'Oh, yes. We're not unique in that regard. We haven't escaped the worst of human nature. You'll rarely see the other side of the town, but it's there, hidden, only to rear its ugly head if good people are prepared to do nothing.'

'But...'

'Everything okay, ladies? Good morning, Grace.' A pretty, dark-haired woman stopped by their table.

'Lovely as usual, thanks, Cleo. Ali, this is Cleo who manages the café. Cleo, this is Ali. She's Adam Holland's sister.'

'Welcome to Bellbird Bay, Ali. I can see the resemblance to your brother. We're very lucky to have a famous author living in our little town. Are you visiting or have you moved here?'

'Visiting for a few months.' As she spoke, Ali realised how pleasant it would be to live here, to become part of this friendly community, to forget all the vying for position, the backbiting, the insults and innuendo she'd been subjected to. It was only here in Bellbird Bay, far from the life she'd grown accustomed to, had taken for granted – even accepted as the norm – that she realised how toxic it had become.

'Well, I hope you enjoy your time here. It's a good place to find peace.'

Ali gazed after Cleo as the woman made her way back to the kitchen. *How did she know?*

'She didn't read your mind, if that's what you're thinking,' Grace chuckled. 'Ruby Sullivan's the only one in Bellbird Bay who can do that, and you'll probably bump into her sooner or later. Cleo was probably talking about herself. She and her daughter came here to make a new life after she lost her husband. And she did. She's made a success of this café, now helps Bev with the weddings, and is in a relationship with Will Rankin, one of our local heroes.'

Ruby Sullivan, where had Ali heard that name?

'She's right about Bellbird Bay, you know,' Grace continued. 'There's something about the place, something in the air.' She paused and shrugged. 'Sorry, I sound fanciful, but it's something I discovered. I know Libby did, too, and I'm guessing your brother…?'

'Mmm.' Ali didn't put much store in such things, but she seemed to recall something Adam had said… or was it Libby? Something about magic and good things happening. Well, she could certainly do with something good happening to her. Then she remembered where she had heard the name before. 'Ruby Sullivan, isn't she the woman who bakes these delicious brownies?' Ali asked to change the subject. She took a bite of the sweet confection which melted in her mouth. 'Yum, they are good.'

'Yes, Ruby bakes the amazing cakes Cleo serves here, but she also has another… talent, I guess you might call it – or gift.'

Ali raised one eyebrow.

'Oh, she's an old woman, some say she's a witch, but she does have this habit of making disconcerting statements. It's as if she can see right into a person, know what they're thinking… and she offers what some consider to be predictions.'

'They used to burn witches.' Ali didn't know what made her say this, but the thought of this Ruby Sullivan made her feel uncomfortable. Even though she didn't believe in such things, she decided to keep out of the woman's way.

Ten

It was only a week before Christmas, and *Bay Books* was filled with customers all intent on finding just the right book to give their friends or family on the big day. There was a festive atmosphere in the shop, helped along by the sound of Christmas carols playing softly in the background – something Neil had persuaded his dad to agree to.

Neil was passing over a book for gift wrapping to one of the students who'd been employed in the lead up to Christmas, when he noticed the woman browsing in the children's section. He felt a prickle of pleasure. It was the same woman he'd seen with Adam Holland in the surf club soon after he arrived in Bellbird Bay.

Surprisingly in such a small town, this was the first time he'd seen her since then. Each time he'd ventured out – to the beach, *The Bay Café*, the art gallery – he'd kept an eye out, hoping they'd bump into each other. But he'd had no luck, not even among the crowds at the lighting of the Christmas tree – a large Norfolk pine on the esplanade – a few weeks earlier.

He was wondering how he could find a moment to approach her when Bronte bounded in. Given the proximity to Christmas, she'd agreed to help out in the bookshop each afternoon when her work with Owen Rankin finished.

Despite his initial hesitation, Neil had discovered that working with the young surfer seemed to fulfil some need in Bronte. She was a different girl from the sullen one who'd spent her time on her phone or her iPad. The few weeks spent helping develop designs for surfboards had transformed her into the lively, enthusiastic girl Neil remembered she used to be.

'What can I do, Dad?' she asked, joining him behind the counter.

Neil quickly glanced around, before saying, 'Can you take over here for a bit?'

'Sure.' Bronte gave him a puzzled look but took his place and smiled at the next customer in line. 'How can I help you?' she asked, as Neil moved through the shop to where the woman was clearly having difficulty in making a decision.

He took a deep breath. 'Having a problem?'

*

Ali turned quickly, the breath leaving her body as she was swamped by an emotion she didn't understand. The man who'd spoken to her was tall, his thatch of grey hair indicating he was close to her own age. She hadn't seen him when she'd come to the shop with Adam on a previous visit to Bellbird Bay. A slight twitch at the corner of one eye revealed he was nervous. What did he have to be nervous about?

The silence which stretched between them was broken only by the sound of a Christmas carol playing in the background. Ali was vaguely aware of hearing a familiar rendition of *I'll be home for Christmas* before saying, 'I'm looking for a book for a six-year-old girl. I'm afraid I'm not familiar with what she might like.' She gestured to the shelf where she'd been searching fruitlessly. Having decided to purchase a book for Libby's granddaughter for Christmas, Ali now realised she knew next to nothing about Clancy's taste in reading, or about what might be appropriate for a girl of her age.

'Let me see if I can help. I'm Neil Simpson, by the way. Harry Simpson, my dad, owns the bookshop.'

'Ali Wells.' Ali didn't know why her hands suddenly felt clammy, and her heart was pounding. She hoped she wasn't going to faint.

As Neil's eyes started to move along the shelves, Ali took several deep breaths, managing to calm herself and regain her composure.

'How about one of these?' he asked, handing her *Charlotte's Web* and *Pippi Longstocking*.

'Oh, I remember these,' she exclaimed. 'What a good idea. Thanks so much. I doubt if I'd have found them myself. I'll take both of them.' She hoped Clancy would enjoy them as much as she had when she was a child. She remembered how she would hide away from the arguments between her parents and lose herself in the stories of other worlds.

She was carrying the books across to the counter, Neil following, when there was a crash and a loud scream. Immediately, several people in the shop sprang into action. Before Neil could reach his dad, the young girl behind the counter, the one who'd screamed, bent down to speak to the old man, one customer pulled out her phone, saying, 'I'll call an ambulance,' while another said, 'I'm a nurse, let me see him. Don't crowd around, give him air,' she said to several others who had stopped browsing the shelves to move closer.

Ali didn't know what to do. She couldn't just leave. She didn't want to get in the way. But she felt, somehow, involved. She reached into her bag for the bottle of water she always carried and handed it to Neil, who by this time was kneeling by his dad.

'Thanks,' he said, glancing up at her.

People began to move away and leave. Then Harry tried to sit up. 'I'm fine,' he said. 'I just need a moment.'

'You're not fine,' Neil said, a tremor in his voice. 'You need to go to hospital to be checked out.'

While the old man was still grumbling and trying to get to his feet, an ambulance pulled up outside the store and two paramedics rushed in. They cleared the shop, and Ali was left with only Neil, Harry, the young girl and the paramedics. She didn't know why she stayed. Maybe it was the idea she could be of some assistance, or maybe it was the link she felt to the man, Neil. She stood there, the two books in her hand, unable to move.

But when the paramedics began to check Harry out, to open his shirt and attach small sticky electrodes to his chest, Ali knew it was time to go. She placed the two books on the counter and slipped out quietly.

*

Neil couldn't believe how quickly things had changed. One minute he was heading to the counter to ring up two books for Ali Wells and trying to figure out how he could get her phone number or arrange to see her again, the next, his dad was lying on the floor, the sound of Christmas carols suddenly louder as the customers in the store fell silent.

He silently berated himself for giving into Harry's objections to seeking medical help before now. Surely this could have been avoided if Neil had insisted. But it was too late now. A customer claiming to be a nurse pushed in, took Harry's pulse and warned others away.

Neil accepted the bottle of water Ali handed him, her concern confirming to him she was someone he wanted to know better. But now wasn't the time.

Dad had to be okay. Neil saw Bronte's face, white with shock, a tear trickling down one cheek. 'Grandad,' she said, her voice barely audible.

'I'm fine.' Harry tried to rise.

'Stay where you are, Dad. You may have broken something.' The gash on his forehead worried Neil. Harry might be suffering from concussion. He unscrewed the water bottle then screwed the lid on again. Should he wait till the ambulance arrived? His knowledge of first aid was minimal, restricted to the playground mishaps of teenagers and the need to be aware of student allergies. But, even at school, there were others more capable than he to take care of such incidents.

It was a relief when the paramedics arrived with their equipment. They confirmed nothing appeared to be broken and set about testing Harry's heart.

'We'll take him into Emergency,' one of them said, seemingly satisfied Harry hadn't had a heart attack. 'Do you want to come with him in the ambulance?'

Neil looked at Bronte who was white and shaking. Ali had disappeared. 'I'll follow in my car,' he said. 'Bronte?'

'Can I come with you, Dad?'

'Of course. I'll need to lock up here first.' Neil went behind the counter on which the two books he'd chosen for Ali were lying. He closed the computer and collected the day's takings, before turning off the CD on which Elvis was still telling them he'd be home for Christmas.

By the time they arrived at the hospital, Harry was already in a bed and was looking a lot brighter.

'There's nothing wrong with me,' he objected. 'This is just a big fuss about nothing, and we're losing business. You should have stayed in the store, Neil. What happened to all the customers?'

'They'll be back, Dad. Don't worry about them. Right now, your health's more important.'

'Hrmph.' Harry leant back on the bank of pillows.

'We were worried about you, Grandad,' Bronte said. 'You gave us a fright, falling down like that.' Now he had regained the colour in his face, Bronte had cheered up somewhat.

It was a couple of hours later, and Neil and Bronte had downed two cups of surprisingly good hospital coffee, when they were allowed back in to see Harry.

'Hey, Dad.'

'Grandad.' Bronte rushed to Harry's bedside.

'I don't know what all the fuss is about,' Harry said. 'There's nothing wrong with me. Can't a man fall down without having to undergo an inquisition?'

'What did the doctor say?' Neil asked. Harry had been moved from the cubicle in Emergency to one of the wards. It didn't look as if he'd be going home any time soon.

'Some claptrap about more tests. I need to get back to the bookshop. It's our busiest time.'

'I can handle the shop, Dad.'

'And I'll help. Owen can do without me for a few days… however long it takes,' Bronte added.

Neil threw her a grateful look. 'So you can just concentrate on getting well, Dad, and on the doctors finding out what's wrong.'

'There's nothing wrong with me,' Harry repeated.

'We'd like to do a few more tests.' The man who entered the room was wearing blue scrubs and had a stethoscope around his neck. 'Make sure Harry is okay before we send him home.'

'Don't talk about me as if I'm not here,' Harry grumbled, but he appeared calmer in the presence of the doctor.

'What tests?' Neil asked, but the doctor didn't elaborate.

'It should only take a few days. You'll be home for Christmas, Harry,' the doctor said.

'Will Grandad be all right?' Bronte asked on the drive home. 'I got such a fright to see him lying there as if... He was so white and still.'

'I'm sure he will be. At his age, the doctors just need to be sure everything's okay. You heard what the doctor said. He'll be home for Christmas. We need to make sure it'll be a special day for him.'

'Right.' But Bronte didn't sound convinced. 'I'll call Owen,' she said. 'I'm sure he'll understand.'

Despite his reassurance to Bronte, Neil was worried about his dad. While glad Harry was finally getting the medical care he needed, Neil wondered what tests they were going to conduct, and what they'd discover. It seemed Harry's heart was strong enough, but there were so many other ailments which could have affected the old man.

Eleven

Back in her apartment, Ali found she couldn't settle. She tried to read the book on her Kindle, the one which had kept her awake for hours last night, but even it couldn't stem the fizz of excitement, the butterflies careering around in her stomach, which had begun in the bookshop.

Glad she had promised to have dinner with Adam and Libby that evening, Ali decided to take a warm bath. Surely spending time relaxing in the scented oils Libby had given her for her birthday would help calm her nerves. She was sure that was all it was. She was uptight from seeing the incident in the bookshop. It was nothing whatever to do with meeting the tall man whose eyes were a distinct shade of blue-green reminiscent of the ocean on a stormy day.

Stop, she told herself. She was acting like a teenager, though Ali had never acted like this as a teenager. She'd never behaved like this. Always the calm sensible one in any group of girls or women, her decision to major in Women's Studies had come as a surprise to those who didn't know her well, didn't know her history – her mother's history.

The bath water grew cold as she relived the afternoon.

After leaving the bookshop, Ali had hesitated outside, wishing there was something she could do to help. Through the window, she could see the paramedics doing their thing, Neil and the young girl – who must be an assistant – standing beside them. The girl was crying.

Realising there was nothing she could do, while feeling strangely reluctant to leave, Ali had gone into the nearby Bay Café *and ordered a coffee, taking a seat at one of the outside tables from where she had a clear view of what was happening at the bookshop. When her coffee arrived, she discovered she was trembling. It was the shock she told herself, the shock of seeing someone collapse right in front of her. But, deep down, she knew it was more than that. Before Harry Simpson collapsed, she had already received a shock.*

Meeting Neil Simpson had disturbed her more than she imagined. She was glad neither Adam nor Libby had been there to say, 'I told you so'. Was this what had happened to her brother when he met Libby, what happened to all those people she'd ridiculed in the past, what she'd assured them could never happen to her? She'd heard of the term coup de foudre, *but never imagined it happening to her. Ali shook her head. What was she thinking? Her brain was addled. Neil Simpson had helped her choose a couple of books for Clancy. Then his father had collapsed. It had been hot in the shop. There had been Christmas carols playing. Nothing else had happened.*

Ali had gulped her coffee, watching as the two paramedics helped the old man into the ambulance which was waiting at the kerb. Then, a few minutes later, Neil and the young girl appeared. He locked the door, and they disappeared in the direction of the car park. There had been nothing else to see; it was over. So why had she still been shaking like a jelly. It had taken another cup of coffee for the caffeine to help her recover her equilibrium.

Rising from the bath, Ali quickly dressed in a pair of beige pants and a blue tunic top, brushed her hair, and added a smidgeon of makeup, grimacing at her face in the mirror. Then she set off to make her way to the boardwalk, only stopping at a bottle shop on the esplanade to purchase a bottle of chardonnay. As she passed the now-closed bookshop, she glanced at it briefly, a tremor passing through her at the memory of what happened there.

'Hey Ali,' Adam greeted her. 'Good day?' He hugged her and gave her a kiss on the cheek. 'Libby will be through in a minute. Glass of wine? This looks like a good one.' He inspected the bottle she handed him.

'Thanks.' Wine was exactly what she needed. She'd been tempted to pour herself a drink and have it in the bath but managed to stifle the urge. Now she was glad she had refrained.

'A strange thing happened to me today,' Ali said, when they were seated around the table enjoying a chicken casserole.

Both Adam and Libby stopped eating and gazed at her.

'I was in *Bay Books* choosing a gift for Clancy when the owner collapsed.'

'Oh, no! Harry's such a nice man,' Libby said. 'Was he badly injured?'

'I don't know. Someone called an ambulance, and it took him off to hospital.'

'I should call in at the bookshop tomorrow to ask about him,' Adam said. 'I wonder who'll look after it till he's well again.'

'There was another man there – he said he was his son – and a young girl.' There had also been several younger girls, but it had seemed to Ali they were only there to gift wrap books for customers.

'I didn't know he had a son. More wine?' Adam picked up the bottle of chardonnay.

'I seem to recall someone mentioning it,' Libby said, holding out her glass. 'He's a school principal… in Brisbane, I think. He must be here for Christmas. I'm glad he was with Harry.'

'Ali?' Adam gestured towards her with the bottle.

'Thanks,' she said. But she was distracted by the conversation, by this added insight into Neil Simpson. A school principal? He seemed too attractive to be a school principal. She'd always felt people who took on that position were… well, not like him.

'I do hope he'll be all right,' Libby said. 'It's such a lovely bookshop and Bellbird Bay needs it. Your brother's books sell well there,' she said to Ali.

'I'm sure they sell well everywhere,' Ali said. She grinned across the table at Adam, relieved the conversation had moved on from Neil Simpson.

'What did you get for Clancy?' Libby asked.

'I didn't. I had just chosen two books – *Charlotte's Web* and *Pippi Longstocking* – when the incident happened. I had to leave them on the counter. I guess I'll go back for them when they open again. I hope they manage to open before Christmas.' And she could meet Neil Simpson again and discover if she experienced another jolt of whatever it had been. She felt herself blushing.

'Are you too hot?' Libby asked, solicitously.

'No, I'm fine. Just a hot flush,' Ali said, in an attempt to explain the sudden reddening of her cheeks, embarrassed lest Libby and Adam should suspect the real reason.

'I'm sure Harry's son will keep the shop open,' Adam said. 'It must be a busy time for them, and a lot of people would be disappointed if they weren't able to get their last-minute Christmas gifts.'

'Talking of Christmas,' Libby said. 'We plan to have it here. Emma, Nick and Clancy will be coming for breakfast. We can spend the morning here opening presents, listening to carols, have a turkey lunch, then go to the beach. It was fun there last year with Grace and her extended family.' She gave Adam a secret smile, making Ali feel uncomfortable.

'Sounds good,' Ali said, trying to hide the embarrassment she always felt at seeing such signs of affection. For the first time, she felt envious of their obvious love for each other, a love which excluded everyone outside their bubble of happiness.

But, in an instant, the moment had passed, and Libby was asking Ali how she was enjoying living in Bellbird Bay and if she'd heard any more from the university.

Answering that she was loving the ambiance of the small town, Ali frowned at the second part of Libby's question. Since leaving Perth, there had been no communication from either Richard or the university HR department. In itself, it wasn't unusual. At this time of year, after all the results were in, the university shut down till mid-January when it geared up again for the new academic year. But Libby's question made Ali wonder if there would still be a place for her when classes started again. Her leave didn't finish till almost Easter, but she'd need to have some indication before that. The memory of Richard's suggestion of early retirement came back in full force. She wasn't ready to retire... not yet. But... could she go back into the position she'd left, face everyone again, knowing how they'd treated her?

*

Ali waited two days before returning to the bookshop. She pushed open the door to hear the Christmas carols were being played much louder than before, the sounds of *Jingle Bells* blaring through the shop which was filled with happy chatter. There were three young people behind the counter attending to customers – the girl she'd seen before, along with another blonde girl and a dark-haired young man. The same group of younger girls as before were busy gift-wrapping books for customers. There was no sign of Neil Simpson.

Stifling the surge of disappointment, Ali waited in line at the counter. When it was her turn, the young girl she remembered from her last visit produced her books from a shelf behind her. 'Dad said you'd be back for them,' she said.

Dad? This must be Neil's daughter. She was around the same age as Chelsea. For a moment, Ali compared the two girls, but there was no comparison. After the incident in Perth, Chelsea had become withdrawn, unwilling to mix with strangers. This girl, while there was a shadow in her eyes, was full of confidence and enthusiasm for her job.

'I was here when the owner collapsed,' she said. 'How is he?'

'Grandad is getting along well. He's been having various tests and is still in hospital. Dad's visiting him right now. He should be home for Christmas. Nate and Han are helping out.' She nodded to where the two other young people were busy with customers.

'I'm glad. I hope you have a good Christmas,' Ali said, before turning to leave.

Twelve

Neil waited impatiently for Doctor Young to come to the point. His dad was looking better every day, eager to return home and get back to the bookshop, but he still hadn't received the all clear from the medical staff.

Today, the doctor in charge of Harry's case had asked for a meeting with Neil, and after popping in to see his dad, Neil was now sitting in a side room to the ward listening while the doctor gave a rundown of the tests they'd conducted on Harry.

Neil wished he'd get on with it, so he could get back to the shop. He felt an obligation to his dad to ensure all was well there. When they heard about Harry's mishap, two of Bronte's new friends offered to help. Nate McNeil, who normally served behind the bar in the surf club – Neil recalled seeing him there – and Hannah Johansen, a teacher on school holidays. They were housemates of Owen Rankin, the young man Bronte was working with. Nate and Hannah – or Han as Bronte called her – seemed like a nice pair of youngsters, responsible and eager to be of help. They were cheerful to have around, and the customers liked them. But Neil had promised his dad he'd take care of the shop while he was in hospital, so didn't want to leave the young people in charge for too long.

Doctor Young cleared his throat. 'It appears your father is suffering from Parkinson's disease.'

Neil stared at him. This diagnosis had never occurred to him, though perhaps it should have, given his dad's tremor and occasional unsteadiness. 'What does it mean?' he asked. He knew very little about the disease.

The doctor leant his elbows on the desk and steepled his hands before speaking again. 'We know that, although people with Parkinson's share symptoms, each person's experience of the condition and response to treatment is different. In your father's case, it appears the disease has progressed to what we call mid-stage. There are various therapies we can pursue, however, you – and he – need to understand as it progresses your father will find significant decreases in his movement and reaction times. If he lives alone, he will eventually find many daily tasks are impossible, and it can be dangerous for him.'

Neil felt his world crash down around him. 'How soon?' he asked, a tremor in his voice.

'We calculate Harry is currently at stage three, what we consider to be a turning point in the disease. He will notice a distinct deterioration when he reaches stages four and five and will require more care. Dementia is also common in these later stages.'

'And the time frame?' Neil held his breath.

'It's difficult to say. Not everyone progresses to the later stages, but in your father's case…' He shook his head. 'The disease itself isn't fatal. He could live with it for years. But injuries that occur because of a fall or problems associated with dementia can be. I'm sorry to be the bearer of bad news.'

'Thanks,' Neil said, not knowing what he was thanking him for and feeling as if he'd been hit by a truck. If… *when* Harry could no longer live alone, no longer go to the bookshop every day, what would he do – what would Neil do?

'Does Dad know?'

'I told him earlier this morning. I must say, he took it pretty well. It's not an easy thing to accept.'

'He runs a bookshop.' Neil was having trouble coming to grips with what he had just heard.

'I know. Everyone in Bellbird Bay loves *Bay Books*… but I'm afraid the day will come – sooner or later – when Harry will be forced to use a walking frame to get around. It won't be easy for him to continue doing what he does now.' His lips turned down. 'I'm sorry,' he repeated.

'When can he go home?'

'We'll be discharging him today. The hospital pharmacy is preparing medications for him to take home and we can arrange for physiotherapy which should improve his movement. It's important he remains active and isn't allowed to fall into depression. We don't recommend surgery in his case.'

'Right.' The good news was his dad was coming home. Neil decided to focus on that and think about the rest later... much later. 'Is that it?' he asked.

'For now. You may want to speak to us again, or to your GP and develop a care plan. Does your dad live alone?'

Neil nodded.

'Then you may want to consider a move to somewhere he can receive more care.'

Neil flinched at the thought of trying to persuade Harry to leave the family home. But he knew the doctor was right. There was no way he could manage to live alone as his disease progressed, not even with Joan popping in every day. He'd need more care than she could provide. Even if they could arrange for someone to come to help him shower and dress, it was a big house to take care of. Then there was the bookshop.

When Neil left the doctor, he was in despair. But he forced himself to put a smile on his face before he saw his dad again.

'He told you?' Harry asked, as soon as Neil entered the room.

Neil nodded.

'He's full of hot air,' Harry said. 'I feel fine. It was just a little fall. But at least they're letting me go home.'

'Dad, you need to pay attention to what Doctor Young said. You have a disease that's likely to worsen. You could...'

'Don't fuss,' Harry interrupted. 'I'm fine now. What's happening with the bookshop? Who's minding it while you're here?'

'Bronte and two of her new friends – Nate and Hannah. But I'll go back once we get you home and settled.'

'I can come with you.'

'I don't think that's a good idea, Dad. The doctor said...'

'Pooh! It's *my* bookshop and it's the week before Christmas.'

'Not today,' Neil said in a firmer voice. 'Let's discuss it again tomorrow.'

'Hmph.'

But Neil could see his dad was weakening.

It took some time for the hospital to process all the paperwork required before Harry was allowed to leave, but they were finally on their way home. At Harry's insistence, they made a detour along the esplanade, driving slowly past *Bay Books* to enable Harry to see the bookshop was busy, and everything appeared to be going well.

'I suppose they know what they're doing,' he grumbled. 'I know Nate and Hannah. They're good kids, and Bronte knows the ropes.'

'They'll be fine, Dad. I'll go in this afternoon, if I can trust you to behave at home.'

Harry only chuckled, but Neil could see his dad was tired and still hadn't regained his full strength. He doubted he'd make it back into work before Christmas.

Thirteen

On Christmas morning, Ali awoke early. She'd given in to Adam and Libby's pleas for her to spend the night before Christmas at their home, and now was glad she had. Instead of wakening in her quiet apartment, even before she opened her eyes, she could hear Christmas carols being played and smell the aroma of freshly ground coffee.

While she was still dressing, there was a loud knocking at the front door, and she heard a childish voice yelling, 'Merry Christmas, Grandma! Guess what Santa brought me?'

When she hurried into the kitchen, Ali was greeted by the whole family. Adam was organising coffee, Libby was making pancakes, and Emma and Nick were watching Clancy attempt to attach a bunch of artificial holly to Milo's collar while the dog stood patiently. Her eyes filled with tears at this picture of family harmony. It was only a year since she'd felt so alone after her mother died. Then she'd been reunited with Adam, been introduced to Libby and met Libby's daughter, her daughter's partner and her granddaughter. Now she was part of this happy family.

Over breakfast on the deck, they reminisced about the surf lifesaving fundraiser the previous day. It was the second time Adam had taken part in the annual swim and surfing event and they all laughed as he recalled his first attempt, the previous year. 'I did better this time,' he said. 'I knew what to expect.'

'Can we open the presents now?' Clancy hopped up and down in excitement. 'You've all finished eating.'

'I guess we shouldn't keep you waiting any longer,' Libby said. 'We can clear up later. Presents first.'

By the time all the presents had been opened, the living room floor was strewn with paper. Clancy was thrilled with the books Ali had chosen, and with the Barbie doll and paint set Libby and Adam had given her.

'There is one more gift,' Adam said, a twinkle in his eye.

Clancy gazed at him in surprise.

'Wait here.' He left the room. When he returned, he was carrying a tiny wriggling creature. 'This is for you, Clancy,' he said, as the little girl's eyes grew bigger and bigger.

'For me?' she asked as if she couldn't believe it.

'Grandma and I know how much you wanted a puppy of your own now you're not living with us and Milo,' he said, handing the spaniel pup to her.

'What's his name?'

'He's a she and she doesn't have a name yet. You can choose her name.'

Clancy rubbed her nose in the dog's fur, giggling as the tiny creature tried to lick her face. 'I'm going to call her Holly,' she said, 'because I got her on Christmas day.'

'What a good idea,' Libby said.

While Emma and Nick took Clancy, Milo and Holly to the beach, Ali helped Libby clear up the breakfast dishes. Adam folded the discarded Christmas wrapping paper and fired up the Weber barbecue ready to cook the turkey.

Ali was helping prepare the salads for lunch when Adam appeared in the kitchen. 'I heard Harry Simpson is home again,' he said. 'Will told me at the fundraiser yesterday. It seems young Owen's housemates were co-opted to help out at the bookshop with Harry's granddaughter, who's a friend of Owen's.'

'Is he back in the shop?' Libby asked.

'Will said not. I guess he's still recovering.'

'Oh, I hope there's nothing seriously wrong,' Libby said. 'Bellbird Bay needs its bookshop, and Harry Simpson *is Bay Books*.'

Adam murmured agreement.

Ali wondered again about Neil Simpson, the man she'd met in

Bay Books. She'd been disappointed when there was no sign of him when she returned to pick up the books, and she'd had no excuse to make another trip there. Not that she wanted an excuse. She wasn't interested in him, was she?

If Sally had been here, Ali could have shared her feelings with her, discussed the stupidity of giving in to her instant reaction, to even consider if what she'd felt was a genuine emotion and not the result of some animal instinct. But Sally was in Perth, enjoying Christmas with her family, and Ali was here in Bellbird Bay.

'Something the matter, Ali?' Libby asked.

'No.' Ali forced a neutral expression onto her face. 'I was just trying to picture a town without a bookshop.'

'Unimaginable,' Adam said.

Further conversation was rendered impossible by the arrival of the rest of the family, back from the beach. Emma and Nick dropped into chairs by the kitchen table, and Clancy danced around the room, the two excited dogs getting under everyone's feet.

Lunch was a jolly affair. They ate on the deck, the two dogs lying under the table to be surreptitiously fed titbits by Clancy when she thought the adults weren't watching. Since it was a special day, no one objected but Ali knew everything would go back to normal when Christmas was over.

After lunch, everyone, including Clancy and the dogs, settled down for a nap, before heading back to the beach.

*

In the house two streets back from the esplanade, Christmas day was a more sedate affair. Neil and Bronte had stocked up on prawns and salmon from the fisherman's market, planning a simple seafood feast. For dessert, Bronte had offered to make a pavlova, saying she'd sometimes made one at home.

After a breakfast of scrambled eggs and bacon, the three unwrapped the gifts they'd bought for each other. Bronte was delighted with the new iPhone Neil had selected, and he grinned with surprise when he unwrapped her gift to him of a Fitbit. 'So you can check your 10,000 steps, Dad,' she told him. Neil and Bronte had combined to buy Harry an iPad, and he had given them both a package of books.

Lunch was a success, during which they all managed to put Harry's diagnosis to the back of their minds and focus on the celebration. To Bronte's delight, Harry declared the pavlova was as good as the one her grandmother used to make.

Despite his insisting he was fully recovered from his collapse, Harry became tired after lunch and agreed to take a rest. Bronte disappeared to catch up with her new friends, and Neil settled down to read one of his new books – *Picture you Dead* by Peter James, an author he wasn't familiar with.

But after a while, he became tired of reading, even the crime thriller failing to hold his attention. He popped his head into the bedroom to see his dad's eyes open. 'Awake, Dad?'

'Almost. Might stay here for a bit.'

'I think I'll take a walk to the beach, try out my new Fitbit. Okay with you?'

'No worries. When I get up, I'll set up the new device the two of you gave me. It'll keep me busy for a bit.'

'I won't be long.'

Neil headed for the esplanade and stepped down onto the beach, deciding to walk up in the direction of the headland. On the way, he glanced up at the row of beach shacks which lined the boardwalk, wondering what it would be like to live there, to waken to the sound and sight of the ocean every morning. It would be very different from his view of the Brisbane River. He suddenly felt dissatisfied with the life he'd enjoyed for the past twenty years. Why was he living in the city when he could have been enjoying a more relaxed pace of life here in Bellbird Bay? Was it only his present challenges at the school affecting his mood, or was it something else?

His mind went to the woman he'd met in *Bay Books*, the one he'd been helping when his dad collapsed. She'd said her name was Ali, Ali Wells, and she was buying a book for a six-year-old. From her lack of knowledge about what the girl might like, he'd guessed it wasn't for a granddaughter. She'd intrigued him, but Harry had collapsed and everything else became unimportant, other than the need to get him to hospital.

Neil had hoped to see her again when she came to collect the books she'd chosen, but she must have come when he was at the hospital, because they'd gone when he checked the shelf. Bellbird Bay was a small town, he reminded himself. He was bound to bump into her again. And next time, there would be no emergency; he'd be able to get her number, discover if she lived here or was visiting. Maybe she even lived in Brisbane, and they could…

Neil was walking along in the shallow water at the edge of the ocean. Lost in a dream, he was imagining all sorts of scenarios in which they met again, arranged to have dinner, discovered they lived close to each other in the city, when he was drenched by what felt like a huge wave. Looking up, he saw a small girl and two dogs, one large, one small. The girl's blonde curls were peeking out from below a sunhat. 'Sorry,' she said.

Then he heard a voice calling, 'Clancy!' and saw Ali Wells running towards him.

Fourteen

At first, Ali didn't recognise the man who had been drenched by Clancy playing with the dogs in the shallow water, then he spoke.

'It's Ali, isn't it? Ali Wells. We met in *Bay Books* just before my dad collapsed.'

'Of course. I'm sorry about…' She gestured to his soaked shorts.

'It's nothing.'

'You're Neil Simpson. How is your dad?' If she'd known she'd meet Neil Simpson on the beach, Ali would have taken more care with her appearance. She was conscious of the old shorts and faded tee-shirt she'd donned after lunch when the trip to the beach was mooted. Then she mentally chastised herself for such vain thoughts. What did it matter what she looked like? She'd never been one to care much for appearances.

'He's recovering slowly, but…' He hesitated as if unwilling to disclose more information. 'You picked up the books?'

'Yes.' Ali pushed a strand of hair out of her eyes. 'Thanks. Clancy loves them.' She gestured to where the small girl was playing with the dogs.

'Your…?'

'She's the granddaughter of my brother's partner.'

'Right.'

'Merry Christmas.'

'Merry Christmas to you, too.'

They stood staring at each other, as if unsure what to say next.

'Ali, you said you were going to have a swim with me.' The little girl appeared between them.

'I did.' Ali looked from Clancy to Neil and back again. There was no way she was going to strip off and expose her tatty old swimsuit and middle-aged body to his eyes. 'In a few minutes, Clancy,' she said, the fluttering in her stomach telling her the jolt she'd felt when she last met Neil hadn't been due to the heat or noise in the bookshop.

'I mustn't keep you.' But Neil still didn't move.

Ali felt as if the next few moments lasted for hours. Time stood still. Clancy was tugging her arm, but she couldn't move.

'I… I wonder if we could meet sometime… for coffee?' Neil asked at last.

'I guess so.' Why couldn't she sound more polite? But she didn't want to sound too eager.

'Can you let me have your number?' Neil took out his phone.

Ali reeled off her number, and he tapped it into his phone. 'I'll be in touch,' he said, and with a grin he was off, striding along the beach away from them.

'Ali!' Clancy said again. 'You promised.'

Now Neil had gone, Ali ran up the beach to where the others were playing a game of beach cricket and arguing over the rules. Fortunately, it appeared they'd been too engrossed in their game to notice what was happening with her and Clancy. She slipped out of her shorts and tee-shirt and ran back down to the edge of the water with Clancy to where the dogs were still frolicking in the waves, Holly following Milo's example.

But as Ali joined Clancy in the water, the feeling of exhilaration which filled her was unlike any she'd experienced before. It was lucky the little girl was a capable swimmer due to swim lessons at school and a year with Nippers, and didn't require Ali's assistance, because Ali's mind was far away. It was with the man who'd invited her for coffee, who'd entered her number into his phone as if it was the most natural thing in the world.

'Everything all right, Ali?' Adam asked, when the game of cricket was over, and Ali and Clancy had re-joined the group. The dogs, having exhausted themselves, were lying on the sand beside them.

'Of course. Why do you ask?'

'Who was that we saw you talking with?' Libby asked.

Damn! Ali had thought them too busy to notice. 'Neil Simpson. Clancy and the dogs managed to send water all over him.'

'Harry's son?' Adam asked. 'Why didn't you introduce us? I'd like to have met him.'

'I thought you went into the shop to ask after Harry. Didn't you meet him then?' Libby asked.

'No, only the granddaughter.' Adam frowned. 'She didn't know very much, only that her grandad was still in hospital. It was Will who told me he was home.'

'Maybe if you go in again, you can meet him and get more news,' Libby suggested. 'I expect the bookshop will be open again after the holiday, and maybe Harry will be back by then, too.'

'Good idea,' Adam said. 'Now, who's ready to go home and have some Christmas pudding with ice cream?'

'Me!' Clancy yelled, to everyone's amusement, as they began to pack up ready to return to the house.

*

What a stroke of luck, Neil thought, as the distance between him and Ali lengthened. He resisted the temptation to look back, to see her in her swimsuit, aware she might feel self-conscious. It had been impossible to stifle the thrill of seeing her again. Even dressed as she was in what were clearly old clothes, Ali Wells was an attractive woman. She still managed to look elegant in the scruffy beach outfit, with her hair flying in the breeze.

And now he had her number, and she'd agreed to have coffee with him.

It was a long time since Neil had felt such a strong attraction to a woman. In recent years, the job had kept him fully occupied during the week and by the weekend he'd been too tired to do much in the way of socialising. There had been the parents, the single mothers who saw him as fair game, whose advances he managed to brush off politely, knowing to give in to one would bring forth a shower of abuse from the others. It was easier to remain single and alone.

Here in Bellbird Bay, it was as if he had a new lease of life. The sight of the woman he now knew was Ali Wells in the surf club had reawakened emotions which had been lying dormant. He couldn't wait to get to know her better and wondered what her connection to Adam Holland might be. Was he the brother she referred to? If so, given she had a different surname was she – or had she been – married? He couldn't wait to set a date to meet her for coffee.

Fifteen

Bay Books was due to re-open for business with the usual Boxing Day sale, and Harry was champing at the bit to get back in harness. Nothing Neil could say would dissuade him and, eventually, he decided it might be worse for his dad's health to insist he stay away from his beloved bookshop. But he did manage to get him to agree to return home at lunchtime.

Bronte made things easier by arranging to help out full-time for a few weeks, too, saying Owen understood. The secret smile as she said it reminded Neil of his twenty-year-old self and his first love, and he wished life and love was still as simple and straightforward as it had seemed back then. Though, he remembered, even then, life hadn't been without its angst. He had no desire to be twenty again.

'When are we going to meet this local hero, this paragon of the surfing community?' he asked at breakfast.

Bronte blushed. 'Da…aad!'

'Don't tease the lass,' Harry said, the knowledge he was going back to work putting a spring in his step and a smile on his face. Looking at his dad's smiling face, the healthy colour in his cheeks, Neil was tempted to discount the doctor's diagnosis. But he knew the disease was still there, lurking, until it reared its ugly head again.

'Owen said he might drop into the bookshop when he finishes today,' Bronte said, blushing again. 'But no interrogation or smart remarks, Dad.'

'Have I ever?' Neil realised he'd never met any of Bronte's boyfriends because she'd been living with her mother.

'There's always a first time. Just don't embarrass me, Dad.'

'Promise.'

'Time to go.' Harry pushed back his chair. 'I'll get my sandals on while you two pack the dishwasher.' He disappeared in the direction of his bedroom.

'You heard the man,' Neil said to Bronte, gathering up some of the dishes.

Once at the bookshop, Harry was quick to take over the reins. He walked around inspecting the displays, tweaking a few books here and there and nodding to himself.

Neil and Bronte held their breath till he said, 'Seems you did a good job when I was laid up, but don't think you can get rid of me like that again.' He chuckled.

Neil felt a pang, at the thought of the future awaiting his dad and hoped it was some time away. He knew they needed to prepare for it. But not today.

Nate and Hannah bounced in a few minutes before opening time to greet Harry with wide grins. 'Great to see you back, Mr Simpson,' Nate said. 'Hope you had a good Christmas.'

'Pretty good, thanks, son,' Harry replied. 'I trust you two know what you're doing.'

Neil hid a smile, knowing how it was only with the help of the three youngsters that he'd been able to keep the bookshop going while Harry was in hospital.

'We're good, Mr Simpson,' Hannah replied, as Bronte went to open the door to a flood of early customers, all intent on securing a bargain.

It was lunchtime before the rush let up, and Neil could see his dad was beginning to wilt. 'How about I drive you home, Dad? I can fix a bite of lunch before I come back.'

Harry opened his mouth to protest, then seemed to think better of it. 'Thanks, son. Good of you.'

'Want me to bring back anything?' Neil asked the three young people.

'No need, Dad. We can get something from *The Bay Café* and take turns to eat out the back,' Bronte replied.

'If you're sure?'

They all nodded in agreement.

Back at the house, Harry dropped into a chair at the kitchen table. Now he was home, it was clear how much the morning had taken out of him. 'No need to make much for me, Neil. I'm not very hungry. I might have overreached myself this morning.'

Neil scrutinised his dad, noting he looked paler than he had earlier. 'I'll just put together a few of the leftovers from yesterday,' he said. 'Then you might want to take it easy for the rest of the day.'

'I think you may be right, son, but it was good to get back to the old place. I'll be back to my usual in a few days.'

Neil frowned and bit his lip. He hoped his dad was right. The alternative didn't bear thinking about.

After a lunch of leftovers washed down with a ginger beer, Harry headed off for a rest, and Neil drove back to the bookshop.

The afternoon proved to be just as busy as the morning, and Neil was tired, too, when five o'clock came and it was time to close up for the day. 'See you tomorrow, guys,' he was saying to Hannah and Nate, when another young man, his face tanned from time spent in the sun, his bleached blond hair tied up in a bun on top of his head and wearing a pair of board shorts and a tee-shirt with the slogan, *Bay Surf School*, appeared in the doorway. His feet were bare.

Neil was about to tell him they were closed, when Bronte rushed out from behind the counter. 'Owen!' she said, grinning happily, 'You came!' So, this was the boy Bronte was so enamoured with, the one who designed and made surfboards.

'Dad, this is Owen. Owen, my dad,' Bronte said, unnecessarily.

'Good to meet you, Mr Simpson. Bronte has told me a lot about you.'

'Neil,' Neil said automatically. Mr Simpson made him feel he was back in the school. 'Good to meet you, too.'

Before he could say any more, Bronte clutched Owen's hand. 'There's a party on tonight, Dad. Okay if I go straight to these guys' place and change there? I brought my gear with me.'

'Fine by me. You know you don't need to ask my permission, Bronte,' Neil said, wondering how he'd managed to miss her carrying an extra bag into the car that morning. He supposed he'd been too concerned with his dad to notice. He saw Owen give her a nudge.

'And I might stay over and come straight here in the morning. So you don't need to wait up for me.' She dropped her eyes.

'No problem.' Neil wondered if this was a common occurrence in Brisbane, and if so, how Pippa handled it. But he wasn't about to start playing the heavy father. Bronte was twenty. She could be living on her own, answerable to no one. He supposed he should feel grateful she consulted him about her movements.

The bookshop seemed particularly empty once the young people had left. As he set about counting the takings, then turning off the lights and locking up, Neil reflected on Bronte's new friends. They were a credit to the local high school. Although Neil loved *Beckwith Boys' College*, he sometimes wondered about the wisdom of single sex schools – especially for boys. But when he'd suggested going co-ed, he'd been outvoted by the school board – the same board which was now in trouble with the law for their dirty-dealing.

Before driving home, there was one more thing he wanted to do. Ali Wells' image floated behind his eyes as he picked up his phone.

Sixteen

It had been a busy two days for Ali, most of them spent with Adam, Libby and Libby's family, the trip on Nick's boat on Boxing Day an unexpected treat. The call from Neil Simpson just as she arrived home had rounded it off nicely.

Now Christmas was over, and the prospect of meeting Neil for coffee was making her feel sick. It was a relief when her phone rang, and she saw Sally's number on the screen.

'Happy Christmas! Sorry I couldn't catch up with you before now. Families!' Sally said, bubbling with usual enthusiasm.

'Happy Christmas. I was tied up with family, too.' Ali couldn't believe the pleasure it gave her to be able to say that.

'How was it?'

'Pretty good. You?'

'Boring as usual. I missed having you around to complain to.'

Ali chuckled. When she was in Perth, the two had always managed to catch up sometime, either on Christmas Day or, more typically, on Boxing Day, when Sally would bemoan the claustrophobic nature of her extended Italian family who all got together at Christmas for a big celebration. Having celebrated Christmas alone with her mother, Ali had always envied her friend, while pretending to sympathise.

'So, you and your brother's new family – tell me about them.'

'Nothing much to tell. There's Libby, who I already told you about, her daughter, Emma, granddaughter, Clancy, and Emma's partner, Nick. He owns a boatyard, and we went sailing yesterday.'

'Wow! Wish I'd gone sailing instead of listening to the olds wondering why I hadn't found a man yet. I swear they'll drive me to drink.'

Ali laughed.

'And how are you enjoying Bellbird Bay?'

'It's good. Quiet after Perth. I've been learning to relax.'

'What's your new place like? Have you room for a guest? I'm taking a couple of weeks off in January and thought I might visit you there. I can always write up a feature on holidaying in Queensland and use the trip as a tax break. What do you say?'

Ali only hesitated for a moment. The thought of having her old friend for company, even if only for two weeks, gave her a buzz. It would be good to have someone who understood her, to be able to share her unexpected feelings about Neil Simpson, to offer advice. 'I'd love you to come, and yes, I do have a spare room. When do you plan to be here?'

'It depends on when I can get a flight. I'll see what goss I can pick up about the uni before I leave town, though it's been pretty quiet.'

'Well, let me know as soon as you can.'

'Will do.'There was a pause. 'Has something happened? You sound different,' Sally said, seeming to pick up on Ali's supressed excitement.

'Not really. I… I'm just about to go out for coffee.' She bit her lip. Sally knew her so well. Ali should have known she'd guess something was up.

'Coffee? As in meeting a man for coffee?'

'Mmm.'

'It's clearly high time I came to visit to find out what you're up to. Relaxing, quiet, my foot. Sounds as if cupid may finally have caught up with Alison Wells.'

'Don't be stupid,' Ali laughed. But, as she ended the call, she thought her friend might possibly be right.

It was almost time to leave. Ali checked herself in the mirror, satisfied the blue and white striped sundress didn't make her upper arms look fat. She slipped on a pair of white sandals, added a touch of lipstick and carefully brushed her hair. She wasn't sure why she was taking so much trouble. Neil Simpson had seen her in her old daggy clothes on the beach. But, if the butterflies in her stomach were to be believed, this coffee might be the start of something special.

The Bay Café looked different this morning. It appeared to be bathed in a radiance which had nothing to do with the sun shining down on it. Neil was seated at one of the bleached wooden tables outside the café, perhaps even the same one at which Ali had sat watching him close the bookshop. It seemed so long ago.

He rose as she approached. 'Good morning. Good to see you.'

Ali smiled and took a seat. 'Morning. Good to see you, too,' she said, feeling awkward.

A waitress appeared immediately, giving Ali only a moment to take in Neil's crisp blue shirt, cleanly-shaven face, the dark hair with only a hint of grey. She was enveloped in a warm glow. 'Can I take your order?'

'What would you like?' Neil asked.

'Cappuccino, please.'

'A cappuccino and a short black – and two of your lovely brownies,' Neil told the waitress, before turning his attention back to Ali. 'I hope you have a sweet tooth,' he said.

'Yes, I... Thanks.'

'Thanks for coming. You must think this a bit odd. I don't normally invite strangers for coffee, but...' he looked down at his hands which were clasped on the table, '...I wanted to get to know you better. At the bookshop...' he pushed a hand through his hair, '... Dad...'

'How is your dad?'

'He's making progress.' Neil hesitated, then added, 'He's been diagnosed with Parkinson's.'

'Oh, I'm sorry.' Ali didn't know much about the disease other than it could cause tremors and falls, and it was what Michael J Fox suffered from. 'Is it...'

'It's not terminal in itself, but it's doubtful if he'll be able to continue to manage in the bookshop in the long term. I guess the time would have come sooner or later. He's not getting any younger. But it was a shock.'

'Oh, I'm sorry,' Ali repeated. 'What will happen to the bookshop?'

'Dunno.' Neil pushed a hand through his hair again. 'But I didn't invite you here to bore you with my family's woes. Tell me about you. Do you live in Bellbird Bay or are you visiting?'

'I'm here for a few months. I live in Perth and I'm taking long service leave.' Her heart plummeted at the reminder of what might await her back in Perth. 'My brother lives here.'

'Adam Holland.'

'How did you know?'

'I saw you with him in the surf club. You look alike. I'm a big fan of his writing.'

'Oh!' It was a new experience for Ali to be identified as Adam's sister. Until recently, she had been unable to claim him as her brother, and in Perth no one knew of her connection to the famous author.

'What do you do in Perth?'

'I'm at the university.' *But for how much longer?* 'I lecture in Women's Studies.' Ali watched Neil carefully for his reaction. In her experience, many men immediately wanted to pigeonhole her as radical when they heard this.

To her relief, Neil said, 'Really? How fascinating. I've often thought there should be more about that in the school curriculum. For my sins, I'm the principal at a boy's college – in Brisbane. It's been difficult to introduce anything new, anything the school board might deem to be extremist.'

Their coffees arrived along with two plates, each with a brownie topped with a strawberry and a serving of cream.

The pair were silent as they took a sip of coffee and bit into a brownie.

'Not bad,' Neil said, putting down his fork.

'You have a daughter,' Ali said. 'I met her in the bookshop when I went back for my books.'

'Bronte. Yes. She's spending the summer with me and Dad.'

'She seemed to be very efficient. Is she a student?' Ali remembered thinking she was the same age as Chelsea – around twenty.

Neil rubbed his chin. 'Not exactly. She lives with her mother. Hasn't seemed to discover what she wants to do.'

'She's working in the bookshop for the summer?'

'No. That was only a stopgap for Christmas – and while Dad was in hospital. But she has found a job. She's been helping design surfboards with a young fellow, Owen Rankin.' He frowned.

'You don't approve?'

'It's none of my business, really. But she seems happy. That's all I want for her. And I suspect – more than suspect – she and Owen... But I dread to think what's going to happen when her mother finds out.'

'*She* won't approve?'

'Pippa has delusions of having a daughter with a degree in business, law, IT... Bronte has been enrolled in all three and dropped out of each of them.'

'Ouch.'

'Indeed.'

They sat smiling at each other, Ali feeling totally in tune with her companion.

'How was your Christmas?' Neil asked, and the conversation veered away from more personal matters to their Christmas Days and their thoughts about Bellbird Bay.

Finally, Ali said regretfully, 'I should go.'

'Must you?'

'Yes. I promised to have lunch with Libby, then we're taking her granddaughter to a movie.'

'The little girl with the dogs?'

Ali chuckled. 'The same. Only one of the dogs is hers – the puppy was a Christmas present. The other – the larger one – belongs to Libby. He looks fearsome but is very gentle.'

They rose together.

'I've enjoyed this. I'd like to see you again.'

Ali smiled. She'd enjoyed meeting him again, too, and was hoping he'd suggest another meeting.

'What are you doing on Saturday?'

'New Year's Eve? I don't know. I expect Adam and Libby will have plans.'

'I noticed the surf club is holding a special evening – dinner, music, the works – and staying open to let everyone bring in the New Year. Can I persuade you to join me?'

Ali thought of all the lonely New Year's Eves she'd spent with her mother, or with Sally, drinking too much and hoping the next year would be better. 'I'd love to,' she said.

Seventeen

The surf club was alive with revellers when Neil and Ali reached the top of the stairs. He was glad he'd had the foresight to book a table, because it looked as if they had all been reserved. He put an arm around Ali's waist to protect her as they pushed their way to the bar where a familiar voice greeted him.

'First drinks are on the house tonight,' Nate said. 'What'll it be?'

'Champagne?' Neil asked Ali.

She nodded.

Carrying the two flutes of sparkling wine, Neil ushered Ali to the deck where their table awaited them. He was glad to get out of the crush. It was quieter out here, the music from the main restaurant only spilling through when the door opened.

'Would you have preferred to be inside?' he asked.

'No, this is perfect.' Ali took a sip of her drink.

'You're looking lovely tonight.' Neil could hardly keep his eyes off his companion who was wearing a turquoise dress in a floaty fabric, the fitted bodice and scoop neckline showing off her figure to perfection. She seemed to have done something different with her hair, too, making it curl around her face and, if he wasn't mistaken, she was wearing more makeup than on the previous occasions they'd met.

He'd made a special effort, too, opting to wear the new shirt Bronte had helped him choose, assuring him the pale blue linen garment with the grandad collar was very trendy. He'd worn it with his favourite chinos and at the last minute, had slapped on some Paco Rabanne aftershave which a former girlfriend had told him was very sexy.

'Thanks,' she said, blushing, and taking another sip of wine.

'What are your brother and his partner up to tonight?' Neil hoped they didn't plan to be here too, though it was quite possible. Most of Bellbird Bay seemed to have crowded into the club to celebrate the end of one year and the beginning of the next.

'They're having dinner with friends, neighbours of theirs on the boardwalk. They said they planned an early night. Not like this crowd.' She glanced around to where everyone appeared to be settled in for the night, tables groaning with plates of food and bottles of wine.

'There'll be a lot of sore heads tomorrow,' Neil agreed. 'We should take it easy if we don't want to join them.'

When they'd ordered their meal, Ali said, 'The barman seemed to know you. Have you been here a lot?'

'Not here. Nate's a friend of my daughter. He was one of the group who helped out in the bookshop till Dad got back on his feet. I'm surprised to see him here tonight. Bronte is off to a party. I thought he'd be there, too.'

'I guess you don't have a choice when you work in hospitality.'

'I guess not.'

'Tell me about your school,' Ali said, after a pause. 'How long have you been principal there?'

'Ten years. I taught history before that.' Neil picked up the napkin containing his cutlery and put if down again. *How much to tell her?* He looked at the trusting grey eyes gazing into his and made a decision. 'I'm not actually sure I still have a job.'

He didn't know what reaction he expected, but not the peal of laughter he heard.

'Sorry,' Ali said. 'I shouldn't laugh, but it sounds as if we're in the same boat.'

'How so?'

'I may not have a job to go back to either.'

'Want to talk about it?'

Ali shook her head, then appeared to change her mind, and began to speak, the words flowing out of her like a torrent.

When she finished, Neil put his hand on hers. 'I'm so sorry. You must have suffered so much.'

'Not as much as poor Chelsea,' she said. 'Imagine if your daughter...'

'I am.' Neil ground his teeth. 'I'd want to get my hands on the bastard. And you say his colleagues supported him?'

'Yes,' Ali said bitterly. 'And tried to make out I was at fault for believing her. But enough about my problems.'

Their meals arrived, and no more was said about Ali's experience in Perth. But Neil couldn't forget about it. He wasn't a violent man, but he would love to have had the chance to show those guys they couldn't get away with treating Ali like that.

They enjoyed the Atlantic salmon served with tiny roast potatoes and salad which both had ordered. Then, as the noise from other diners, combined with the music drifting through the ever-opening door to the restaurant, became louder and louder, Neil said, 'Why don't we get out of here? I bet it's a lot quieter down there on the beach.' He gestured to the deserted patch of sand below the deck, lit only by the spotlight in one corner and the moon which was shining brightly.

'Good idea.'

A few minutes later, one hand grasping Ali's, the other carrying a bottle of champagne he'd purchased at the bar, Neil drew Ali down the steps to the beach. Ali was giggling and carrying the two champagne flutes Neil had begged from Nate, promising he'd return them. Ali had removed her sandals which were now dangling by their straps from one wrist.

Once they left the main beach which was set up for the midnight fireworks, they reached a spot where they had the beach to themselves, apart from a group of young people who had lit an illegal fire and looked as if they intended to spend the night there. Hoping Bronte wasn't among them, Neil skirted the group, and Ali and he walked on, neither speaking, content in each other's company, till they found a private spot.

When they sat down on the sand, heedless of their good clothes, Ali turned her face up to the sky. 'This is magic,' she said, gazing at the stars which glistened like diamonds in the dark night sky.

'Different to what you're used to?' Neil asked.

'Very different from Perth.'

'From Brisbane, too.'

'You grew up here. Did it never occur to you to stay?'

'Take a teaching position in Bellbird Bay? I've been asking myself that recently, since I came back for Christmas. Bronte likes it here,' he said, as if talking to himself.

'Your daughter? It sounds as if she's found her calling – and a boyfriend, too.'

'Hmm. You're right there.'

'Is it a problem?'

'Not for me, but as I said, her mother might have something to say about it.'

'What were you doing when you were twenty?'

'Good question. One I asked myself not too long ago, too.' Neil realised he'd been engaging in a lot of introspection this holiday season. *Was it his dad's failing health making him re-evaluate his life?*

'And?' Ali asked lazily, leaning back on her elbows, and staring at him, her face glowing in the moonlight.

'You don't want to know,' he chuckled.

Suddenly there was a loud noise from the direction of the surf club.

'Must be close to midnight.' Neil checked the time on his phone and proceeded to open the bottle of champagne.

They both laughed as it spilled over onto the sand before he had time to fill their glasses. Then there was another noise, followed by loud bangs and the sky lit up with myriad colours. The firework display had begun.

'Happy New Year!'

'Happy New Year!'

They toasted each other, then, taking Ali's glass from her and placing both glasses on the sand, Neil took Ali in his arms, something he'd been wanting to do all evening.

Neil didn't know whether the way his heart leapt and the buzzing in his ears came from the ongoing firework display, or the woman in his arms, as their lips met and held for what seemed like an eternity.

Eighteen

Ali felt her head was filled with flashing lights and, when Neil finally released her, she wasn't surprised to see the sky filled with flashes of colour. It matched her mood exactly. Neil's kiss had been a revelation, leaving her weak at the knees. She was sure, if he hadn't still been holding her, she'd have collapsed in a heap onto the sand.

'A new year, our first together,' he murmured into her hair.

For a moment, Ali allowed herself the comfort of his arms. Then her innate common sense reasserted itself, and she pulled away. The kiss had been good – more than good – but Neil Simpson was still practically a stranger. All the stories she'd heard, read about – even written about – flooded back to make her question her feelings.

'A new year, certainly,' she said, brushing the sand from her dress.

'Another drink?' Neil asked, picking up the bottle which had been lodged in the sand.

'Mmm.' Maybe another drink was what she needed to dispel the emotions which were running rampant, emotions she'd often ridiculed in others, emotions which she knew could lead the unwary into a trap. Look what had happened to her mother, to countless other women who'd allowed their emotions to sway them, to lead them into an unwise alliance.

But... she glanced at Neil, his profile clear in the moonlight and the glow of the New Year fireworks and felt her heart thud unexpectedly... perhaps Neil was different.

As suddenly as they had started, the fireworks ended – with one last burst of colour – and there was silence. Only the gentle lapping of the waves and the distant sounds from the surf club met their ears. Even the group of young people had disappeared, gone home or to some other more attractive location, their fire extinguished.

'I guess I should get you home,' Neil said, holding the now empty bottle upside down.

Now it was time to leave, Ali found herself reluctant to do so. Here, alone on the beach with this attractive man, for just a short time she'd been able to put her worries to rest. She wanted to hold on to the feeling for as long as she could. Once she returned to the real world, she knew they'd all come rushing back.

Neil held out his hand, and Ali, picking up the sandals which she didn't remember discarding, allowed herself to be pulled up from where she'd been sitting on the sand. She slipped the sandal straps over her wrist again and picked up the two empty glasses. Then they made their way back along the beach to where the light from the surf club shone down on them. From the noise drifting down from the building, it seemed the party there was still going on.

'Wait a moment,' Neil said when they reached the doorway. He disappeared with the two glasses and the empty bottle to return almost immediately. 'Let's go.' He took her hand again.

There was something comforting about having her hand in his. It made Ali feel safe in a way she hadn't for some time. It took her back to her childhood, before she and her mother left, before she was aware of the tension in the house, before the arguments. It reminded her of the times she and her big brother had snuck away on what they called their adventures.

But Neil was no big brother. He was an attractive, sexy man who Ali realised she was becoming to care for more than was wise. For one thing, her life was in Perth – on the other side of the country – and his was in Brisbane. This – no matter how pleasant – could only be an interlude.

Back in Ali's apartment, they stood gazing at each other, Ali's stomach churning, her heart beating madly. Then, before Ali could offer the coffee which she'd mentioned in the doorway, the reason for inviting Neil in, he pulled her into his arms.

'I've wanted to do this all evening,' he murmured into her hair.

Ali felt her insides melt. She knew she wanted it, too. While part of her wanted to resist, another part was aching for more. As their lips met in a searing kiss, and their bodies melded together, the surge of desire caught her unaware, and she was helpless.

*

Next morning, Ali wakened with a smile on her face. She stretched her arms above her head, remembering how Neil had kissed her gently at her door before leaving in the early hours of the morning. She turned her face into the pillow which still held his scent.

To her surprise, she felt no regrets. It had seemed so natural when they arrived back at her apartment, to invite him in. Then everything seemed to happen at once.

Neil was an accomplished lover. Although shying away from commitment, Ali was no coy, retiring virgin. She'd had lovers in the past, not many and always men she knew posed no threat to her avowed single status. Neil was different.

It was difficult for her to identify exactly how he had managed to push through the barriers she'd erected, the ones which had helped keep her safe from the wave of emotion such as she was now experiencing. Thank goodness Sally would be here soon. She needed to discuss this with someone who would understand her dilemma. In the meantime, she would just live in the present and enjoy the journey.

She was in the shower when she remembered her promise to call round to see Adam and Libby today, to celebrate the new year with them. They were planning a luncheon barbecue with a few friends, and she'd promised to provide something for dessert.

Showered and dressed in a pair of white cargo pants topped with a black and white top, Ali made herself some breakfast and mentally flicked through her standard desserts, finally settling on the Donna Hay banana upside down cake which would use up the bananas she'd bought on her last shopping trip. Knowing it would take over an hour to cook, she quickly finished breakfast and donned the apron Clancy had given her for Christmas.

Ali had just popped the cake into the oven when her phone pinged with a message. A smile lit up her face when she read Neil's message inviting her to dinner again that evening.

Love to, thanks, A, she replied, her heart thudding in anticipation.

The next message was from Sally. Her friend wanted to wish her a Happy New Year and to ask if she could arrive on the fourth.

Ali texted back to say she was looking forward to Sally's visit, a tiny part of her wondering how it might affect her newly formed relationship with Neil. But perhaps it was just as well. It would do no harm to put it on hold while her friend was here – give her time to reflect on the wisdom of becoming involved in something in which there could be no future – even though this had never deterred her before. But Ali knew already she'd never before felt what she did for Neil Simpson.

Arriving at Adam and Libby's, Ali was almost knocked over by Clancy, Milo and Holly playing a game of tag in the yard, accompanied by another small girl and dog. 'Careful,' she warned, balancing the cake in one hand while opening the gate with the other and trying to avoid the group of small people and animals.

'Clancy!' Libby called out from the open door when she saw Ali coming through the gate. 'I see you've met Mia. She's Clancy's friend. Come in and meet the rest of the family. Let me take that. Mmm, it looks delicious.' She relieved Ali of the cake. 'Mia's dad is Bryan Grant. Remember Bev and Iain? Bryan is Iain's son.'

With the names swirling around in her head, Ali followed Libby into the yard where a crowd of people were already milling around, several of whom she'd already met. Libby knew so many people in Bellbird Bay, it wouldn't have surprised Ali to see Neil there with his father. To her relief, he wasn't. She wasn't ready to go public with a relationship which had barely begun.

The barbecue followed the usual pattern with most of the men congregating around the barbecue, and the women forming groups on the other side of the yard. It was one of the things Ali had always hated about social events in Perth. As a staff member at the university, on such occasions, she was neither fish nor fowl, belonging neither to the group of men throwing meat on the grill or the wives gossiping about their children.

Here it was slightly different. But she had little in common with either group, and everyone seemed to be part of a couple. Ali was feeling distinctly *de trop* and wondering how soon she could slip quietly away. For the first time in her life, she wished she was part of a couple, too. She was hugging the knowledge of Neil to herself, when a voice said, 'Not enjoying yourself?'

Turning quickly, Ali found herself meeting an amused pair of eyes. 'Sorry?' she asked.

'You're looking as if you're wondering how soon you can escape.' The woman chuckled. 'We can be a bit overpowering. I know how you feel. I felt a bit like that, too, when I first came to Bellbird Bay.' A shadow crossed her face to quickly disappear. 'But you get used to it, and everyone is really friendly – though maybe that's the problem?'

'No... it's just...'

'Sorry, I don't think we were properly introduced. I'm Ailsa. I'm with Martin, the tall guy with the blond hair.'

'You're...' Ali tried to remember where she'd heard the name.

'Martin Cooper.'

'The photographer? Of course.' Adam had mentioned the world-renowned photographer who had returned to live in his hometown. There was something else. 'You recently married, didn't you?'

'We did. You may have met my son,' Ailsa continued. 'Nate works behind the bar at the surf club. He prides himself on knowing everyone who walks in.' She chuckled again.

'I believe I have,' Ali said cautiously, remembering the dark-haired young man from the surf club the previous evening, the one Neil said had helped out in the bookshop and was a friend of his daughter. 'He's not here?' She glanced around.

Ailsa shook her head. 'Not his scene. He and his housemates are having a party of their own today. I suspect it'll be a lot livelier than this one. He shares a house with Cleo's daughter and Will's son.' She gestured to where her husband was chatting to another blond man – this one with his hair tied back in an untidy ponytail had his arm around a dainty woman with a cloud of dark hair who Ali remembered meeting in the café at the garden centre. 'Come and meet them.'

To her surprise, Ali found herself following Ailsa across to where the others were standing.

They welcomed her into the group where she discovered the

young people were the topic of conversation. It appeared Nate and Hannah, Cleo's daughter, were a couple and they were predicting an engagement might be imminent. Also, Will and Cleo had recently become engaged, but hadn't set a date for the wedding.

'I hear Owen has found himself a girlfriend now, too,' Martin said, giving Will a nudge. 'Better look out. The youngsters might beat you two to it.'

Cleo blushed, but Will only laughed. 'She's helping him out at the workshop,' he said. 'Seems a nice girl. They met when she hired a surfboard from me. Bronte. Comes from Brisbane and is here for the summer.'

The conversation moved on, but Ali savoured the comment and stored it up to share with Neil later.

Nineteen

Neil spent New Year's Day with his dad. Bronte had disappeared immediately after breakfast, wearing a pair of brief shorts and a tee shirt that looked as if it was about to fall off one shoulder, muttering something about a party and being late home. Neil had no idea when she'd returned the previous evening, certainly before he tiptoed into the silent house in the early hours feeling like a teenager again.

It had been a surprise – an extremely pleasant one – to find himself in Ali's bed, to make love till they were both exhausted, to awaken with her in his arms, her hair tickling his cheek. It had been a long time since he'd felt this way. For too long he'd played the part of the staid school principal, keeping women at bay, only surfacing for the odd dinner date, never to be repeated. Now, he wanted to yell from the rooftops, to tell the world he'd found... what? Was it love or lust that had overtaken them?

One thing Neil did know – he wanted to see Ali again, to repeat last night's experience, to discover if this was more than just a flash in the pan.

To his delight, she'd agreed to have dinner with him again tonight and he'd managed to book a table at what was touted as one of the best restaurants in Bellbird Bay. He'd walked past *The Beach House* several times and had been impressed by the tall glass and timber structure built on an outcrop of rock and seeming to stand on top of the sea. He was looking forward to discovering if the meals lived up to his expectations.

It had been a lazy day, the New Year's Day public holiday giving Harry a well-needed rest after his insistence on going to the bookshop every day. While Neil had sat in the sun reading, Harry had spent the day relaxing, though refusing to stay in bed, insisting he wasn't sick. But Neil could already see signs of deterioration in his dad's health and was worried about him.

'Going out?' Harry asked, when Neil walked into the living room wearing a new short-sleeved navy shirt with cream pants, and a noticeable scent of aftershave.

'I'm having dinner at *The Beach House*.'

'With the lady who kept you up till the small hours?'

Neil flinched. Despite the disease which was eating away at him, Harry didn't miss much. Neil hadn't thought his dad was still awake when he got home.

'Who is she?' Harry asked, clearly determined to find out.

'Ali Wells,' Neil said. 'You know her brother, Adam Holland, the author.'

'I know the lady, too. I remember she came into the bookshop with her brother on one of her visits. Doesn't she live in Perth?'

Neil sighed. Trust his dad to be well-informed. 'She does. She's spending a few months in Bellbird Bay.'

'Hmmm. It's about time you found a new woman. I never did think much of that one you married.'

'Pippa…'

'Bronte is the only good thing that came out of that marriage. You've been on your own too long, son. You need a good woman, one who'll love and respect you. Your mother and I had a good life together. Life hasn't been the same since she went. I'd like to see you settled with a relationship like we had before I go.'

Was that a tear in his dad's eye?

'Ali and I have only just met, Dad.'

'Sometimes you can tell right away. I know how I felt when I met your mother. It was like a bolt of lightning. And our love never faltered until the day she died.'

A shiver ran down Neil's spine remembering his first sight of Ali. A bolt of lightning described it pretty well. He looked at his dad with more respect. 'Thanks, Dad. I'll remember your advice.'

'See you do. If she's the one, don't let her get away. Don't let the distance from Brisbane to Perth stand between you. There's always a way if you look for it.'

Neil grinned, suddenly feeling ebullient. There was nothing wrong with his dad's mind – not yet, anyway. 'I'll be off, then,' he said.

'And don't forget what I said. If she's the one, you need to hold on to her.'

The smile was still on Neil's face as he walked out the door.

*

Ali was glad she'd been too busy all day to think about dinner with Neil. But now she was back in her apartment, the evening dinner date loomed ahead of her. As she stood in the shower, the water cascading over her, she shivered with delight at the memory of the night they'd spent together. Was what she felt real, or the result of too much champagne and the romance of New Year's Eve on the beach, fireworks overhead, and being in the arms of an attractive man?

Surely she wasn't so easily swayed from her avowed intention never to let a man too close, never to give into emotion, never to allow herself to get into the same position as her mother?

Ali was glad Sally was arriving soon. She needed a dose of her friend's common sense to keep her on track. Meantime, she intended to enjoy the evening. She dressed in a new black and white spotted dress she'd purchased in the boutique, *Birds of a Feather*, on the esplanade, brushed her hair which was growing and curling around her face, and touched up her makeup. She couldn't stifle the burst of excitement which sent butterflies careering around in her stomach.

It was a perfect evening, and Neil was the perfect companion. He looked so smart, and Ali enjoyed the thrill of her hand in his as they walked along the esplanade to the restaurant. It was one she hadn't been to before, though she'd heard Adam mention it.

When they arrived and walked inside, Ali was immediately struck by the tall glass walls reaching to the ceiling, through which she could see the dying rays of the sun casting a yellow and pink glow across the horizon.

'This place is amazing,' she said, when they'd been shown to a table so close to the window, she felt as if they were right on top of the ocean. 'How did you manage to get a table?' she asked, seeing how crowded the restaurant was.

'I was lucky. They had a cancellation. I didn't think it would be as busy as this.'

'It's New Year's Day. I guess everyone wants to celebrate.' She blushed, remembering how they had already celebrated the new year.

'I'm glad to be celebrating it with you.' Neil smiled, his eyes crinkling in a way Ali had come to recognise.

A warm glow suffused Ali. Her stomach fluttered. 'Me, too.'

A waiter appeared and handed them menus, deflecting her embarrassment, and they spent the next few minutes studying the large selection of dishes on offer.

Once they'd ordered, choosing the seafood platter for two, and had been served the champagne on which Neil insisted, saying, 'It is New Year, after all,' Ali settled back to enjoy the evening.

When they left the restaurant, it was completely dark outside. Neil threw an arm around Ali's shoulders and pulled her towards him. Automatically she looked up, raising her face for his kiss. The screech of a night bird startled her, and they broke apart. 'What was that?' she asked.

'An owl. I remember hearing them when I was growing up here. Haven't heard one for years but you never forget the sound.'

Ali shivered. It had been an unearthly sound. She was glad it was only an owl.

They walked on, reaching the entrance to her apartment block after only a few minutes.

Stopping under a strategically placed streetlight Neil turned to face Ali, put one finger under her chin and tipped her face up.

Ali shivered with anticipation.

'Last night was wonderful,' he said, 'but I know we had a lot of champagne. I hope you won't think I'm being presumptuous if...' His finger moved to trace Ali's lips.

She shivered again, an ache for him growing somewhere deep inside. 'Would you like to come up?' she asked.

Twenty

As soon as she awoke next morning, just as the sun was beginning to peek through the curtains, Ali realised she was not alone. This time, Neil hadn't left in the early hours to return home. He had stayed all night. Ali reached out a hand to gently stroke his jaw, enjoying the feel of his overnight stubble.

Neil awakened with a start, seemingly surprised to find himself in bed with her. 'What time is it?' he asked, pushing himself up. 'I have to be at the bookshop.'

Not the most romantic way to begin the day, Ali thought, but of course there was his dad's shop to consider. She checked the time. 'It's only half-five,' she said.

'Oh!' Neil sank back against the pillows. 'I must have fallen asleep.'

'We both did. Would you like breakfast before you leave?'

'Better not. I need to check on Dad, shower and change. Sorry.' He dragged a hand through his already dishevelled hair, making Ali want to run her fingers through it.

Disappointed, Ali rose and pulled on a towelling robe. 'At least have a cup of tea or coffee before you rush off.'

'Okay.' Neil was pulling on his clothes as he spoke. 'I didn't intend to stay all night. Wonder when Bronte got home?' It was clear Neil's mind was far away. His day had already begun.

Her eyes still blurry with sleep, Ali made her way to the kitchen and filled the kettle, dropping herbal teabags into two mugs.

By the time Neil joined her, the tea was ready.

'Thanks,' he said, drinking it down in two gulps. 'Sorry to dash. Can we meet for lunch? *The Bay Café* at one?'

'Sure.' Ali accompanied him to the door where, with a quick kiss, he was gone.

Left alone, Ali wandered back into the kitchen where she made herself toast, liberally spread it with the local honey she'd become addicted to and took it and her tea back to bed.

With nothing to do until she met Neil for lunch, Ali decided to go for a walk on the beach, and perhaps have a swim. But when she got there, the sight of the van bearing the sign, *Bay Surf School* and offering surf lessons and surfboard hire was too tempting to resist. Ever since she arrived in Bellbird Bay, she'd been meaning to take up surfing again, but till now the opportunity hadn't presented itself.

Recognising the blond man she'd met at Libby's barbecue the day before, Ali headed in his direction.

A few minutes later, she was paddling out into the ocean, recapturing the feeling she had almost forgotten of being at one with the elements.

But it had been some time since Ali had spent time in the surf and, before long, she was glad to return to the shore and hand back the surfboard.

'Out of practice?' Will Rankin asked with a grin.

'I'm afraid so, but I'll be back.'

'No worries.' He turned to his next customer, preventing any further conversation.

As she wandered further up the beach, the waves lapping at her feet, Ali wondered if Neil surfed. It would be fun to ride the waves together. She must ask him.

'Ali! You're out early this morning.'

Ali looked up to see Libby coming towards her, Milo at her heels. She smiled. 'Not so early. I've already been surfing. It's such a glorious day.'

'It is indeed. Adam was still asleep when I left. We had a pretty late night, so I decided to let him enjoy his rest. Have you had breakfast? Why don't you come back with me to have a bite to eat?'

Ali felt as if it had been ages since she had eaten the toast in bed, and the mention of breakfast made her realise she was hungry. 'Thanks, I'd like that.'

'Adam should be up by now, too,' Libby said.

Back at the house, the enticing aroma of freshly brewed coffee met them at the door.

'Ali, wondered if we'd see you today. Are you joining us for breakfast?'

'Libby was kind enough to invite me.'

'You don't need an invitation. You're welcome any time.'

'Of course you are,' Libby agreed. 'You're family.'

Ali took a seat on a high stool by the kitchen bench, overcome by an unfamiliar emotion. This is what it would be like if she lived here, she realised. She would always have somewhere to come if she was feeling down. It was something she'd missed since her mother died. And this was different. This was Adam, her brother, the one person she'd been able to confide in as a child, the one person she'd trusted never to leave her, never to let her down. She'd been the one who'd left when she and her mother fled around this time all those years ago.

'Hey!' Adam was standing close and smiling. 'Come back!'

'Sorry.' Ali pulled herself together 'Just thinking how glad I am we're together again. I know we did all this last year, but it just hit me again how lucky I am to have you as my big brother – and you, too, Libby,' she said, grasping Libby's hand.

At that moment, Milo broke the mood by pushing his head between Ali and Libby and licking their hands. 'And you, too, Milo,' Ali said with a laugh.

'Now, breakfast,' Libby said, moving away and taking bacon and eggs from the fridge while Adam poured coffee.

After a delicious breakfast of bacon, tomato and scrambled eggs, washed down with lashings of coffee, while seated on the deck, Ali leant back in her chair. 'It's so peaceful here,' she said, gazing out at the ocean. This morning the white-capped waves were pounding on the shore, the turquoise hue of the sea glistening in the sunlight.

'That's why we like it,' Libby said, almost smugly. 'It's why my husband and I chose to retire here and why, even after he died, I came by myself.'

Ali reddened. She'd forgotten about Libby's sad past, a past Libby must be reminded of every time she passed the bench she'd arranged to have erected in her deceased husband's memory. Libby, it seemed, had no fear of commitment, not like Ali – or Adam. Adam had overcome his fear, and he and Libby were happy together.

'What did you do last night?' Adam asked. 'You rushed away from the barbecue. Most of the others stayed till late.' He yawned.

'Your brother is no longer the solitary animal he was when we met,' Libby chuckled. 'You should have seen him last night...'

'Too much wine,' Adam said, but he was laughing, too. 'But there's something about Bellbird Bay... You haven't said why you left,' he said.

'I had a dinner date.' Put like that, it sounded important. Perhaps she should just have said she went out to dinner.

'With Harry Simpson's son?' Adam asked. 'How is the old man?'

'Yes, and Harry seems to be recovering.'

'Did you go somewhere nice?' Libby asked.

'*The Beach House.*'

'Ooh, lovely! Adam took me there on my birthday.' Libby threw Adam an affectionate glance.

'You saw him on New Year's Eve, too, didn't you?' Adam asked, eyebrows raised.

Ali blushed again.

'No need to be embarrassed, Ali,' Libby said frowning at Adam. 'We're not about to judge you. I'm glad you've made a friend here. Maybe even...? You and Adam allowed the situation you grew up with to ruin your lives for too long. I'm glad your brother finally saw sense.' She smiled at Adam again. 'Maybe now it's your turn.'

'I don't think so.' Ali shifted awkwardly in her seat, then checked the time on her watch. 'Sorry, I need to go now. Thanks for breakfast. You must let me return the favour.'

'That would be lovely,' Libby said, glaring at Adam who appeared about to speak. 'Off you go and enjoy your day.'

'Thanks.' Ali hugged Libby and Adam and patted Milo on the head before leaving to walk down the boardwalk. She would just have time to go back to the apartment and freshen up before it was time to meet Neil.

As she took a quick shower, Ali considered how her life had changed since coming to Bellbird Bay, even in the past few days. It was partly due to being close to Adam, but also to having met Neil Simpson. Almost with no effort, he'd wormed his way into her life here and she wasn't sure it was a good idea. At least Sally's arrival in a couple of days' time would put a halt to their meetings and give her time to reflect on what to do about him.

*

Ali broke into a smile as she approached the café to see Neil was waiting for her. He stood, took her by the arm and kissed her on the cheek, sending a thrill through her – right to her toes. She remembered Libby's words and tried to stifle the sensation which threatened to destroy all her good intentions.

'You look lovely, as always,' Neil said, making Ali glad she'd decided to wear the strappy candy-striped sundress which flattered her figure, despite her concern it made her upper arms look flabby. Mentally chastising herself for being so easily swayed, she took a seat and picked up a menu.

'There's a good selection of salads,' Neil said. 'I'm having the Thai chicken one.'

Trying to still the tremor Neil's presence always seemed to provoke and telling herself it was only a normal physical reaction to an attractive man – and one she had spent the last two nights with – Ali studied the menu avidly. But although she tried to pretend her entire focus was on the menu, she was very aware of the masculine presence sitting across the table.

This morning, Neil was wearing a white tee-shirt with the logo *Bay Books* emblazoned on it in royal blue. The tee-shirt was tightly stretched across his chest, showing off his broad shoulders, and the whiteness of the garment emphasised the tan he'd managed to acquire since coming to the coast. Ali swallowed.

'Have you decided?'

Ali realised she had been staring blindly at the menu and had no idea what was written on it. Focussing quickly, she picked an item at random. 'I'll have the prawn salad… with a cappuccino.' Relieved to a have made a decision, she put down the menu to see an amused expression on Neil's face. 'What?' she asked.

'You looked as if you were far away,' he said, chuckling. Then, as the waitress appeared he gave her their order.

'Sorry I had to dash off earlier,' he said when they were alone again. 'I've promised Dad to help out for a bit… just till he's a hundred percent again, though…'

'Will he get well again?'

'The short answer is no... he'll continue to deteriorate. But he should regain some of his strength, enough to allow him to keep going in the bookshop for a bit longer. Then...' Neil opened his arms, '... we'll need to find another solution.'

'It must be hard.' Ali put a hand on his.

'Yeah.' Neil sighed. 'I suppose eventually he'll have to sell. Some of the bigger chains have been sniffing around already. It would make good sense, but... It's always been a family business and Dad will want to hang on till the bitter end... whenever that might be.' He muttered the last few words under his breath.

Pity welled up in Ali. She wished there was something she could do to lessen the hurt Neil was suffering. But no one could halt the passing of time, or the progress of this cruel disease.

Their meals arrived, and Ali decided to change the subject. 'I went surfing this morning,' she said. 'I'd forgotten how much fun it is. Do you surf?'

'It's not really my thing.' Neil looked uncomfortable.

Ali stared at him in surprise. 'But you grew up here.'

'We didn't all turn out to be surfers. I was more interested in books, spent a lot of my time in the bookshop. I *can* surf, but it never grabbed me in the same way as others like Will Rankin and Martin Cooper.'

'I hired a board from Will Rankin.'

'Yeah, he's made a living from the sport and good luck to him. You said you're here till Easter?' he asked.

'Possibly. It's when my leave's up. But I may need to go back before then to check...' Ali's heart plummeted at the thought of what might await her. 'I may need to start applying for other positions. It won't be easy once the academic year has started. You?' Ali realised Neil had never actually explained why *he* might not have a job to go back to. The school year began earlier than the academic one.

'You must be one of the few people who haven't read about the scandal that rocked *Beckwith Boys' College*,' he said bitterly.

Stunned by his changed tone of voice, Ali did recall reading an article outlining how a school board had mishandled funds. 'That was your school?'

'The same.'

'But...' she tried to remember what she had read, '...you're the principal. Weren't you exonerated?'

'By the police, not the parent body. And the matter still has to go to court. It's not clear whether the school can survive financially – or whether I can survive the fallout even if it does. Meantime...' He spread his hands.

'...you're helping your dad,' Ali said.

'That wasn't my intention when I came here, but I couldn't let the old man down. Speaking of which, I should be getting back. I should stay home tonight to keep Dad happy but maybe we can connect again later in the week?' He raised one eyebrow suggestively, and Ali almost succumbed.

Only the knowledge of Sally's arrival prevented her. 'I'd love to,' she said, her voice filled with genuine regret, 'but I have a friend arriving from Perth on Wednesday. We normally spend New Year together, but she had to spend it with her family this year. She'll be staying for two weeks.'

'Oh!' The look of disappointment on Neil's face was almost enough to persuade Ali to text Sally to tell her to stay in Perth, but she knew it was out of the question. And it would do them both good to cool what had started to become more than Ali wanted to cope with.

Neil made a quick recovery. 'Perhaps I can take both of you to dinner,' he suggested.

'Perhaps.' But as Ali watched him walk away, she wondered if that was such a good idea.

Twenty-one

'You'll never guess, Dad.' Bronte arrived home from work bubbling with enthusiasm.

She had certainly changed since they arrived in Bellbird Bay, whether as a result of working in design or meeting Owen Rankin, Neil wasn't sure, but suspected it was the latter. Since meeting the young surfer, Bronte had become part of the group of young people Owen lived with. He'd met them and they seemed a decent bunch of kids. He knew their parents, and they were good people, too. 'I suppose you're going to tell me,' he said with a grin.

'I've been thinking about Owen's business. He's designing surfboards, but his customers love everything connected with the surf. So...' she took a deep breath, '...I had the idea of surf gear. You know, tee-shirts, caps... that sort of thing. I talked with Owen about it, and he likes the idea.'

'Well done.' It seemed her foray into business studies hadn't been completely useless. 'What happens next?' Neil took a sip of the beer he'd poured as soon as he got home from the bookshop.

'I already have some designs I've been playing around with, and I've researched a few companies which produce tee-shirts and caps. We can start with those and work up to other items. If they go well, we could set up an online store and...'

Neil laughed. 'Sounds as if the summer might not be long enough for you.'

Bronte became serious. 'No, Dad, it won't. I'm really enjoying being here, working with Owen. I feel fulfilled in a way I never did studying that stuff Mum forced me to enrol in. Owen has suggested...'

'Steady on, sweetheart,' Neil interrupted, not wanting to hear what Owen had suggested. 'I'm happy you're enjoying what you're doing. It's always good to feel fulfilled. But remember, this is just a summer gig. We'll both be going back to Brisbane at the end of January. Your mother...'

'I don't care what my mother wants or expects me to do. I've had enough of doing what she wants. I'm not a kid anymore. Now I plan to do what *I* want and neither of you can stop me.' She stormed out, leaving Neil staring after her.

'You should listen to her, son.'

Neil glanced around quickly. He'd forgotten his father was there.

Harry was sitting quietly in his favourite armchair, a glass of beer in his hand. 'Bronte has a point, Neil. She's twenty, and stubborn like you were at her age. You should be grateful she's found gainful employment with a decent young man. She could have got herself mixed up with the wrong sort.'

'I know. I am. But...' Neil shook his head.

'What's your problem?' Harry was beginning to sound testy.

'Pippa.' Neil knew exactly what his ex would say if Bronte chose not to return to Brisbane and resume a degree course.

'Poof! What did she ever do with herself other than swan around?'

Neil couldn't hide his amusement. It was true Pippa had been a model when they met, and not a very successful one. But she did come from one of the wealthier Brisbane families and her father was a member of state parliament which boosted her delusions of importance. 'I guess you're right, Dad. It's more important Bronte is happy.'

'I know I am. I want you to be happy, too.' Harry peered at him. 'This woman you're seeing... is she making you happy?'

Neil shifted uncomfortably in his seat and took another sip of beer. His dad had brought up Ali before. He remembered what Harry had said then, but he didn't feel comfortable discussing her with him. He made a sudden decision. 'Think I'll go for a walk, Dad. You be okay? What about dinner?'

'I'm not an invalid,' Harry said in a testy tone again. 'I'm quite capable of making myself something to eat.'

Wondering if it was his illness making him so grumpy, if he was suffering more than he was willing to share, Neil bit back the retort that came to his lips. 'Right. I'll be off, then.'

Glad it was a clear evening, Neil set off to walk towards the esplanade. He paused when he reached the bookshop to admire the window. He'd prevailed on his dad to allow him free rein with the display, and it looked good. In a better frame of mind than when he'd left the house, he walked on, musing that he could have been seeing Ali tonight. Despite planning to remain home, his dad's questions and irritable mood had forced him out. Now he wasn't sure where he was heading.

Suddenly, Neil found himself in front of the surf club. Its familiar atmosphere was exactly what he needed to cheer him up.

As soon as he reached the bar, he saw Will Rankin leaning against it, a glass of beer in one hand and gesticulating with the other. He grinned. Will never changed. He still looked like the disreputable surfer he had when they were at school. He had been happy then, and he looked happy now. Despite what life had thrown at him – Neil knew he had lost his wife and son in quick succession – Will still had a smile on his face.

Neil recognised the barman, too. It was Nate, one of the young people Bronte had befriended who had helped out in the bookshop before Christmas.

Both spoke at once.

'Hey, Neil. I heard you were back.'

'What'll you have?'

Neil answered Nate first. 'A pot of light beer, thanks, Nate,' he said then, turned to Will and offered his hand. 'Good to see you, Will. I'm here for the summer and have been giving Dad a hand.'

'Nate said.' He paused, took a drink. 'I hear your daughter has made an impression on Owen.'

'So it seems. She's loving working with him... and...' He picked up his beer.

'Join me?' Will gestured towards the door to the deck as a crowd of guys surged towards the bar.

Once out on the deck, Neil felt himself relax. The familiar sound of the waves and the cries of the seagulls took him back to his teenage years, years when he hadn't a care in the world, when anything seemed possible.

'Was that your school I read about?'

Will's question brought him back to the present with a thud. 'Probably.'

'Didn't sound good. There's too much of that sort of thing going on. Discovered corruption in our own town council recently. The bugger scarpered interstate, but the police caught up with him before he could get any further.'

'Oh!' For a moment, Neil had thought he was about to be interrogated about his part in the mess at the school.

'Yeah, not what we expect in Bellbird Bay, but greed is everywhere.' Will took another swig of beer. 'Heard your dad's sick, too. Must be hard.'

Neil gazed down towards the beach where he could see several figures walking along at the edge of the water just as the sun was setting, its golden glow reflected on the ocean.

'Yeah. It's Parkinson's,' he said.

'Bummer.'

The two sat in silence.

Thoughts were whirling through Neil's head – his dad, Ali, the mess with the school, his own future. But foremost was what to do about Ali.

It was comfortable in Will's presence, like pulling on an old shoe, one he'd forgotten about, but which he knew well, one which still felt the same as it used to. He glanced at his companion. While they'd never been close friends at school, Will was one of the good guys... and he'd been married. And Neil had heard he was now in another relationship. 'Can I ask you something, mate?' he said at last, hoping Will wouldn't rubbish him.

'Sure.'

'I need some advice. It's about a woman.'

'Isn't it always?' Will laughed, but not unkindly. 'Not sure I'm the best person to ask but go ahead.'

'Trouble is, I'm out of practice... Oh, not with that aspect of it,' he added with a chuckle when Will's eyes widened.

'Thank Christ for that.' Will chuckled too. 'Though maybe I could give you a few pointers in that direction.'

Neil felt himself redden. 'Since Christmas, well, New Year, really, I've been seeing this woman. I thought we were good together, but now she tells me she has a girlfriend coming to stay for two weeks so wants to cool it. I need to... do you think... is she tired of me? Is this her way of letting me down gently? Or is she being kosher?'

'Women!' Will rubbed his chin. 'I was married to one and am living with another, and I'll never understand them. But what I do know is this.' He leant forward across the table. 'They're unpredictable. What I suspect is...' he paused again, '...she likes you but has cold feet. It's not uncommon with women when they get to our age. I'm guessing she's in her fifties?'

Neil nodded.

'Do I know her?' Will asked suddenly, surprising Neil.

'I don't know. Maybe. Ali Wells. She's Adam Holland's sister.'

Neil suddenly felt uncomfortable discussing Ali like this. He wished he had never mentioned it. But now he had, he was stuck with the conversation.

'Tall, slim, elegant, greying hair?'

'Sounds like her.' Now Neil was really embarrassed.

'We met at a barbecue, and she hired a surfboard from me. Good-looking lady.'

'Yes.' Now Neil remembered Ali talking about surfing. It seemed everyone in Bellbird Bay swam into Will Rankin's orbit at one time or another.

'Sorry I can't be of more help.'

'It's okay, thanks. I shouldn't have asked.' *And wish I hadn't. Now there's one more person who knows my business.*

'You'd probably be better asking one of the women. My partner, Cleo, and Ailsa, Martin's wife, should be here later.'

'Thanks, but I should be getting back.' No way was Neil going to open himself up to the ridicule of a couple of women. He must be needing his head read to have mentioned his concern to Will in the first place.

Twenty-two

'When does your friend arrive?' Libby asked.

The two women were enjoying coffee in *The Pandanus Café* after Libby had been on a spending spree in the neighbouring garden centre.

'Tomorrow.' Ali couldn't wait to see Sally again. Libby was becoming a good friend and, as she got to know her better, she could understand how she had managed to break down all Adam's preconceived ideas about commitment. But Ali wasn't ready to confide in her about Neil… not yet. Sally was a different matter. Sally would understand Ali's reluctance to become too involved, combined with the strong pull of attraction she felt towards him.

'You've known each other a long time?'

'It seems like for ever. We met when we started high school. I was still fairly new to Perth, still smarting from having left home and Adam, and Sally… it was as if she took his place. Not really, of course,' she chuckled. 'No one could do that. But she'd been born in Perth, knew the city well and took me under her wing. We went everywhere together.' Ali smiled remembering how it was as if the pair of them were joined at the hip. 'She's my best friend,' she said simply.

'Good friends are important,' Libby said nodding. 'I lost my best friend in Brisbane earlier this year. Cancer.' Her eyes clouded for a moment, then they brightened again. 'But I've made some good friends here in Bellbird Bay, even though it's not so easy to make friends as we get older.'

'Finished, ladies?' the dark-haired manager of the café stopped by their table. 'Looks like you're going to be busy, Libby,' she said, gesturing to the trolley laden with plants and bags of fertiliser.

'We are, Cleo. And you're right. A lot of my old favourites suffered from the intense heat over Christmas, and I need to replace them. I'm hoping Ali might help me put these in.' She smiled at Ali as she spoke.

'Of course, I'd be happy to. I used to love pottering around in my mother's garden. I miss it.' Ali could see the garden of the Perth house in her mind's eye, could almost smell the fragrance of the lavender and jasmine her mother tended so carefully, scents which would always remind her of her mother.

'Enjoy your gardening. I wish I had more time for ours,' Cleo said laughingly as she picked up their cups and walked off.

'You don't have to help if you don't want to,' Libby said when they were alone again, 'if you need to get things ready for your friend.'

'No, I'd be happy to, really. There's not much to get ready. The shopping's done, the bed's made. It's a small apartment to keep tidy. And a few hours of gardening is exactly what I need.' Ali almost added, *to keep my mind off Neil Simpson*, but caught herself just in time.

*

Ali was right. The time spent with her hands in the soil was calming. There was something about a garden. Didn't she read something somewhere about being close to God in a garden? Regardless, it was rewarding to see the garden come to life as she and Libby dug and planted. When they sat back on their heels and surveyed the result of their work, they both smiled.

'Looks good, doesn't it?' Libby asked.

'It's beautiful. Where's Adam?' Ali asked, realising there had been no sign of her brother.

'Locked up in the study with Jay Bolton,' Libby said, referring to the hero in Adam's new series. 'He's working to a deadline and I daren't disturb him. He won't emerge till dinner time. You'll join us for dinner, won't you?'

'Thanks, I'd love to. Meantime...' She looked down at her hands which were covered in soil.

'Why don't you clean up and take a walk till dinner's ready? It should be lovely up at the headland at this time of day.'

'Are you sure I can't help?'

'I'm sure. You've been a big help already, and dinner will be no trouble. You look as if you need some fresh air in your lungs.'

Although they had been in the fresh air all afternoon, Ali understood what Libby meant. She did need some time to herself. Family was good, but it could get claustrophobic at times to always be with someone. Was she becoming antisocial, she wondered. Then she dismissed the notion. She just needed some time to herself.

It was beautiful up on the headland. Ali stood looking out at the wide expanse of ocean, down to where a group of surfers were only black spots on the surface of the dark blue water, then out to the horizon where the sky met the sea. In the face of such majesty, her own worries paled to insignificance.

Ali was turning away from the edge, preparing to walk back down the boardwalk when a strange figure appeared. The woman was wheeling a green bicycle with a large basket attached to the back of it. She was wearing a wide-brimmed straw hat and her face was creased with wrinkles. She peered at Ali.

'You're at a crossroads,' she said in a voice so soft Ali had to strain her ears to hear. 'Follow your heart and the way will open up for you. The past is over. Don't be afraid to take a new direction.'

Before Ali could reply, she was gone, wheeling the bicycle through the white gate of a shabby high-set house Ali hadn't noticed earlier. She read the sign on the gatepost. *Headland House.*

Feeling bewildered, Ali continued on her way, glad when she reached the safety of Adam and Libby's house where Milo padded out to greet her and lick her toes. Libby was setting the table on the deck and Adam was opening a bottle of wine. It was all so normal.

'Everything okay? Did you have a nice walk?' Libby asked.

'Ye...es. I met this strange woman who said...' Ali frowned, trying to remember exactly what the woman had said, '...something about a crossroads and following my heart. It was weird. Then she disappeared into a tall house before I could ask her what she meant.'

'Oh, you met Ruby,' Libby said with a smile. 'We've all been subject to her strange utterances at one time or another.'

'Ruby Sullivan – the woman who bakes the delicious cakes and…?' Suddenly Ali remembered what Grace had said about her. She was a witch. Ali shivered.

'You don't need to worry about her. She's harmless,' Adam said, grinning. 'Wine?' He held out the bottle he'd just opened.

'Thanks.' Ali took the glass and a gulp of the wine, the icy cold liquid sending a jolt through her.

'Though she often hits the mark,' Libby said, accepting a glass of wine, too. 'I can remember when…'

'Not now, Libby,' Adam said. 'Let Ali enjoy her wine.'

'No, I want to know,' Ali insisted, dropping into a seat. 'Grace said she was a witch.'

Libby chuckled, 'Not exactly. Those who grew up here have tales of how they used to tease her when they were kids. But…' she said, becoming more serious, '…her odd sayings often have a ring of truth.' She threw a glance at Adam. 'She counselled me to have patience and she told your brother his destiny lay here in Bellbird Bay. How prophetic was that?'

Ali shivered again. She *was* at a crossroads, but one she could handle. If she had to move universities, it wouldn't be the end of the world. But as for following her heart… That had never been in her plan.

'You're freaking her out, Libby,' Adam said, refilling Ali's glass, which she had no recollection of emptying. 'Is dinner ready?'

'Of course.' Libby went into the house, followed by Milo, no doubt hoping some titbits would come his way.

By the time Libby returned, carrying a platter of cold meats and a bowl of salad, Ali had regained her equilibrium and was able to help Libby place the dishes on the table. 'I'll fetch plates,' she said, rising to go to the kitchen. Milo followed her, still hoping for something to eat.

'He's already been fed,' Libby called after her. 'Don't be tempted to give him anything.'

'Did you hear that?' Ali asked the dog who was looking at her pleadingly. 'Don't tell Libby,' she whispered, dropping a piece of ham which was left on the benchtop.

Milo swallowed it quickly and looked up for more.

'Sorry, that's all.' Ali showed the dog her empty hands, then collected the plates and carried them outside, Milo following and settling down at Adam's feet.

Dinner was a relaxing affair, Ali noting yet again how compatible Adam and Libby appeared to be. It almost made her want to have the same sort of affectionate relationship they did. Almost... but she knew her distrust of relationships was so ingrained it would be difficult, if not impossible, for her to achieve the same sense of oneness the pair possessed.

'No word from the university?' Adam asked when Libby had gone inside to make coffee.

Ali shook her head, all the memories of her humiliation flooding back. 'No, but I didn't expect to hear anything yet. Sally has her feelers out and may have news for me. But...' she sighed, '...I need to start looking around to see what positions are available elsewhere. I have contacts I've made at conferences.' She knew she could have contacted these people before now, but had been delaying in the hope that... what... that Richard might change his mind? She knew there was as much chance of that as Hell freezing over. 'Maybe I can find something closer to Bellbird Bay,' she said.

'We'd love that. Libby and I are both enjoying having you here. It's been like a breath of fresh air to be in the same town as you again for weeks at a time, Ali. Those short visits last year didn't cut it.'

'It's been good for me, too, Adam.' Ali fell silent, remembering how much she'd missed her big brother when her mother dragged her away, how for weeks, months even, she'd cried herself to sleep at night wondering if she'd ever see him again, wishing he would appear as if by magic. It had taken over forty years – a lifetime – for her wish to be granted.

'There is a university in the hinterland,' he said.

'But they don't offer Women's Studies. We discussed that last year,' she reminded him.

'No.' It was Adam's turn to sigh.

'Something the matter?' Libby returned with the coffee just as Adam sighed.

'We're just discussing Ali's future prospects,' Adam said. 'Not every university offers the discipline she lectures in.'

'Maybe you need to become an author like your brother,' Libby joked.

'I wish, but fiction isn't my bag. I could publish some of the papers I've written but I doubt they'd appeal to a wide audience. And I love teaching, making a difference in women's lives.'

The topic of conversation changed to Adam's next book and the television series based on one of his earlier novels, the first episode of which was due to be shown in a few weeks' time.

'It's been delayed so often, I'll believe it when I see it,' Adam said, 'though I don't intend to actually watch it.'

'Why not?' Ali asked. 'I can't wait to see Phil Hanlon on the small screen.'

'Me neither,' Libby said.

But Adam shook his head. 'I couldn't bear it.'

The two women laughed.

'On that note, it's time I went home,' Ali said. 'Thanks for dinner and for allowing me to share in the gardening, Libby. I enjoyed it.'

'Thank *you*.' Libby hugged Ali and gave her a kiss on the cheek. 'Any time you want to help out, you don't have to ask.'

'Goodnight, sis.' Adam pulled Ali into a hug, too. 'We love having you here. It's a real pity you can't stay.'

'I'm here till Easter. You'll probably be tired of me by then,' Ali laughed as she pushed open the gate, making sure Milo stayed inside.

Walking down the boardwalk towards the esplanade on her way home, Ali pondered her brother's words. Would she stay here in Bellbird Bay if she could? She remembered having asked Neil that same question.

He hadn't replied.

Twenty-three

Ali's heart was light as she drove to the airport to pick up Sally. Despite having a restless night troubled by thoughts of Neil and the uncertainty of her future career, the prospect of her friend's company made her want to burst into song.

Arriving in plenty of time, she grabbed a coffee and settled down to await the plane's arrival. She was about to check the arrival board, when her phone pinged with a text. It was from Sally to tell her the plane had landed.

Soon the pair were hugging, delighted to see each other again.

'I've missed you,' Sally said when they drew apart. 'I'm dying to see this little town you've told me about and to meet your brother.'

'It's nothing like Perth,' Ali said. 'Do you have luggage to collect?'

'No, this is it. I travel light.' Sally pointed to the small case sitting at her feet.

'Let's go, then. I have a bottle of chardonnay cooling in the fridge and your favourite pizza in the freezer.'

'I can't wait. Lead on.'

'Wow, the coastline is spectacular.' Sally twisted her neck to gaze down at the stretch of sand and ocean on the way back to Bellbird Bay. 'No wonder your brother chose to move here.'

'I think Libby had something to do with it,' Ali said with a grin.

'You said he was just as determined as you to avoid commitment. What happened?'

'I guess Libby happened.'

'She must be pretty special.'

'She is.' Ali thought of the kind woman who had managed to steal her brother's heart. 'It's been lovely spending time with them.'

'Not thinking of staying yourself?' Sally shot Ali a wary glance.

'No chance.' Ali laughed but couldn't help remembering Adam's words.

An hour later Ali and Sally were seated on Ali's tiny balcony with glasses of chardonnay.

'I can see why you like this place,' Sally said, stretching out her legs. 'I would too. But don't you miss the city?'

Ali thought for a moment before replying, 'No, not really. Though I probably would after a while. It's a different sort of life.' She took a sip of wine. 'Now, tell me the goss. What's been happening at the university since I left?' She knew her friend would have had her antennae out – and they mixed in the same circles.

Sally's forehead creased. 'You're not going to like what I heard at a Christmas party.'

'Tell me.'

'Richard has announced his retirement, and Hugo Martin is running around town like a dog with two tails. Now you appear to be out of the picture, he's sure he'll be named the new Head of School.'

Ali's heart plummeted. The coil of fear she'd been trying to suppress tightened. 'But… I'm still on staff,' she stammered.

'Tell that to the arrogant bastard. You need to come back to Perth if you want to stand any chance of getting Richard's position.'

'Oh!' The thought of returning to enter the contest for Head of School was daunting. Did she really want to jump through the hoops it would entail, open herself up to further humiliation only to be pipped at the post by Hugo Martin?

Seeming to read her mind, Sally said, 'If you don't, you're letting him win, letting a man get the top job again. What sort of message does it send to your students?'

'If I have any students left,' Ali said bitterly. 'The last thing Richard said to me was that he was cutting Women's Studies.'

'Well, it's your call. Word is Richard will stay for one more semester and they won't start advertising his position till close to Easter. That's when your leave finishes, isn't it?'

'Mmm.'

'Have you heard from the student who…?'

'Chelsea? Yes, she's transferring to her local university. At least she's able to continue her studies.'

'While Hugo gets off scot-free and may even get the promotion he's been angling for. It's not fair.'

'Life isn't fair.' Where had Ali heard that said? But it was true, and life was often less fair for women than for their male counterparts. It was one of the reasons she'd chosen to study, then lecture in Women's Studies. But had she done enough? Little had changed and the very university where she'd taught was still the bastion of male dominance.

'So, you'll apply?'

'Oh, I don't know, Sal. I need to think about it.' And consider what it might be like. Even if she was successful, she'd still have to deal with the same sort of prejudice she'd experienced over the situation with Chelsea. Was she really prepared to put herself through that again just to prove a point?

'You're not going to let them win?' Sally sounded aghast. 'After all you've said and written about women's rights and…'

'I know, I know, but… now I'm away from it all, I've had time to think, to distance myself.'

'And…?' Sally persisted.

'I'm not sure it's what I want.' Ali surprised herself with the admission the senior position she'd coveted for the past ten years might not be what she really wanted after all.

'Time for a refill, and where's the pizza you promised me?' Sally asked, rising and holding up her empty glass.

'What's been happening with you?' Ali asked. 'How was Christmas?' It was sometime later. The bottle of chardonnay was empty, and the remains of the pizza were strewn across the coffee table.

Sally made a face. 'Oh, the usual. All the rellies came to Mum's and the celebration seemed to go on for days. I only managed to escape to Belinda's party by the skin of my teeth,' she said.

Ali was sorry to have missed that particular event. Belinda Allen had been at school with both Ali and Sally, but instead of staying around in Perth, had headed off to Europe as soon as she finished Year Twelve, returning three years later to wow them all with her elegant makeover. Now, she owned a top-of-the-market wine bar in the city where she threw a marvellous party every Boxing Day.

'I suppose that's where you heard about Richard and Hugo,' she said. 'Were either of them there?'

'You must be joking. I doubt Belinda's bash would interest Richard, and Hugo could never score an invite. But they were the topic of conversation in one group.' She tapped her nose.

'Roland,' Ali guessed, grinning when Sally nodded. Roland Granger had been at school with them, too. Older than the three women, his partner taught drama at the university and was renowned for his sharp tongue and addiction to gossip. He was also no friend of Hugo Martin.

'I'm bushed.' Sally yawned. 'Might be time for me to turn in. You haven't said much about this man you've met,' she said, giving Ali a piercing look.

'There's plenty of time for that,' Ali said, yawning, too. Now Sally was actually here, she discovered she wasn't so keen to talk about Neil Simpson.

Twenty-four

Neil was enjoying a coffee break at *The Bay Café* and wondering how soon he could leave the bookshop to his dad again when his phone rang. Seeing Pippa's number on the screen he was tempted to ignore it but knew his ex-wife. If she wanted to speak to him, she wouldn't give up till he answered. He hadn't forgotten their last call and suspected this one would be about Bronte, too.

With a sigh, he pressed to accept the call. 'Pippa.'

'Neil. I'm guessing you know why I'm calling.'

'I presume you've heard from Bronte.'

'What were you thinking to allow her to...'

Neil held the phone away from his ear as the invectives flowed, becoming louder and louder. When there was silence at last, he put the phone back to his ear. 'Are you finished?' he asked as calmly as he could.

'Finished? Bronte's the one who'll be finished when I get hold of her. How can she throw away her future in a tinpot town like Bellbird Bay?'

'You seemed to think it was okay for her to spend the summer here.'

'That's different. I wanted her to realise... Damn you, Neil Simpson. Why do you always have to sound so... so....'

Neil smiled. It wasn't often Pippa ran out of words.

Her silence didn't last for long. 'You're her father. You need to make her realise she's ruining any chance to make something of herself if she doesn't re-enrol in a degree course. I don't know what's wrong with the girl. I've given her so many chances… and she's thrown away every one of them. She could have been almost finished her degree by now if she'd stuck at it.'

'A degree you'd chosen for her. Did you ever consider asking Bronte what *she* wanted to do?'

'What would she know? I'm her mother. I know what's best for her.'

'Well, it hasn't worked so far, has it?'

Pippa emitted an expletive.

Neil could imagine her enraged face.

'Bronte's happy, Pippa. She's happier than I've seen her for years. She went along with the degrees in business, law, IT, to please you, but she was never invested in them. Now she's…'

'Working with a surfer… designing surfboards… What sort of life is that? You've spent your working life with young people, preparing them for university. Surely you of all people realise her mistake.'

Her words hit Neil like a bolt of lightning. Had he, as a teacher and principal, been doing exactly what he was accusing Pippa of? Had he been so intent on shoehorning his pupils into university places, he'd completely ignored their own wishes and aptitudes? Surely not. But at least he could ensure his daughter followed her dream.

'Bronte has always been artistically gifted. This is giving her the opportunity to use her gift. And she's doing more than designing surfboards. She's using the skills she developed in her business and IT studies to help Owen expand his business into other lines and to develop an online business.'

'And who is this surfer, this Owen Rankin she raves about? What sort of guy spends his life with surfboards? Some sort of no-hoper and layabout,' she said, answering her own question.

'Actually, Owen is a pretty decent guy. I've met him, and his friends – the ones Bronte is spending time with. I was at school with his father, and Owen is a chip off the old block. Will Rankin is a respected member of the community, runs the local surf school, the surfing carnival committee and…'

'Exactly as I thought,' Pippa said. 'Sounds as if you've gone native, too. I should never have allowed Bronte to go to Bellbird Bay.'

Neil had to bite his tongue to prevent him from reminding Pippa it had been her idea for Bronte to spend the summer with him and his dad.

'Now the least you can do is talk some sense into her,' she said, before ending the call.

'And goodbye to you, too,' Neil said to the silent phone, before slipping it back into his pocket. He picked up his coffee and took a sip, grimacing when he discovered it had gone cold. Then he returned to the bookshop.

Try as he might, Neil was unable to forget Pippa's call as he went about his daily tasks in the bookshop. He knew he hadn't been remiss in allowing Bronte to follow her dream, but had he been guilty of stealing the dreams of other students by funnelling them into university places?

He was still pondering when, in the early afternoon, Bronte breezed into the bookshop, Owen trailing behind her. Her long blonde hair was tied up in a topknot remarkably similar to Owen's, and both were dressed in cut-off denim shorts and white tee-shirts bearing the slogan *Bay Surfboards* inscribed on a surfboard, a design he'd seen Bronte playing around with a few nights ago. The sight of them brought a smile to Neil's face. They could have been twins.

'Like the tee-shirts. How did you get them done so quickly?'

'We discovered this guy who sells his tees at the markets and had him mock up a couple for us. Cool, aren't they?' Bronte pulled hers tight across her chest to give Neil a better look.

He averted his eyes.

'I wish your grandma was here to see you,' Harry chuckled. 'She'd have been first in line for one.'

'Grandma surfed?'

'My word. We all did.'

'We've decided to take the afternoon off and go surfing,' Bronte said. 'Owen thinks I need more practice and he wants to start training for the surfing championships. They're held on Easter weekend.' She grinned at her companion who grinned back.

They were the epitome of young love, reminding Neil of his own first forays in that direction. For a fleeting moment he wondered what Myra Dennis was doing now.

'Your mum called,' Neil said to Bronte.

She made a face. 'What did she want? I emailed her to let her know I plan to stay here and work with Owen.' She clutched the boy's hand as if it was a lifeline.

'She said she's not pleased, Bronte. Thinks you're ruining your life.'

'What would she know? All she wants is to be able to boast about me to her friends. "My daughter the lawyer" or some such thing. I'm old enough to decide what I want to do with my life, and this is what I want to do.' She swung the hand in Owen's.

'Don't you think she deserves more than an email? Perhaps a phone call?'

'No way.' Bronte sighed. 'I know how it would go. She'd want to lay all these guilt trips on me, make me feel I had let her down, that I was an ungrateful daughter, yadda yadda. You know what she's like, Dad. I don't need all that.'

'You heard the girl, son,' Harry said. 'Let her make her own decisions. You certainly did when you were her age.' He chuckled.

'Neither you nor Mum tried to run my life,' Neil said, but he understood where his dad was coming from. 'Okay, Bronte. But don't blame me if...' What could Pippa do? Bronte was right. She was an adult, capable of making her own decisions. The only problem was that Pippa would blame him. Well, he had broad shoulders and, after the first flush of their relationship, when had Pippa's opinion ever bothered him? 'Enjoy your surf,' he said.

'We will.'

The pair left, laughing before they went out the door and making Neil wonder if he was overreacting to Pippa's complaints.

'She's all right, Neil,' Harry said when the door closed after the youngsters. 'It does my heart good to see a young couple making something of their lives. If I was fifty years younger, I'd wear one of their tee-shirts myself. Pippa should be grateful Bronte has some direction in her life. I'm willing to bet *Bay Surfboards* has a prosperous future ahead of it.'

'Hmm.' Neil didn't comment, but he thought his dad could be right. And it was good to see Harry more like his old self. Some days it was difficult to believe he was really ill, others it seemed as if he didn't have much longer to go. It was a pernicious illness, one Neil knew would eventually take away the man he knew and loved.

Twenty-five

'Now, who's this man who has you tied in knots? What's so special about him?' Sally asked, when they were enjoying a breakfast of coffee and chocolate croissants on Ali's balcony. It was the third day of Sally's visit and, although the two of them had sat up late each night sharing gossip, Ali still hadn't broached the subject of Neil with her friend.

'He's…' Ali hesitated, trying to work out what it was about Neil Simpson that set him apart from other men she'd dated, '…different,' she finished.

'Different how?' Sally asked, biting into her croissant and sending pastry flakes all over the balcony. 'Sorry, I can never eat these without making a mess. They're yummy.'

Ali was distracted for a moment, then responded, 'Different to the men I … we… knew in Perth.'

'That doesn't tell me anything. Am I going to meet him?' Sally peered at Ali over the top of her coffee cup.

'He did suggest we have dinner.' Ali wasn't sure it was a good idea. Sally could sometimes appear quite offensive with her smart remarks.

'Good idea.'

'I don't know. Sal. As I said, he's not like the guys we meet in Perth. There's something about him… he has a daughter, a father who's sick. He's caught up in a scandal in the school where he's principal, he's helping out in his dad's bookshop…'

'So? None of that tells me why you've got your knickers in a knot.'

'He lives in Brisbane, and I'll be going back to Perth.'

'So it's a holiday romance. Perfect... no?' Sally appeared puzzled.

'No. It's not that simple.'

'You mean...?' Sally's eyes widened. 'Don't tell me Ali Wells is in danger of breaking all her own rules where men are concerned.'

'Not exactly.' Ali shifted uncomfortably in her chair and stared out over the ocean wishing she'd never thought she could ask advice from Sally.

Sally waited patiently.

'It's all happened so fast, Sal. I've never felt this way before. It's as if I've fallen from a cliff. I'm in freefall and I don't want to stop. I don't know what to do.'

'My, you have got it bad.' Sally peered at Ali again and her voice softened. 'Look, why don't you just see what happens. As you said, you live on opposite sides of the country, but...' she took a deep breath, '... if this is the real deal...' She held up both hands. 'I know, I know. We've both always said love wasn't for us; we didn't believe in the romantic balderdash peddled by the movies and the romance novels. But what if... just what if it *can* happen to us? What if not every relationship ends up the way your mother's did, the way of all those women you write about, lecture about? What if there was a way you could have it all – career, marriage, independence, happiness? Might it not be worth giving up your avowed intention to avoid any sort of commitment?'

'You've changed your tune.' Ali's eyes widened in amazement.

'Maybe I have. Maybe it's time. Since you left Perth, I've given a lot of thought to the future – my future – and I don't like what I see. Being with my family over Christmas... oh, it was the usual Italian family catastrophe. But this year, it hit me that my sister, my brothers, they all have someone... all except me. I'm fifty-five, Ali, and what do I have to show for it? A career that keeps me busy from dawn to dusk, that exhausts me. Relationships that go nowhere – from my choice, it's true. But for how much longer can I find men willing to go along with that? Most of the guys I – and you – meet these days are married, looking for a brief fling. And while it suited us when we were in our twenties, thirties, even forties, for how much longer? Soon we'll be sixty, then seventy. All of our peers will have settled for someone while we...'

Ali was stunned by Sally's rant. She'd always assumed they'd grow old together – two career-minded women who didn't need anyone else in their lives – especially a man – to find fulfilment. She'd expected Sally to tell her she was imagining the feelings she was experiencing with Neil... not this.

'Sorry to shock you. Now, about this man of yours...'

'He's not mine... but he's nice,' Ali said dreamily, picturing Neil's face on the pillow next to hers, his bronzed chest, his...'

'You're blushing!'

Ali's hands automatically went to her cheeks which did feel warmer than the morning warranted.

'Anyway,' Sally brushed the remaining pastry flakes from her lap, 'what's on the agenda today?'

'We're meeting Libby for lunch,' Ali said. 'She's buying more plants – though I don't know where she's going to put them all – and wants to meet us in the café attached to the garden centre. I've been there with her before and it's pretty good. Adam will join us if he can spare the time.'

'I like your brother and his partner,' Sally said. 'Didn't you say he was totally opposed to commitment, too, until he met her?'

'Don't you start. I get enough of that from Libby. I've been counting on you to back me up.'

'All I said was we're not getting any younger and perhaps we should start thinking about our old age.' But Sally giggled as she spoke, making Ali grin.

'Old age! Listen to the woman. We're not in our dotage yet, and even when we are, we won't need a man to make us feel validated.'

'If you say so. What are we going to do till lunchtime?'

'Maybe have a swim?' Ali stretched her arms above her head. 'And I want to introduce you to a great little boutique on the esplanade. It's called *Birds of a Feather.*'

'Sounds good to me.'

*

After a refreshing swim, Ali and Sally made their way to the esplanade where, after casting a glance towards *Bay Books* and wondering if Neil was working there today, Ali led the way to the boutique.

'What do you think?' she asked her friend as they stood at the window filled with brightly coloured garments.

'It looks amazing. You've been in already?'

'Bought a snazzy black and white outfit, but I'm tempted to splurge on one of the more brightly coloured ones. It is summer, after all.'

Laughing together, the two entered, to be greeted with a smile. 'Back again,' Greta said.

'My friend's visiting from Perth and we're both in the market for something different... something bright.'

'I can certainly help you there. Why don't you have a look around and see what appeals to you. Those over here...' she gestured to where, along one wall, a collection of dresses in tropical prints were on display, '...are new arrivals. I'll leave you to browse. Let me know if you need any help.'

Half an hour later, each carrying a bag emblazoned with the *Birds of a Feather* logo, Ali and Sally left the boutique. They were both smiling delightedly, and their credit cards were markedly lighter.

'Who'd have thought you'd find such an amazing shop in a small town like this,' Sally said as they made their way to Ali's car. 'Time for lunch?'

Ali checked her watch. 'We should go straight there,' she said. 'I'd hate to keep Libby waiting.'

Libby was already seated at a small table when the two women arrived at the café.

'This is amazing, too,' Sally said, her eyes sweeping around to take in the large pandanus tree in the centre and the small tables artistically placed among a series of low bushes and towering palm trees. In the far corner, the kitchen was neatly hidden from view by a screen of grevillea.

'Beginning to change your mind about Bellbird Bay?' Ali asked, waving to Libby and making their way towards her.

There was no time for Sally to respond before they reached Libby, who rose to give each of them a kiss on the cheek.

'Sorry, Adam isn't going to make it,' Libby said. 'He's waiting for a call from his agent. I don't know why he can't call him, but it is what it is.' She spread her hands. 'Anyway, what have you two been up to? How are you enjoying our small town, Sally?'

A waitress arrived before they had finished filling Libby in on what they'd been doing, and they interrupted their conversation to check the menu and place their orders. Both Libby and Ali chose quiche with salad, while Sally decided to try the salad of the day which was a pear and walnut salad with crumbled blue cheese. All three ordered an iced latte and a slice of a decadent chocolate Bavarian cake for dessert.

'Now, where were we?' Libby asked.

'We were up to our visit to *Birds of a Feather*,' Ali said with a grin. 'It was Libby who told me about the boutique,' she said to Sally.

'I'm sure Greta looked after you and didn't let you leave empty-handed,' Libby chuckled. 'We are in a book club together. I have a few of her outfits now.'

'We did buy a couple each,' Ali admitted with a conspiratorial grin to Sally.

'And now you need an occasion to wear them.' Libby nodded. 'Adam suggested we all have dinner at the surf club tonight. Another gem in Bellbird Bay,' she told Sally. 'Everyone ends up there at some time or other.'

'I'm up for that. Ali?' Sally said.

'Sure,' Ali said. 'It's a lovely spot.' But she was wondering if she might see Neil there, remembering him telling her it was where he'd first noticed her.

*

Arriving at the surf club dressed in the garish dresses purchased that morning, Sally appeared unimpressed. Ali led the way inside and, as they made their way upstairs, recited the story of Ted Crawford, the man whose image appeared on the mural and who had been local surfing champion three years running. Sally was still unimpressed.

However, when they entered the restaurant, Sally said, 'Wow!' her eyes going to the view from the deck, the gold and red glow of the sun disappearing below the horizon, and Ali felt an unexpected thrill of pride which she quickly suppressed. It wasn't *her* surf club. *She* wasn't responsible for the magnificent view.

'There they are.' Ali pointed to where Adam and Libby were

standing at the bar chatting to another couple. Ali recognised them as Martin and Ailsa Cooper, the pair who had married a few months ago. She stifled a sigh. Another loved-up couple. Bellbird Bay seemed to be full of them.

When Libby and Adam had greeted Ali and Sally with hugs and kisses on their cheeks, Libby turned to Sally. 'These are friends of ours, Ailsa and Martin Cooper.' Then, turning to Ailsa and Martin said, 'Sally is a friend of Ali's visiting from Perth.'

There were handshakes all round then Sally stared at Martin in awe, 'Not *the* Martin Cooper?' she asked. 'I've followed your career. I love your work.'

'Thanks.' Martin looked embarrassed.

'You didn't tell me Bellbird Bay was home to *two* famous men,' she said to Ali.

It was Adam's turn to look embarrassed.

'We won't keep you. Here are Will and Cleo now,' Ailsa said as Will Rankin and his partner, Cleo, appeared at the top of the stairs.

'We have a table reserved on the deck,' Libby said, adroitly guiding Ali and Sally outside and to a table overlooking the ocean which was now a dark heaving mass.

Once all four had ordered and been supplied with glasses of white wine, Ali asked Adam, 'Your agent called?'

'He did. Julian can be a hard taskmaster, but he's on board with my new series and making noises about another television series. That's what he wanted to talk with me about – that and a book tour.' He grimaced. 'I'm hoping to get out of it. I don't want to spend weeks on the road away from Libby.' He gave Libby's hand a squeeze.

Ali looked away. While she was happy for Adam, glad he'd found someone to spend the rest of his life with, she didn't need to watch them being affectionate with each other. Though there was something touching about it. It was something that had been missing from their parents' marriage, something that made her wonder if Sally was right.

Sally started asking Adam about his writing and how he found his agent, and Ali let her mind wander, only surfacing when she heard Libby say, 'Isn't that Harry Simpson over there? Is the man with him his son?'

Twenty-six

This was the first day Harry had gone to the bookshop on his own, insisting he didn't need Neil's help and, while Neil was concerned about how his dad would manage, he knew it would be a mistake to say so. Harry could easily lose his temper these days, be quick to take offence, and Neil had worked out it was best to let him be. He'd find out soon enough if things started to go wrong.

But with Harry at the bookshop, and Bronte at Owen's workshop, Neil was alone in the house with time to think. Uppermost in his mind was what to do about Ali. Her friend would have been in Bellbird Bay for a few days now. Was it time to contact her again, to suggest they all meet for lunch or dinner – or should he give them more time together? This is where he'd hoped Will might be of help. But his old school friend hadn't come up with the goods, so he'd been left to his own devices. He wished he knew Adam Holland well enough to approach him. Maybe Ali's brother would know how his sister's mind worked. Or maybe, as Will suggested, he needed to ask the advice of a woman. The trouble was, apart from Ali, he didn't know any women in Bellbird Bay.

He'd seen Ali at the surf club the previous evening. He and his dad had gone for an early dinner. They'd been about to leave when he'd spotted her at a table at the far end of the deck. She was with her brother and the woman who must be his partner. They were accompanied by a younger woman with short dark hair – presumably her friend. He'd been tempted to go over to say hello, to introduce himself to her family and friend, but something had held him back. They appeared to be enjoying a family dinner together and he didn't want to intrude. It was only on the way home, when Harry said, 'Wasn't that your lady friend at the club?' that he cursed his lack of courage.

Neil was still puzzling over this when an email arrived from his friend Barry in Brisbane. In addition to being a good friend, Barry was Neil's deputy principal and, as such, was well aware of his situation. He also had a son at the school, about to start year ten. Neil hadn't heard from Barry since leaving Brisbane, apart from a card at Christmas. He opened the email.

Neil,

Hope things are going well for you on the coast. Thought I should bring it to your attention that those board members not caught up in the corruption scandal plan to meet late January to discuss the future of the college. I've been invited, along with several others of the parent body, but not sure if they've contacted you. As you are no doubt aware, your involvement in the business is still undetermined in their eyes despite police deciding otherwise. The attached article in the local press – which may have escaped your notice – hasn't helped your case.

I'm happy to go in to bat for you, but you may want to put your own case. I can forward you more information on the meeting as it comes to hand.

Cheers,

Barry

Curious, Neil opened the attachment to read the headline *Local Principal Leaves Town in the Wake of Scandal.* He flinched. It was only the local rag, the one distributed free in the community, not the Courier Mail. Neil's eyes skimmed the article which made much of him leaving Brisbane to spend time 'sunning himself on the coast while others stayed to face the music'. He closed the article in disgust, unwilling to read any further. These hacks would print anything. Did they know he'd been advised to take leave till the fuss died down, that his father lived here where he'd grown up? Probably. But it made no difference when they thought they had a story that would attract their advertisers – the only way a free paper could make money.

The article wasn't what worried Neil. The board meeting was. As principal, he would normally be invited to their meetings as an *ex-officio* member. The fact he hadn't been informed of this one, that members of the parent body – including his deputy principal – had, was a real cause for concern.

He closed the computer with a sigh. Barry had promised to keep him informed. Maybe it was time to go back to Brisbane, to face the remaining board members, to reiterate his innocence, his ignorance of any knowledge of the wrongdoing. But what would it achieve?

Neil slumped in his chair.

His reverie was interrupted by his phone ringing. Seeing his dad's number, Neil answered quickly, hoping all was well with Harry and the bookshop.

'I thought you might be interested, son,' Harry said. Neil could hear the amusement in his voice. 'Adam Holland is dropping in to sign copies of his latest book. If you'd like to meet him…' Harry let his voice trail off.

'I would.' Neil wasn't sure how meeting Adam when he was signing books in *Bay Books* would further his knowledge of what was going through Ali's mind, but he was willing to try anything. 'See you soon, Dad.'

*

To Neil's disappointment, there was no sign of Adam Holland when he reached the bookshop. 'Have I missed him?' he asked Harry, staring around the almost empty store.

'He's in the back room.' Harry chuckled. 'Adam's not one for publicity. He'd prefer to be incognito. He should be finished soon, and I'll introduce you. In the meantime, you can take care of these for me.' He gestured to two boxes of books on the floor near the counter.

'Sorry, Dad. How are you coping?' Neil realised he should have asked that first. Instead, he'd been too wrapped up in his own concerns.

'I'm fine as always. Maybe a tad slower than I used to be, but you will be too when you reach my age.'

Neil peered at his dad in an attempt to identify any sign his condition had deteriorated further, but he still looked the same as always, albeit his hair was whiter, his face more lined. There was no sign of the insidious disease lurking in his body. Today there wasn't even any sign of the tremors Neil had noticed before Christmas. He picked up the boxes and carried them through to the back room where Adam Holland was seated at a small table with a pile of books.

'Hello?' Adam stopped what he was doing and looked up with a smile.

Neil stretched out a hand. 'Neil Simpson. I'm Harry's son. It's a pleasure to meet you. I'm a big fan.'

'I think you're something else, too,' Adam said with a chuckle. 'I believe you know my sister.'

'Ali? Yes. She's mentioned me?'

'To Libby, my partner, more than me.' He picked up his pen again. 'Maybe we can have a coffee when I finish here… if you have the time?'

'I'd love to. I just have a few things to take care of for Dad,' Neil lied.

'So you met him?' Harry asked when Neil returned.

'You old devil. You knew I would when you asked me to take care of those boxes of books.'

'And?'

'We're going to grab a coffee when he's done here. In the meantime…' he said, unconsciously echoing his father's words.

'You can take over here while I take a short break,' Harry said, walking towards the door. 'I won't be long.'

True to his word, Harry had returned by the time Adam emerged from the back of the store rubbing his wrist. 'Glad I don't have to do that too often,' he said grimacing.

'I appreciate you doing it for me. My regular customers now know I have signed copies and it's always a nice surprise for visitors,' Harry said.

'Happy to. It's not a problem, Harry, even though I may complain a bit. I'm ready for that coffee now.' He looked at Neil.

'Okay if I leave you to it, Dad?' Neil asked.

'Off you go. As you can see, we're not overrun with customers today.' He gestured to the few people browsing among the shelves and the mother whose two children were seated in the beanbags in the children's corner and looked to be settled there for some time.

'I'll look in again before I go home.'

Harry waved him away.

'Here, okay?' Adam gestured to *The Bay Café*. 'The coffee is good, and they know me. I used to have breakfast here every day before Libby and I got together. Now I only do it when she's working.'

'Perfect.' It had become a favourite with Neil, too, being so close to the bookshop.

Both ordered black coffee and sat for several moments in companionable silence.

'I hear Harry's sick,' Adam said at last. 'He has a good bookshop. I'd be sorry to see it go.'

'It hasn't come to that, yet,' Neil sighed, 'but even Dad can't go on for ever.'

'What will happen to it when he can no longer cope?'

Neil rubbed his chin. 'That's the problem. So many small independent bookshops are going to the wall these days. Dad's been able to hang on because of a good local following – and there's the tourist trade. It may be attractive to one of the larger chains, but...'

'It would lose the delightful atmosphere your dad has created.'

'Yeah.'

Their coffees arrived and Neil took advantage of the interruption to take a sip, wondering how he could bring the conversation around to Ali.

It was Adam who brought her up. 'My sister has mentioned you.'

Neil felt the tips of his ears turn red. 'We've met a few times. She... I enjoy her company.'

'Hmm.' Adam fixed Neil with a piercing look. 'Libby thinks there's more to it than that.' He took a sip of coffee and leant across the table. 'I don't want to come over as the heavy older brother. We're none of us kids anymore, and Ali would probably kill me if she could hear me, but...' He stirred his coffee and took a deep breath. 'You have to understand. We lost touch when we were young and only got back in contact a year ago. To me, Ali's still the little sister I knew when I was twelve.' He cleared his throat. 'We didn't have it easy growing up. Dad...' He paused. 'Dad was a bully.' He thrust a hand through his hair – the hair which was so like Ali's. 'Our mother left, taking Ali with her. She was too afraid to keep in touch and it wasn't till she died that Ali…' His eyes moistened and he brushed away an incipient tear. 'Sorry. Our home situation affected us both. I guess, like me, Ali is afraid of what a marriage – any sort of commitment – can be like. I need to be sure…' He gave Neil a piercing look again.

It suddenly all began to make sense to Neil. 'I'm no bully. I'd never let her down,' he said. 'I've never met anyone like Ali. I'd never hurt her.'

Adam seemed to relax. 'You seem like a genuine guy. I'm glad. *I* avoided commitment like the plague until I met Libby. She showed me what a relationship could be like. We both want that for Ali, too.'

'Me, too,' Neil said, suddenly tongue-tied.

'Look, she has this friend staying with her for a couple of weeks. The two of them are coming round for dinner tonight. Why don't you join us? I'm sure Libby would like to meet you, too.'

'Thanks, I'd like that. It's kind of you.'

'Good. I'd better be off. I have a deadline to meet for my agent. See you tonight around six?'

Neil nodded.

Adam gulped down the remains of his coffee and strode off, leaving Neil staring after him in surprise and wondering how Ali would react to seeing him at her brother's dinner table.

Twenty-seven

Ali and Sally were visiting the Botanic Gardens and had just decided to have lunch in the café there when Ali's phone rang. Sally wandered off to take a look at the Japanese Garden while Ali answered the call.

'I thought I should warn you,' Libby said. 'Adam met Neil Simpson this morning. He was signing books at the bookshop and the two got together. He's invited him to dinner tonight.'

Ali felt herself blush. 'Thanks for letting me know, Libby,' she said.

'Problem?' Sally asked when she re-joined Ali at the door of the café.

'Not really. Looks as if you're going to get your wish, after all, Sal. My brother has invited Neil to dinner this evening.'

'I didn't realise they knew each other.'

'They don't... didn't. I guess they do now.' Ali wasn't sure how she felt about it. It was as if she'd had matters taken out of her hands, had lost control of the situation. She realised it was foolish to think like that. There was no reason why the two men shouldn't have met – Adam wrote books, Neil's dad sold them. But she felt as if fate was conspiring against her. Adam and Libby were family. Neil was... what was he? A ship that passed in the night? No, he was more than that. She remembered how he made her feel, how she couldn't get enough of him, how...

But to have dinner with him in the bosom of her family... was she ready for that?

'Good.' Sally seemed unaware of Ali's misgivings. 'I'm looking forward to meeting him. Now, what shall we order?' They had entered the café by this time, and Sally was studying the blackboard menu.

Ali gazed at it, but it was all a blur. All she could think of, was that she'd be seeing Neil again that evening. But in the company of not only Sally, but also Adam and Libby, not to forget Milo. How would it be? She hoped he liked dogs – and that Milo liked him. According to Libby, the ungainly creature was a good judge of character.

'Ali!' Sally's voice brought Ali back to the present. 'I'm tempted to try the rocket and avocado with roast beef and Dijon mustard on rye. What about you?'

'Sounds good. I'll have it, too,' Ali said, without being aware what she had ordered.

By the time they'd chosen a table and placed their orders, Ali was feeling more like herself.

'Are you okay? You seemed a bit spaced out. Was it something Libby said?'

'It was everything she said, Sal. My big brother invited a man I've been seeing to dinner without even asking me how I felt about it. How embarrassing is that? My dates have never met my family – not ever.'

'Oh, is that all?' Sally laughed. 'Chill. It's not as if you have a big Italian family like mine, one which will want to set the wedding date and plan the wedding before he sits down at the table. That's why I don't take anyone home to meet them. Adam and Libby are more... restrained.'

'Restrained!' Ali snorted. 'You should have heard Libby before you arrived in town. She was instructing me on the joys of a relationship. Just because she and Adam have found *true love*,' she made quotation marks with her fingers, 'she thinks everyone else should be part of a loved-up couple. It's this damned town,' she fumed. 'It seems to be a haven for older people to find romance. Why, even...' She fell silent remembering Ruby Sullivan's words about following her heart.

To her surprise, her friend didn't immediately support her. 'Don't you think you're being a bit unfair, Ali? Libby and your brother are clearly very happy together. Is it wrong for her to want the same for you?'

'Not when you put it like that,' Ali said grudgingly, 'but... I hate the idea of sitting there with the two of them – maybe you, too,' she said glaring at her friend, 'wondering about us and imagining… all sorts of things that aren't true.'

'I think the lady doth protest too much.' Sally grinned.

'Oh, you!' Suddenly Ali saw the funny side of it. What was she getting so worked up about? She was a grown woman. Why should she be concerned because her brother had invited a perfectly nice man – one she was already fond of – to dinner? 'You're right,' she said. 'Let's eat,' she added, seeing their meals arriving.

*

That evening, as she discarded one outfit after another, trying to decide what to wear, Ali knew it was a big deal. It was akin to taking a man home for approval. Both Adam and Libby knew she was seeing Neil. She suspected they knew more about their friendship than she was willing to admit to them, maybe even to herself. And Sally would be no help. She, and her irrepressible sense of humour, would no doubt milk the situation for all it was worth. Ali would be glad when the evening was over.

Finally settling on one of the dresses she'd purchased from *Birds of a Feather* – a bright blue dress with white patterns which reminded Ali of the ocean, and a deep v-neckline. She applied a little more makeup than usual, fluffed her hair and was grimacing at herself in the mirror when she heard Sally call, 'Ready?'

Her friend was waiting for her wearing a white dress patterned in red poppies – another of their new purchases. 'Wow!' she said when she saw Ali.

'Is it too much?' Ali frowned, ready to change or to wipe off some of her makeup.

'You look perfect. Neil Simpson won't know what's hit him.'

'Hmm.' Ali wasn't sure she agreed but was satisfied with Sally's reaction. 'Shall we go? We can walk up. It's a lovely evening.'

On the way along the esplanade and up the boardwalk, Ali was trying to work out how to greet Neil. It was a strange feeling, almost as if they were going on their first date – though their first date had been nothing like this. When did it all become so complicated?

'There's nothing to be worried about,' Sally said, sensing Ali's mood. 'It's only dinner. Adam's your brother. Libby likes you. Neil's your...' she gave a chuckle. 'Well, it is a bit odd, I guess. It would seem better if you'd been the one to invite him.'

'Exactly. I feel as if I'm being set up with someone who I've already... Oh, heck, Sal. What am I going to do?'

'Grin and bear it. It can't be too bad, can it?'

By this time, they'd reached the gate to Adam and Libby's house and could see three figures sitting on the back deck. Neil was already there. Ali took a deep breath and pushed open the gate to be greeted by a wet tongue. Thank goodness for Milo, she thought as she stooped to pat the dog, whose tail was wagging furiously to welcome her.

*

Neil's heart leapt at the click of the gate latch. He'd been trying to concentrate on his conversation with Adam who was describing how he'd come to Bellbird Bay to fulfil a friend's deathbed request. But his mind hadn't been on what Adam was saying. Ever since he'd been invited to dinner, Neil hadn't been able to stop thinking of Ali. Now she was here.

He stood up as the two women came through the gate, Ali was wearing a stunning dress which took his breath away. He couldn't see her face. She had bent down to talk to the dog. The huge brute of indeterminate breed which seemed friendly enough had padded over to greet the two women. and Ali was making a fuss of him. Was she avoiding meeting him?

Eventually, she stood up and their eyes met. He was sure the spark flying between them must be apparent to everyone else, but no one commented as Adam introduced him to Sally, the friend from Perth, the one who had commandeered Ali's presence for the past week.

Neil barely noticed her, his entire attention focussed on Ali. His eyes drank her in. remembering every last detail of their times together, her lips on his, her soft skin, her hair tickling his cheek, her... He swallowed and found his voice. 'Good to meet you. Good to see you again, Ali.' He wanted to give her a kiss on the cheek. Who was he kidding? He wanted to pull her into his arms and never let her go. He made do with shaking her hand along with Sally's and watched enviously as Adam hugged her.

It was a light-hearted evening. Dinner was superb, and Neil learnt more about Ali's life in Perth and the ups and downs of working in a university, making him glad he'd stuck to school teaching. But despite it all, Ali seemed to enjoy it – and to enjoy living in Perth. It made him wonder if there could be any future to their relationship. The friend, Sally, was a livewire, sharing stories, which must be exaggerated, of her life as a journalist with a women's magazine. But she kept them all laughing till, seeing Libby suppress a yawn, Ali said, 'It's time we went and let you two get some sleep.'

Checking his watch, Neil was surprised to see it was almost midnight. Where had the time gone? 'I'll walk you two ladies home,' he said to Ali and her friend as they all rose to leave.

After hugs and handshakes and promises to get together again, the three left to walk down the boardwalk arm-in-arm. Neil thrilled to feel Ali snuggle into him on one side, while Sally kept a respectable distance on the other.

All too soon they arrived at the entrance to Ali's apartment block.

'I'll see you up there,' Sally said, winking before she pushed open the door, leaving Neil and Ali together outside.

They stood there, their arms still entwined, the roar of the waves in their ears, the tangy scent of the ocean wafting up to enfold them. Then, Neil did what he'd wanted to do all evening. He pulled Ali close.

'I've missed you,' he murmured into her hair, inhaling her scent. 'You look wonderful tonight.' His lips drifted across her forehead to her eyelids, then glided down her cheek till they met her lips; lips that were just as soft and sweet as he remembered, making him ache with desire.

'I've missed you, too,' Ali murmured between kisses.

'When does your friend leave?' he groaned.

'Another week.'

'Damn.'

Neil's lips found hers again, and it was as if time stood still.

Twenty-eight

Ali felt as though she was walking on air, encased in a warm glow when she walked into the apartment. She had almost forgotten about Sally, so it was a shock to see her friend sitting on the sofa with a glass of wine.

'Wow, you didn't tell me what a hunk he was,' Sally said with a grin.

Ali blushed. 'He's okay.'

'Only okay? He's gorgeous, and he seems really nice with it. I see what you meant about him being different. If you don't want him…'

'Sal!'

'Okay, okay.' Sally held her hands up defensively. 'Only saying. So what if he lives on the other side of the country? That would never have stopped you before. It's not as if you're falling for the guy, is it? And these things can always be worked out? Wine?' Sally held up a glass.

'Thanks.' Ali accepted the glass and took a gulp of the icy liquid.

'You're not, are you?' Sally peered at her.

'Not what?'

'Falling for him.'

'Of course not.' Ali took another gulp of wine. 'As if…' She let out a laugh which didn't come out quite right, but Sally didn't seem to notice.

'Well then, enjoy it while you can. Is he as good in bed as…?'

'Sal!'

'Okay, only asking.' Sally grinned again. 'I guess you've answered me.'

The pair were silent for a moment and Ali hoped Sally had finished with dissecting her relationship with Neil. She had.

'I like your brother and his partner,' she said. 'They're good together. It makes you think, doesn't it?'

'Think?'

'Some people seem to manage to find what's called their soulmate.'

'Hmm.' Ali yawned, reluctant to continue this conversation. 'I'm going to turn in. See you in the morning. Don't forget we've promised to meet Adam and Libby at the beach in the morning to watch Clancy in Nippers.'

To Ali's relief, the rest of Sally's visit passed without further references to Neil, apart from her final comment at the airport that Ali shouldn't let him slip through her fingers.

*

It was a week since Sally had left and Ali missed her friend's company. She had been busy updating her CV and shooting off queries and applications. She'd also contacted HR in her own university to enquire as to the status of the Head of School position. Now with them all done, she found herself at a loose end. There were only so many walks and swims one could take, and only so often she could have coffee or lunch with Libby, or disturb Adam's writing schedule. Most evenings were spent with Neil. Ali remembered Sally's advice and decided to enjoy his company while she could, without worrying about what the future might bring.

Ali was drinking coffee on her tiny balcony one morning, gazing down at the ocean and wondering how to spend the day, when she remembered her conversation with Grace Winter about the women's centre. While at the time, she'd dismissed the idea of volunteering, now it made sense. At least it might be worth finding out more about it.

A quick call to Libby to get Grace's number and she was keying it into her phone.

Grace appeared delighted to hear from Ali. 'I'm minding my granddaughter this morning,' she said, 'but both Isla and I would be delighted to see you. She's tired herself out on the beach already and is due for her nap. And Tiger can only take so much of her teasing him before he runs off and hides,' she added, referring to her cat. 'You know where I am. I have freshly made scones and I'll put the kettle on.'

Grace's granddaughter was still running around when Ali arrived and was interested in the new arrival, but before long, she began to wilt and was happy for Grace to put her down for a nap. As soon as she had gone, Grace's tortoiseshell cat appeared as if by magic and, purring loudly, began to wind himself around Ali's ankles.

'I see you've made a friend. I hope you like cats,' Grace said with a chuckle when she returned to the kitchen, where Ali was seated at the table. 'Let me boil the kettle again and we can take our tea out to the deck. It's much pleasanter out there on a day like this. We practically live outside in summer. I usually have herbal tea. Does fennel and cardamon suit you?'

'Sounds lovely.'

'Can you carry out the scones?' Grace gestured to a plate of scones which had already been cut in half and liberally spread with jam.

Grace was right. It was lovely out on the deck. Her house was similar in style to Libby's, both looking out onto the ocean which today was calm, the water changing colour from turquoise to blue as the depth changed.

'I'm glad you called,' Grace said when they were settled. 'You've decided you want to know more about the women's centre?'

'I do. I've done all the sight-seeing I want to, and I'm at a bit of a loose end.' She stared at Grace. 'I know Libby works at the library, but what do you do with your time? How often do you volunteer?'

'Not as often as I'd like. I work part-time at the library, too... and I have a secret vice.' She chuckled. 'I write children's books.'

'Wow! And Ted?' There was no sign of her husband.

'He paints... pastels usually. You can see some of his work in *The Bay Gallery*. And, in turtle season he volunteers with TurtleCare protecting the hatching turtles.'

'Gosh, you're a busy pair.' Ali was impressed. Somehow, before coming to Bellbird Bay, she had the impression it was filled with older people, people who'd retired and spent their time... doing what? Ali had no idea. Instead, everyone she'd met so far led a busy, active life.

'So, the women's centre. What would you like to know?'

'Last time we spoke, you said it included a rape centre and a women's refuge. How does it all work?'

'Let me give you a bit of background. I only came to know about it when I arrived in Bellbird Bay, but the centre has been operating in one form or another since the 1990's. It's been successful in obtaining several rounds of government funding and has become adept at raising funds through various local initiatives. I believe Will Rankin has been involved to some extent. Maxine Henderson is the current director and she's totally dedicated to the centre, has been for as long as I've been here. These days, the centre is located in two purpose-built buildings on the outskirts of town and offers a variety of services to women – not only those who've experienced rape or are suffering from domestic abuse.' She paused and took a drink of tea.

Ali, who had been listening avidly, took a sip of tea, too. 'What else does it offer?'

'The centre itself deals with sexual assault, homelessness and women's health. And it runs a number of workshops. Then there is the women's refuge which is located separately to provide the security its clients need. It's run by Eleanor Walsh who has personal experience of what her clients have suffered.'

'What's your role?'

'I'm involved with one of the workshops. I run a writing group from time to time, and others run sessions for yoga, music, gardening, cooking. The list is endless.'

Ali's heart fell. 'I'm not sure what I could offer.'

'The centre attracts women of all ages. Some are students, or looking to gain entry to university but who, for one reason or another, have found it difficult to study. You wouldn't believe how, in some homes, further study is frowned upon.'

'I would.' Ali recalled one student she'd counselled a few years earlier, a mature student whose husband was so opposed to her studying that he locked away all her course materials. 'So you think I could offer them assistance in…' She tried to think how her range of skills and experience could be put to best use.

'Perhaps you could mentor some young people, help them see what options they have, assist them through the application process, give them study techniques.'

'I could do that.' But Ali felt a sense of disappointment she wouldn't be able to take a more hands-on approach.

Seeing Ali's expression, Grace said, 'At least you can start with those. Maxine may have other ideas of how your skills can be used. You're only here for a short time, aren't you?'

'Till Easter.' Which would come around before she could blink. Ali knew she really needed to be more proactive. Sending out her CV and emails were all very well but, as she knew, there was nothing like personal communication. She needed to make some calls.

'Would you like me to take you along, introduce you to Maxine? I'm sure she'd be thrilled to meet you, to have another pair of hands. My daughter, Mel, will be picking up Isla after lunch. We could do it this afternoon. I'm afraid I'm not free for the rest of the week.'

'Oh!' Ali wasn't prepared to make the visit so soon, but why not? It wasn't as if she had anything else to do until she met Neil for dinner. 'That sounds good. What time should I come back?'

'I can pick you up... around two? I'll give Maxine a call and tell her to expect us.'

'Thanks.' Ali jotted down her address. 'I'm on the other end of the esplanade, a new block of apartments.'

'I know where it is. Ted and I watched them being built. You have a good view of the harbour there.'

Ali headed off down the boardwalk hoping she was doing the right thing.

*

By two o'clock, Ali was ready and waiting at the entrance of the apartment block. Deciding she should look more professional, she'd changed the shorts and tee-shirt she'd been wearing all morning for a smart shirtdress in pink cotton, the waist cinched with a wide white belt which was matched by her sandals. A white shoulder bag over one shoulder completed her outfit.

She didn't have long to wait. Grace arrived on time, driving up in a little blue car. Ali piled in, and they set off.

'I called Maxine,' Grace said, 'told her about your background. She's looking forward to meeting you. I suspect she already has lots of ideas as to how you can contribute. Don't let her steamroller you. She tends to get excited about the centre; it's been her baby for the past twenty-odd years. I can't imagine it would have been so successful without her hand at the helm.'

Ali didn't reply. She was wondering about the woman she was going to meet. Who was this paragon who had gained Grace's admiration and respect?

She was still wondering when they drew up in a spacious car park close to two long single-storey buildings surrounded by trees and bushes. A man on a ride-on mower was making short work of an extensive lawn. There was a sign pointing to the office, and a board which appeared to show a map of the centre. Ali would have liked a closer look, but Grace hurried her toward the building which housed the office.

The woman who rose to greet them was nothing like Ali had expected. She'd imagined the director would be around her own age, but Maxine Henderson was older. She must be older even than Grace, her white hair cropped short, her eyes bright with intelligence. 'Welcome to *Bellbird Women's Centre*,' she said, offering her hand. 'You must be Ali Wells. I'm delighted to meet you.'

'Thanks for agreeing to meet me,' Ali said, unable to stifle her surprise.

'I know, you expected someone younger. Everyone does.' Maxine gave a throaty chuckle. 'Take a seat and I'll have Joy rustle up some tea.'

At that moment a young woman dressed much as Ali had been earlier, appeared in the doorway. Her dark brown hair was cut in a fashionable bob, and she was smiling. 'Peppermint tea okay?' she asked. 'We've run out of most of the others, though I could duck across to see if…' She glanced at Maxine who raised an eyebrow at Grace and Ali.

'Peppermint sounds lovely,' Grace replied, taking a seat and indicating to Ali to do the same.

While they were waiting for tea to arrive, and Grace and Maxine were catching up on news of people Ali didn't know, Ali gazed around the room which was so different to the office she was familiar with in the university, the only similarity being the wall of shelves overflowing with books. This one was spacious and held a sofa, a low coffee table and several plants in colourful pots. On one wall were a series of watercolours which Ali would love to have examined more closely, and a number of framed photographs. It was a comfortable room with a lived-in feel.

Tea arrived, and Maxine got down to business. 'Grace tells me you have a background in women's studies in university and have time on your hands,' she said with a smile.

Ali nodded.

'Well, we can always do with help at the centre, and with your experience and undoubted skills, you'd be an asset to us.' She chatted on about the history of the centre, the activities it provided and the clientele it served. Ali was interested in the women's refuge too and was pleased when Maxine suggested she could visit it later in the week.

When they had finished their tea, Maxine offered to show Ali around, an offer Ali gratefully accepted.

'I won't join you,' Grace said. 'I want to check my next writing workshops with Joy. I'll be here when you get back, Ali.'

Maxine led Ali off, chatting all the time and providing more information than Ali could grasp. She was fascinated with how the centre had become established and how it had survived in such a small town.

'Oh, we don't only cater to residents of Bellbird Bay,' Maxine laughed. 'We wouldn't need all this space for that. Our clients come from all over the coast. We've developed quite a reputation,' she said proudly, 'and we even get women referred to us from Brisbane, women who need a fresh start away from whatever is causing their situation. It's aways preferable that they find a refuge in a location where they're unlikely to meet anyone who knows them.'

'Right.'

As they moved from one room to another, seeing the vibrant young women who composed the staff, Ali became even more impressed. She began to wonder how she could possibly contribute.

'Grace said she'd suggested you might offer study skills and the like,' Maxine said when they were walking back towards the office.

'Yes.' Ali tried not to sound dispirited.

'I have a better idea if you're agreeable.' Maxine peered at her through eyes that were all-seeing. Not unlike those of Ruby Sullivan, Ali thought, but kinder, softer.

'What would that be?'

'We don't have time now. Grace is waiting for you. But why don't you come back tomorrow? Come around one and join us for lunch, meet some of the others properly. We always have a communal lunch on Fridays and share the good and bad moments of the week. Then, after lunch, we can talk, and I'll explain what I have in mind.'

'Thanks. I'd like that.'

'Seen enough?' Grace asked when they walked back into the office where Grace was petting a Siamese cat.

'Oh, I see Simon found you,' Maxine said. 'He can always tell a cat lover.'

'He's a beauty,' Ali said. 'Yes, I'm ready to go now, Grace. Thanks so much for the tour, Maxine. I'll see you tomorrow.'

On the way back in the car Grace asked, 'Did Maxine discuss how you can contribute?'

'Not yet. She wants me to go for lunch tomorrow to meet everyone and talk then. It sounded as if she may have something special in mind.' Ali was beginning to feel a curl of excitement at the thought of spending time in the centre.

Grace chuckled. 'If I know Maxine, she has already sussed you out and knows exactly what she wants you to do. But remember what I told you. Don't let her push you into something you're not comfortable with.'

'I won't.' Ali couldn't imagine being coerced into doing anything she didn't want to, but Maxine had given the impression of being a strong and forceful woman when she put her mind to it. Well, Ali could be strong and forceful, too. Tomorrow should be interesting.

Twenty-nine

Neil checked his emails again, but there was still nothing from the school. Barry had already sent him a copy of the agenda for the board meeting, prominent on which was the future of the school. He should have been invited, unless there were still some who believed him to be guilty – at the very least of turning a blind eye to the corruption. But, like a fool, he'd trusted the chairman of the school board... and his offsider who handled the finances. And look where that trust had got him.

He grated his teeth. There was nothing for it. He'd have to start applying for other positions, though the chances of finding another principal's position at this late stage were slim. But at least he could still find a teaching job, even on a casual basis.

He sighed and checked the time. It was too early to meet Ali. She had arranged to meet with the woman in the women's centre for lunch and hadn't been sure how long it would last. They were to meet in the surf club at seven so she could tell him all about it. He was pleased she was excited about an opportunity to work in her chosen field, albeit in a volunteer capacity and in a more practical role than she was accustomed to, but it made his own lack of purpose all the more annoying.

Tired of his own company, Neil decided to head to the surf club anyway. Maybe a beer in the familiar surroundings would take the edge off his disappointment.

He had just ordered a beer from Nate when someone slapped him on the shoulder.

'On your own tonight?' Will Rankin asked, raising a hand to Nate who, seeming to understand the gesture, proceeded to pour him two beers. 'Martin and I are on the deck. Join us?'

'Thanks.' Neil picked up his drink and followed Will to where Martin Cooper was sitting alone and staring out at the ocean.

'Look who I found at the bar,' Will said, as they joined him.

'G'day. On your own?'

'I asked him that, too,' Will said.

'I'm meeting Ali for dinner,' Neil said awkwardly. Did everyone know about them? He had confided in Will but had hoped he'd keep it to himself.

'Ailsa saw you together,' Martin said. 'You can't keep a secret in this town. You should remember that.'

'True.' Neil did remember. He had a flash of the time he and a mate had thought no one knew they had borrowed his dad's car to impress two girls. It turned out the whole neighbourhood knew, and his dad had been standing on the kerb waiting for his return.

'You'll be returning to Brisbane for school starting again?' Martin asked.

Neil flinched. 'Hopefully. I...'

'I saw the news item,' Martin said. 'But you were cleared.'

'Tell that to the remaining board members and some of the parent body,' Neil said bitterly, downing half his beer in one gulp.

'Sorry, mate. What will happen?'

'Christ knows.' Neil dragged a hand through his hair. 'I'll need to find another job somewhere. I guess there are always openings for teachers.' He gave a sigh.

'But...' Martin began, before Will put a warning hand on his arm.

'I'm sure something will turn up,' Will said. 'It usually does.'

'Thanks, Will.' Neil remembered life hadn't been kind to Will either. He remembered Ruby Sullivan's words. *The road ahead may not be the route you expect, but it will bring you more happiness than you have ever imagined.* Had they been closer to the truth than he thought? But how could losing his job bring happiness?

'Here they are.' Will's voice brought Neil back to the present. Looking up, he saw two women walking towards their table. One was tall with greying hair, the other shorter with a cloud of dark hair on her shoulders. Both were carrying glasses of wine.

Neil rose to leave.

'Don't go,' Will said as the women reached them. 'This is Cleo,' he gestured to the shorter woman, 'and Ailsa, Martin's new wife. Neil is joining us for dinner. His lady will be along soon.'

'Oh,' Neil shook hands with the women and sat down again, wondering how Ali would react to their dinner for two being highjacked.

The women kissed their respective partners on the cheek and settled down.

'You're Harry Simpson's son, aren't you?' Ailsa said. 'I saw you in the bookshop before Christmas. I heard he'd been ill.'

'Yes.' Neil wasn't sure which question he was answering.

'Did you grow up with these two reprobates?'

'I'm afraid so.'

'Do we know your lady?' Cleo asked.

'Ali Wells. She doesn't live here. She…'

'She's Adam Holland's sister,' Will said.

'Of course. We met at Adam and Libby's barbecue, and she's been in the café a few times with Libby. I manage *The Pandanus Café* in the garden centre,' she said by way of explanation.

Just then, Neil's phone pinged with a text. 'She's here,' he said with a smile, glad to be excused from any further interrogation.

*

Ali stood at the top of the stairway and stared across the restaurant, but there was no sign of Neil. She checked her watch to see it was just after seven. Maybe he was on his way. Taking out her phone, she sent a brief text. *Just arrived at the club. A.*

She had barely time to return the phone to her bag, when she saw Neil come through the door from the deck.

'Ali!' Neil gave her a kiss on the cheek, her heart giving the now familiar lurch as, his hand on her waist, he guided her towards the bar. 'I'm with Will and Martin and their partners. I hope you don't mind. They invited us to join them for dinner.'

'Of course not,' Ali said, though she felt a sense of disappointment they wouldn't be eating alone. But she'd met Will and Cleo – and Martin and Ailsa – and liked them. Maybe it was selfish to want to keep Neil to herself. But they were going to have so little time together, she wanted to store up the memories to take with her back to Perth or wherever she ended up. 'White wine, please,' she said to the barman, when they reached the bar.

Out on the deck, there was a light breeze blowing in from the ocean, bringing with it the salty scent of the sea. Ali did love it here and would be sorry when it came time to leave. But it wasn't her home.

The four others on the deck welcomed her and they were all soon engaged in a discussion around a fundraiser Will was organising for the surf lifesaving club. 'It started a few years ago to raise money to send Owen to the championships in Hawaii, and we did so well it was decided to make it an annual event,' Will said with a grin.

'He sells himself short,' Ailsa said. 'Will is a local hero. Not only is he one of Bellbird Bay's surfing champions, he's now a member of the council, chairs the surf lifesaving committee which runs the championships and the triathlon, and supports several local charities.'

While Ailsa was speaking, Will's face was becoming redder and redder.

Ali felt sorry for him but was impressed.

Neil said what both of them were thinking. 'Impressive, mate. Who'd have thought you'd become so respectable when we were all in our teens, and you and Martin were vying for the championship – and the girls.'

'Anyway,' Will said, 'the long and short of it is, the fundraiser is on Saturday, and I hope you'll both be there.'

Neil looked at Ali who gave a brief nod. 'Sure will,' he said. 'Where...?'

'Right here in the club. It's closed to everyone else, but most of the town will be there. There's food, drinks, door prize, raffles, a silent auction, music... all the usual stuff. Money raised goes to the surf club, the breast cancer association and the women's centre.'

Ali's ears pricked up at the mention of the women's centre. 'I was there today,' she said.

Will seemed not to hear, continuing to talk about the fundraiser, but Ailsa and Cleo took notice.

'What were you doing there?' Cleo asked.

'Grace Winter suggested I might want to volunteer,' she said. 'She took me along to meet the director yesterday.'

'Maxine.' Cleo nodded.

'She invited me back today to meet everyone and to suggest I act as her assistant while I'm here – only part-time, of course, and in a volunteer capacity. What she's done there is remarkable.'

'It is. It helped me when I arrived in Bellbird Bay.'

Ali and Ailsa both looked at Cleo, a question in their eyes.

'One of the activities they provide is grief counselling. I'd just lost my husband. Without the help I received at the centre – and the position at the café – I don't know how I'd have coped. Hannah was a teenager at the time and missed her dad dreadfully. We both did.'

'I'm sorry.' Ali put a comforting hand on Cleo's arm.

'Who's ready to eat?' Will's question changed the atmosphere, and they all picked up the menus which were lying on the table.

By the time they had ordered and been served – the club's famous burgers and chips for the men and salads for the women, plus more drinks for everyone – the conversation had moved on again. Martin and Ailsa were asking Will and Cleo about their wedding plans, making Ali feel uncomfortable, and wonder if Adam and Libby planned to go down that route, too. Though, in her mind, they were almost as good as married already.

What was it about this town? Everywhere she went, she seemed to meet yet another couple who had found their soulmate in later life. It made her glad she would be leaving at Easter.

Though, she reminded herself, not everyone was part of a loved-up couple. Otherwise, there would be no need for the women's centre. Ali thought again of these dedicated women she'd had lunch with. Of different ages and different backgrounds, they had common goals and were committed to the centre and its director. And while she hadn't visited the women's refuge yet, from what Maxine had told her, it was run by equally dedicated women, many of whom had themselves experienced domestic violence.

The evening proved to be more enjoyable than Ali anticipated. After her initial disappointment that she was to share Neil with two other couples, she discovered they were good company and knew Ailsa and Cleo could become good friends. Though she'd hardly be here long enough to make friends.

When she and Neil left, with promises to meet again at the fundraiser, she tucked her arm into Neil's as they sauntered along in the direction of her apartment. This was one of the advantages of Bellbird Bay, she reflected. Unlike Perth, almost everywhere she wanted to go – except the women's centre – was within walking distance. She barely needed her car, though it had come in handy when she and Sally were exploring the countryside.

'Enjoy tonight?' Neil asked, as they left the esplanade behind for the section of boardwalk which led to her apartment block.

'I did. They're nice people. You grew up with Will and Martin?'

'Yes, though we weren't close. We all knew each other back then. It was a different time. A lot of water under the bridge. It's good to catch up with them again.'

Ali wondered what it must be like to have spent all your growing up years in one spot. To be able to return decades later and pick up these earlier friendships. She had been so young when she left her childhood home, she had no memory of friends there, only of Adam. There had been one girl at school who... but she couldn't even remember her name. Arriving in Perth, it had taken her ages to fit in. It hadn't been till she started high school and met Sally that she had anyone she could call a real friend.

'Penny for them?' Neil said.

'Oh, just thinking how different your childhood was from mine. Adam and I stuck together. He tried to protect me from all the stuff going on at home. Then in Perth...' she shook her head. 'You were lucky.'

'I guess I was. But you have Adam again now. You have your career. And you have me.' He swung her around and hugged her tightly, kissing her soundly on the lips till she begged him to stop. They were still on a main thoroughfare. It was too public. Anyone might see them.

'We'd better go inside, then,' Neil said, when she voiced her objections.

Ali's heart began to beat faster, a flash of desire shooting through her at the thought of spending another night in Neil's arms.

Thirty

'Nate said you had dinner at the surf club the night before last, Dad, with his mum, Martin, Will, Cleo… and another woman.' Bronte was eating breakfast on the run as usual. She was leaning against the sink, a slice of toast and vegemite in one hand, a mug of coffee in the other. 'Is she the one you've been spending all your time with? When are we going to meet her?'

'Umm.' Neil and his dad were seated at the kitchen table enjoying a breakfast of fried eggs and bacon, along with toast and coffee. Surprised at her questions, Neil was slow to reply.

Harry did it for him. 'She's Adam Holland's sister. You know, the local author, the one whose book's been made into a television programme. It *is* time you brought her home to meet us, Neil. Otherwise, she might think you're ashamed of us… or her.'

'I'm ashamed of neither.' Neil hadn't considered inviting Ali to their home… to meet his dad and his daughter. An invitation like that might send her running to the hills – or back to Perth. It smacked too much of a serious relationship. He remembered what Adam had told him about their childhood, about how both he and Ali had been scared of commitment, how Ali probably still was. 'I don't think it's a good idea, Dad.'

'Well, when are we going to meet her?' Bronte persisted, then said, 'I know. How about the fundraiser at the surf club on Saturday. You'll be there, won't you, Dad?'

'Will twisted my arm. You're going?' Neil hadn't thought it would appeal to the younger set.

'Of course. Nate will be behind the bar as usual, and Owen, Han and I have been roped in to manning the door, selling raffle tickets and handling the silent auction. Will has organised everyone to help out. It sounds like a lot of fun. Owen says the first one raised money to send him to Hawaii where he took out the championship, then he came home and won it here, too,' she said proudly.

Neil grinned to himself, amused how these days, Bronte's conversations were all peppered with what Owen said or did.

'Sounds like a plan, son,' Harry said. 'I presume Ali will be there with you.'

'Yes.' Neil sighed. Perhaps it would be okay if she met his family in a neutral setting. 'Sounds good, Dad. I didn't know you intended to go. You haven't mentioned it.'

'Of course I'll be there. I've donated a bag of books to the raffle, and the silent auction is always good value. There won't be many of the old crowd in Bellbird Bay who'll miss out. It's one of the highlights of the year.'

The longer he spent back in Bellbird Bay, the more Neil came to realise there were a lot of highlights – more than he remembered from when he was growing up here.

'Need any help in the shop today, Dad?' Neil asked, as Bronte glanced at the clock and, dropping her mug in the sink, wiping her mouth, and picking up her bag, called, 'I'm late. See you tonight,' and dashed out the door.

The two men chuckled as they heard the sound of her wheeling her bicycle out the gate then the swish of the tyres as she rode off.

'I'm expecting a delivery, so you could give me a hand… if you have a mind to and aren't otherwise occupied.' Harry winked.

'Happy to, Dad. And if you're referring to Ali, she'll be busy. She's going to be volunteering at the women's centre a few days each week.'

'She could do worse. Maxine does good work there. It might do your girl good to see the other side of things. Not everyone has the sort of marriage your mother and I had.'

Neil bridled at the term "your girl" but said nothing. It was his dad's way and may have been an attempt to rile him – or find out more about his relationship. He wouldn't rise to the bait. But his dad's words hit home. Ali had never known the stable home life he'd enjoyed here in Bellbird Bay. He needed to tread gently with her if he wanted them to have a future together.

He wasn't seeing Ali that day or evening as it happened, not till the fundraiser on Saturday. She told him she was having a family dinner which included Adam, Libby and Libby's daughter and granddaughter. The daughter's partner, Nick, would be there, too, but there was no way Ali would want to include him in such a close family evening. He knew the evening he'd already spent with her at Adam and Libby's had been a strain for her.

He cleared away the breakfast dishes and got himself ready for a day in the bookshop.

*

The morning passed uneventfully. The delivery arrived – six boxes of books from various publishers. By the time Neil had moved them into the back office, unpacked them and entered them into the inventory he was ready for a break.

'Okay if I duck out for a coffee, Dad?' he asked Harry, who was engaged in chatting to an old friend by one of the bookshelves.

'No problem. Bring me one back.'

'Sure you don't want me to relieve you then?'

'No. I can drink my coffee just as easily here as I can in any damned coffee shop.'

'Okay.' His dad would never change. Neil hoped he wouldn't. There was something comfortable about the familiar, old guy, something that reminded Neil of growing up here in Bellbird Bay with no worries other than who was going to top the soccer league or come first in the class test.

He headed out to find his usual seat in *The Bay Café* which had become almost like a home from home. Ordering a black coffee and, suddenly feeling peckish, a ham and cheese roll, Neil leant back to enjoy the passing traffic.

When he returned to the bookshop carrying his dad's coffee, it was empty apart from a tall thin man in a suit and tie talking to Harry. He looked different to the normal run of customers in Bellbird Bay, so

Neil studied him as he walked in and made his way towards the two men. As he got closer, he heard the man say, 'You won't get a better offer. You need to understand we mean business,' before he turned, gave Neil a dismissive glance and strode out of the shop, the door banging shut behind him.

'Who was that, Dad? He didn't look or sound like a customer.'

'He was no customer.' Harry's face was red with suppressed anger. 'One of the lackeys from *Wham Bam Books* trying to intimidate me into selling. I'll go to my grave before I sell out to those guys.' Harry was trembling, whether from anger or whether it was his illness making its presence felt again, Neil wasn't sure.

'Look, Dad. Why don't you go back and have your coffee.' He placed the takeaway coffee on the counter. 'I can manage here.'

'I...'

Neil thought his dad was about to refuse, but saying, 'Thanks, son,' the old man nodded, picked up his coffee and stumbled into the back office, leaving Neil feeling helpless in the face of this new challenge. While he was aware Harry couldn't manage the bookshop for very much longer, the thought of it in the hands of the large chain of cut-price books wasn't something he wanted to contemplate. But what other option was there? It was extremely unlikely anyone would want to buy the bookshop as a going concern, and most of the other chains were cutting back on their outlets. *Wham Bam Books* seemed to be the only one which was expanding. But Neil dreaded to think of it turning *Bay Books* into one of the tacky blue and orange monstrosities he'd seen in other places.

By the time Harry returned, he appeared to have calmed down and the rest of the afternoon proceeded without incident. But Neil couldn't forget the dreadful image of the bookshop his father loved, the shop which was his life, being turned into a cheap and nasty eyesore which would ruin the appearance of the Bellbird Bay esplanade with its brightly coloured façade and windows covered in cut-price stickers.

Thirty-one

Ali had enjoyed the family dinner. It had been good to spend more time with Emma, little Clancy and Emma's partner, Nick. Adam had become part of Libby's family so quickly, it was difficult to believe they'd been together for less than a year.

It was good to see her brother so happy, too, so different to the haunted boy she remembered. The transformation was amazing. She supposed much of it had probably taken place in the years they'd been apart, the years when he'd forged his career, first as a journalist, then as a best-selling author. But, looking at him and Libby, at the way they shared affectionate glances, at his hand on her arm, at their smiles when they thought no one was looking, she knew Libby had contributed to Adam's current state of mind.

The meal had been delicious – Libby was an excellent cook – and it had been fun to hear Clancy call Adam Grandad, and to have her say to Ali, 'I need a special name for you. What should I call you?'

After much discussion, they finally decided on Aliya for no real reason other than Clancy liked it.

It was a different experience for Ali to be part of this warm family atmosphere, one she wanted to relish. And the thought that Adam could experience this every day was something she'd never forget.

Today was Saturday, and tonight she was attending the fundraiser in the surf club with Neil. He'd called yesterday, after her first stint at the women's centre and before the dinner at Adam and Libby's, and the memory of their conversation made her heart zing. He was such a kind, gentle man, so considerate of her feelings, so different in that regard from anyone she'd ever known – man or woman. Except perhaps Adam.

Neil had warned her his dad and his daughter wanted to be introduced to her. He'd tried to pretend it was nothing special, that it would be odd if they didn't meet since they'd all be at the fundraiser, but Ali had felt a tremor of discomfort. It was, she felt, a step towards a more serious relationship than she was prepared for.

But she put it out of her mind as she headed to the beach for an early morning surf. This morning, the sea was perfect, just the right sort of waves, and Ali was soon lost in the joy of the sport. She was still hiring a board from Will Rankin and, although tempted to buy one of her own, knew it was an unnecessary indulgence when she didn't intend to stay here. Back in Perth – or wherever she ended up – she'd be too busy developing courses and marking assignments to have time to enjoy this sort of activity.

Ali wiped the saltwater from her face, handed back the board and dried herself off. She slipped on her shorts and tee shirt and made her way to *The Bay Café*, her mouth watering at the thought of a cappuccino. It was still early, and the shops on the esplanade were not yet open. She idly wondered if Neil would be working in the bookshop that morning, if he was still helping his dad out. That thought led to his dad's illness and what would happen to *Bay Books* when Harry could no longer cope. For a few moments, she allowed herself to imagine a scenario where she and Neil worked together in the bookshop, a time when the worries and stresses of the university didn't have the power to affect her. Then her coffee arrived, and she came to her senses.

Half an hour later, she was back home, showered and dressed in a fresh pair of shorts and tee-shirt, prepared to spend a lazy day reading and catching up with her emails.

*

The entrance to the surf club was crowded when Neil ushered Ali inside at a few minutes past seven. She felt very self-conscious knowing she was about to meet his family, even though she'd already seen Harry and Bronte in the bookshop. Glancing down at her carefully chosen outfit – a loose blue sleeveless dress with a handkerchief hem – she hoped it would meet with their approval. It had certainly met with Neil's. His eyes had lit up when he saw her. He'd exclaimed, 'Wow!' before he picked her up, swung her around and kissed her.

Looking around, Ali could see there were a variety of dress styles present. Some people were dressed to the nines in elaborate outfits, while others – mostly men – looked as if they'd come straight from the beach.

They climbed the stairs to be greeted at the door of the restaurant by a cheerful girl wearing a white tee-shirt with a surfboard logo, her face free of makeup except for a smear of lip gloss, her long blonde hair carelessly pulled up in an untidy bun on top of her head. She was accompanied by a young man who looked like her twin but was around a foot taller and more tanned. Ali recognised the girl as Bronte, and the young man looked vaguely familiar, too.

Ali clutched Neil's hand tightly as he said. 'Bronte, this is Ali. Ali, my daughter, Bronte.' She needn't have worried.

'I'm so pleased to meet you properly at last. We've been wondering who Dad has been spending all his time with.'

Ali blushed. She took Bronte's outstretched hand. 'I'm pleased to meet you, too. Your dad talks a lot about you.'

It was Bronte's turn to blush. 'This is Owen,' she said, to hide her embarrassment. 'His dad's running this show.' She grinned at the young man.

'We should move on,' Neil said, and Ali became conscious of the line of people behind them waiting to gain entry. 'See you later, Bronte,' he said as they walked on into the club.

Once inside, music blaring in their ears, they pushed their way to the bar, Neil's hand on Ali's waist giving her a sense of security with which she was unfamiliar. Accepting their complimentary drinks from the darkhaired barman Neil called Nate, and who Ali remembered seeing in the bookshop, too, they managed to find their way out onto the deck which was less crowded and not as noisy.

'Over here!'

Looking towards where the voice came from, Ali saw Libby and Adam standing with Grace and Ted at the edge of the deck which had been cleared of tables for the evening.

Neil raised an eyebrow and, taking a deep breath, Ali nodded, and they went over to join them.

'Neil.'

'Adam.'

The two men nodded to each other while Ali kissed cheeks with Libby and Grace.

'Hello again, Ali,' Ted said. 'And this is…?'

'Neil Simpson,' Ali said.

'Harry's son. Of course, heard you were back. Your dad will be glad of your help. He hasn't seemed himself the last few times I've been in the bookshop. Is everything all right with him?'

'He's getting older, like us all,' Neil said.

Ali threw him a quick glance but realised he didn't want to share his dad's diagnosis tonight.

'How did you go with Maxine?' Grace asked, drawing Ali aside, and leaving the others to chat.

'Good. Thanks for the introduction. Sorry I didn't get back to you.' Ali realised she should have called Grace again after the lunch at the centre. 'Maxine wants to utilise my organisational skills and have me act as her assistant a few days each week while I'm here. I'm really looking forward to it. It should be challenging. I'm to visit the women's refuge with her next week and I'm looking forward to that, too.'

'I'm so glad it's working out for you. I knew Maxine would see how you could fit in and come up with something.' She smiled.

'Oh, look! Something's happening.' Libby was pointing back into the restaurant where the music had stopped and, on a small stage set up for the occasion, Will Rankin was holding a microphone.

From where they were standing, it was difficult to hear what was being said, but it was obviously some sort of welcome speech. When it ended, there was a loud applause, and the music started again.

Soon, surf club staff were moving around with platters of finger food, and other young people were approaching everyone, intent on selling raffle tickets. Neil insisted on purchasing several for a protesting Ali, then took her hand as they followed the others in the group back into the main room to investigate the articles on display for the silent auction.

While Ali was hesitating over bidding for a surf lesson with Will Rankin or a photoshoot with Martin Cooper, finally deciding on neither, she noticed Neil place a bid on a picnic basket. 'How much did you bid?' she asked, only to see Neil grin and tap the side of his nose.

'Are you going to introduce us, Neil?' Harry asked, appearing at their elbow.

'Dad, you old devil. I didn't see you. This is Ali. Ali, my dad.'

'I'm pleased to meet you, Mr Simpson,' Ali said with a smile, while inwardly quaking.

'Harry to you, my dear. So, you're the young woman who's been keeping my son out. You've made a good choice, son. She's a keeper.'

Ali blushed. This is what she had been afraid of, why she'd always preferred to keep men at arm's length and never, never to meet their families.

'Harry!' someone called, and with an apologetic smile, Harry wandered off.

'Sorry about that,' Neil said, clearly embarrassed by his dad's words.

'No worries.' At least it was over now, and they could enjoy the rest of the evening.

The next few hours seemed to pass in a flash. Ali and Neil ate, drank, chatted with people and danced. They chose the slow dances where Ali could rest her head on Neil's shoulder, and he could bury his face in her hair and inhale her delicate fragrance.

All too soon, it was over. Will took to the stage again to thank everyone for coming and for their contributions to the fundraising which, this year, had raised a greater amount than ever. Then he announced the winners of the silent auction and Neil gave a whoop of delight when he discovered he'd won the hamper he bid on. It had been donated by a local café, *The Greedy Gecko*, and could be picked up, filled with goodies, any time in the following twelve months. There were cheers, too, when a young man won a wedding event from *Pandanus Weddings* and immediately got down on one knee to propose to his surprised girlfriend.

It was after midnight, when Ali and Neil made their way back to her apartment, his arm slung around her shoulders as she snuggled into him. Once there, they didn't hesitate. Kicking off their shoes, they tore off their clothes to fall onto the bed together in a wave of passion such as Ali had never known. As she drowned in the heat of their lovemaking, Ali forgot all her inhibitions, all her former fears and wished she could stay there in his arms for ever.

Thirty-two

The sun was shining through the window when Neil leant over to kiss Ali on the forehead. When she opened her eyes and smiled, his heart leapt. Neil knew he'd never felt this way before. The emotions Ali aroused were a million times more powerful than any he'd experienced with Pippa. Theirs had been a flash of desire which had produced Bronte, then the attraction had waned for both of them. Bronte had been the only thing which made the marriage last as long as it had.

'Good morning, beautiful,' he said, sliding down the bed beside her. It was some time before they left it.

They were seated in Ali's kitchen enjoying a coffee after breakfast when Ali asked, 'You're okay with going out on the boat today?'

'I am if you are.' Neil tried to interpret Ali's expression. 'I'm perfectly happy to stay here if you don't want to go.' When Libby introduced Neil to her daughter, Emma, and partner, Nick, the previous evening, Neil had been aware of a slight tension in Ali's manner. It was only apparent for a moment, but he was only too aware how she seemed uncomfortable with him meeting more of her family. He'd enjoyed talking about boats with Nick, who owned a boatyard up the coast and who invited them to join him and Emma to go sailing today, along with a few other friends. Had he been too quick to accept for both of them?

'No, I'm fine with it. It might be fun. You'll probably enjoy it. It's just... Adam and Libby... they want to pair us off. I'm not sure...'

'Hey, it's okay.' He gave her a hug and stroked a strand of hair from her forehead to tuck it behind her ear. 'Will they be there today, too?'

'Probably.' She sighed. 'We all went out on Nick's boat on Boxing Day. Little Clancy will be there, too. She's cute. I guess I'm just not used to this family thing. It was just Mum and me for so long, and I never...'

'You never took your men friends home?' Neil guessed.

'No.' Ali picked up her cup, clasping it in both hands. 'I don't want...'

'Promise I won't give the wrong impression if that's what worries you.' Not the time to declare his undying love, Neil decided.

'Thanks.' Ali gave him a grateful smile, and a kiss on the cheek. 'I'd better get ready.'

*

It was a glorious day to be out on the water and, once they boarded Nick's yacht, Ali seemed to be more relaxed. Neither Adam nor Libby appeared to be drawing any conclusions about his and Ali's relationship, or if they were, they were hiding it well. Emma and Nick were fun to be with, and little Clancy kept them all amused.

There were others there, too. Bev and Iain, friends of Libby and Adam, along with their son Bryan and Bryan's daughter, Mia, who was best friends with Clancy. Neil remembered his dad telling him some tale about Bev, who owned the local garden centre, something about a long-lost son. Was Bryan the son? If so, how could he be Iain's, too? Their relationship appeared to be fairly new judging by the way they kept touching each other.

When this occurred to him, he glanced around quickly to see if anyone was watching him and Ali who were behaving in exactly the same way. Fortunately, no one was. They were all too engrossed in their own affairs.

Neil and Ali were leaning on the boat rail, the wind in their hair, when Ali said, 'School starts next week. You'll be going back to Brisbane.' It wasn't a question, and Neil couldn't tell if Ali was pleased or regretful.

'Umm, no,' Neil said, unwilling to go into more detail. He thought of the call he'd received from Barry early that morning. He'd slipped out of bed to avoid disturbing Ali and had taken the call on her small balcony overlooking the harbour filled with fishing boats and yachts.

'Sorry to be the bearer of bad news, mate,' Barry had said. 'You'll be getting official notification, but I wanted to let you know.'

'The meeting was yesterday, wasn't it?' Neil had had a premonition the news wouldn't be good but had kept hoping.

'Yeah. Seems there's been a mass exodus of students; parents unwilling to keep paying fees after the debacle last term. Anyway, it's been decided to keep the school going with a skeleton staff and…' he cleared his throat, '…they've asked me to take over… for the time being, until… until everything's sorted out.'

Neil knew what it meant. The remaining board members and those parents who'd been present didn't believe he was innocent. They wanted to wait until he'd been cleared in court, even though he wouldn't be on trial, he'd only be appearing as a witness. 'Right,' he said, a sigh escaping. 'Thanks for the heads-up.'

'What'll you do now?'

'What I've been doing, look for anything going in the meantime.'

'Got anything lined up?'

Neil sighed again. His efforts to find another position had been fruitless. 'Not yet.'

'Sorry, mate. Well, I'll let you go. Sunday morning, you know.'

Neil did know. For those like Barry with teenagers, Sunday morning was taken up with ferrying kids to and from sporting events. He remembered what it had been like with Bronte for a while, before she discovered boys and gave up sport.

It was too late now to find a position for the first term, but he could start looking for something for term two. He was still officially on extended leave and on full pay which made things easier, and it would give him the opportunity to keep his eye on his dad's health. But Neil irked at the enforced inactivity. He didn't grudge Barry the position; he'd make a good principal. The worry was that the school would decide to keep him there and dispense with Neil's services altogether.

'So, you'll be here a bit longer?'

'Looks like it. It's called extended leave.' He tried to laugh it off, but it didn't come out right.

'But you *will* be going back?' Ali persisted in asking.

Neil shrugged. 'The corruption case will be going to court. I'll have to testify, then we'll see.'

'Oh!'

Neil could see Ali wanted to ask more but was afraid it would annoy him. He was glad when Nick called out, 'Grub's up. There's beer and sandwiches available', and everyone moved to congregate where the food had been set out.

There was no time for any further private conversation and, by the time they reached shore again, Ali seemed to have forgotten their discussion. But Neil hadn't. Barry's call and its implications preyed on his mind. He couldn't wait till the court case was over to discover his future. He needed to take action, and any action he might take would have the potential to spell the end of any future for him with Ali.

Thirty-three

Ali couldn't think why she'd been so concerned about Neil being included in yesterday's sailing party. It had been a lot of fun, and no one had made any comments about seeing them together. Maybe Sally was right, she thought, for what must have been the hundredth time.

But there was no future in it. She'd be going back to Perth – or to some other university – and Neil would be somewhere else, probably Brisbane. She knew that. She'd gone into this with her eyes wide open, just like all of her other friendships with men. So why did she feel so bereft at the thought of what they had together ending?

She was glad to be alone this morning. After snuggling up together on her sofa last night, Neil had regretfully left, saying he'd been leaving his dad on his own too often and was worried about him. It all made sense, and she was accustomed to being alone, to waking up alone. But this morning, she missed his warm presence in her bed, his gentle kisses, his conversation over breakfast.

Pulling herself together, Ali reminded herself that today she was to visit the women's refuge, and it was time she took a shower and dressed if she didn't want to keep Maxine waiting. It was good of the older woman to take time to show her around.

Half an hour later, dressed in a pair of blue linen pants and a loose white shirt, Ali shrugged the satchel containing her laptop and a few personal items over her shoulder and set off. She had arranged to meet Maxine at the women's centre, from where they would drive to the refuge.

This morning, Maxine was dressed more casually than before, in an outfit not unlike Ali's. On the way to the refuge, Ali peppered her with questions about the work of both the centre and the refuge, intent on obtaining as much information as possible. She was aware how valuable this would be to her future students, some of whom might choose to undertake placements with similar groups.

The trip took longer than Ali had anticipated, but eventually Maxine stopped outside an unremarkable building set back from the road.

'This is it,' she said. 'I told Eleanor you were coming. Monday is usually a busy day for her. The weekend often makes women realise their need to leave a difficult situation. It will be good for you to see it like this, though Eleanor may not have a lot of time to talk with us.'

She led Ali to the building where they were met by a short, slim woman with fading red hair wearing knee-length denim shorts and a tee shirt. 'Good to see you, Maxine. This must be Ali.' She offered her hand which Ali shook. 'You're lucky. Thankfully, it's been a slow weekend,' she said. 'Come in and I'll show you round.'

Ali followed the two women inside to where several women and small children were engaged in various activities. They all looked up when the women walked past, several eyes filled with fear.

'It can take some time for them to recover,' Eleanor said, when they reached the room she used as her office but was more like a comfortable living room. 'What we do here is provide a safe environment, away from the stress and fear that has been part of the women's lives, often for years.' Seeing Ali's eyes widen, she added, 'Yes, it can sometimes take years for a woman to pluck up the courage to leave. I know. It did me.' She stopped for a moment and gazed into space.

'We have twelve women here at the moment,' she said, in response to the question in Ali's eyes, 'and seven children ranging in age from six months to eight years old. We all share the cooking and cleaning, and everyone does her own laundry. There's a large vegetable garden out the back which provides for most of our needs in that regard, and many of our residents find it therapeutic to work in it. It helps take their minds off what brought them here – for a short time at least.'

While Ali would love to have talked with the women, heard their stories, she realised that, as a stranger to them, it would be inappropriate. She could only hope, if she was around for long enough, she might be able to gain their trust.

'Ali is going to be helping me out for a few months,' Maxine said, when they were enjoying cups of tea provided by one of the women who Eleanor said had been there longer than any of the others. Ali wondered what her story was. She felt humbled and not a little ashamed to realise how for years, she'd lectured about women's rights, the prevalence of domestic violence, without ever seeing the results, how women who had escaped violent relationships received help and managed to survive.

'Well, what did you think?' Maxine asked, when they were driving back.

'I'm impressed with what you and Eleanor have established there. Those poor women... their eyes...'

'Yes. It's dreadful to think what they must have gone through, and the courage it's taken them to leave and seek help. I just wish we could do more, help more women take that step. But sadly, many never do. They fall into the habit of acceptance, of thinking it's their fault, that in some way they deserve the way they're being treated. What we do is a small drop in the ocean.' Her lips tightened, forming a thin line. 'But we do what we can. We do our best. It's all we can do.'

For the rest of the morning, Ali helped Maxine with her administration work which was not unlike some of her own admin at university – scheduling courses and planning timetables. She saw Grace's name there, along with the writing group she conducted, and to her surprise, that of Bev Cooper who she'd met, too. It appeared she ran gardening sessions.

Ali looked up at Maxine. 'I see Bev Cooper's name here. I've met her. She owns the garden centre.'

'Yes, Bev helps our gardening group. Some have never spent time in a garden before coming here. She explains about planting, maintaining a garden and harvesting. She's really good with the women. Cleo, who runs the café at the garden centre, volunteers, too. She gives cooking lessons. It's surprising how many of the women in Bellbird Bay help out.'

'I've met Cleo, too,' Ali said, remembering the woman with the cloud of dark hair at *The Pandanus Café*.

'Have you visited *The Pandanus Garden Centre and Café*?' Maxine asked. 'It's a very special place.'

'Yes,' Ali said, remembering that peaceful place and vowing to go there again.

*

It wasn't till a week later that she had the opportunity to make good her vow. As it happened, it was Libby who initiated the visit, suggesting they meet there for coffee on a day when both were free. Libby was very mysterious about her reason for visiting the garden centre but promised all would be revealed when they met.

It was easy for Ali to find her way there again. As on her earlier visits, she was impressed when she drew into a large car park and saw the arched entrance with the sign *The Pandanus Garden Centre and Café* in large, green lettering. Parking alongside a host of other cars, she made her way through the entrance and into a large area filled with trees and plants of all shapes and sizes. She gazed around at the people busily selecting plants and pushing trolleys, the professional looking staff in their green aprons with the pandanus logo and realised it was indeed the special place Maxine had referred to. Ali hadn't expected to find such a large garden centre in this small coastal town. And there was the café, too!

Peering through the rows of plants and shrubs for sale, Ali saw the sign for the café, almost hidden in the far corner of the centre by a tall, blue plumbago hedge. She walked through the gap in the hedge and into the secret oasis she remembered. Tables and chairs were scattered among low bushes and towering palm trees, everything built around the large pandanus tree. Libby was seated at one of the tables and, seeing Ali, she waved.

'This is quite a place,' Ali said as she took a seat opposite Libby. 'How can it survive in a town the size of Bellbird Bay?'

'Amazing, isn't it. Bev built it up from scratch. It's been her whole life for years. But now she has Iain and Bryan, too. I'm so pleased for her.'

'What's the story there?' Ali asked. 'Yesterday, on the yacht, it seemed as if Bryan was her son, but Iain's his father and he and Bev only met recently. Did they know each other years ago, then part...

or…?' What happened?' Other people's lives always fascinated her.

'You'll have to ask Bev. It's not my story to tell. Once you know her better, she might tell you.'

'Oh!' Then Ali's mouth fell open as she saw Adam walking towards them, and she forgot all about Bev.

'Am I late?' he asked. 'Julian went on and on. The television company are pleased with the viewing numbers and want to option the rest of the series. He's hopeful about the Jay Bolton series, too, and is making suggestions for actors to play him.'

'Adam was on a call to his agent when I left,' Libby explained.

'I didn't know you were going to be here, too,' Ali said to her brother. This was becoming curiouser and curiouser – as Alice would say, she thought, one of her favourite childhood stories coming to mind.

'It'll all become clear shortly,' Adam said annoyingly. 'Have you ordered?'

'Not yet,' Libby said, just as a smiling waitress appeared at their table.

'Black coffee for me,' Adam said. 'Ladies?'

'Cappuccino,' Ali said without thinking.

'Lemon and ginger tea for me,' Libby said, 'and does Cleo have any of Ruby's brownies left?'

'I'll see what I can do.' The waitress smiled and disappeared into the kitchen in the corner of the café.

They chatted about the fun they'd had on the boat, Libby saying how nice it had been to meet Neil again, with a knowing smile at Ali, till their order arrived. Then, just as Ali was preparing herself for an interrogation about her relationship with Neil, Adam cleared his throat and took Libby's hand.

'We have something to tell you,' he said, his eyes meeting Libby's for a moment before he turned to face Ali again.

Ali's stomach dropped. She felt sick. He wasn't going to say… She saw the light in his eyes, the answering one in Libby's. He was.

'Libby and I are going to get married,' Adam said with a proud smile at his partner. 'We decided last night and wanted you to be the first to know.'

Ali swallowed. 'That's… wonderful,' she said, after a pause she knew had been too long. It was one thing to be happy that Adam and

Libby had found each other, but marriage? That was another ball game entirely. 'When's the happy day?'

It was Libby who answered. 'Later in the year. We're in no rush. We want you to be there, of course, so we'll plan for university holidays. And we want to have the ceremony here. I'm not sure if you've heard of *Pandanus Weddings?*'

'Yes. At the fundraiser.' The image of the young man dropping to his knee was etched into Ali's subconscious.

'Of course. Wasn't it a romantic gesture, and so generous of Bev,' Libby said, unaware of Ali's inner turmoil.

But Adam seemed to sense how she was feeling. 'It's not like Mum and Dad, Ali,' he said. 'We're not them. Libby and I love each other. We're happy together. Marriage won't change that. We want...' he gazed at Libby with affection, '...we want to make a public declaration of our love.'

'Okay.' The one word was all Ali could manage. The word stuck in her throat; her mouth was dry.

'We'll be sisters, Ali,' Libby said gently, appearing to realise Ali's distress.

'Of course. I'm sorry, it was a surprise. I'm happy for you both.' This time she managed a genuine smile.

'We wanted to tell you here. We're meeting Bev. She's going to show us what she calls the wedding arbour. We'll understand if you don't want to hang around.' Adam gazed at her, a concerned expression marring his previously smiling face.

'No, it's all right. I'd love to see it,' she said, trying to sound enthusiastic.

'Good. Let's drink up. Bev should be here shortly.'

Ali took a gulp of coffee and a bite of a brownie which she was sure was delicious, but the chocolate confection tasted like cardboard. It'll be fine, she told herself. She'd been to several weddings in Perth, weddings of friends and colleagues. They had never affected her like this, only reinforced her determination never to follow their example. But this was her brother. He knew how even the best of marriages could turn out. Her mother had often told Ali how much in love she and Ali's dad had been, how their first few years had been like a dream. Then it started to go bad. She thought of the women she'd met at the women's refuge. What guarantee did anyone have?

Bev arrived to join them, giving Ali no time to change her mind. She listened while the three discussed wedding plans, a flower-covered arbour, and the meal Cleo could provide. Then Bev said, 'Shall we go to see the area we have allocated for weddings? I know you attended Martin and Ailsa's wedding there, but it's different when it's your own.'

'I remember Clancy scattering rose petals,' Libby said with a smile. 'I hope she'll agree to do it again.'

'I'm sure she will. She loved being the centre of attention,' Adam said.

Ali tried to close her ears. All this talk was making her feel distinctly uncomfortable. But she'd agreed to stay, so plastered a smile on her face and pretended to listen.

Together, the four made their way to a corner of the garden centre. There was nothing to see, apart from a plexiglass covering and an archway devoid of any decoration. This was it?

'You have to remember what it can be like, picture how it will look on the day,' Bev said, warming to her subject. 'The archway will be covered with flowers, there will be a small table for the celebrant, rows of chairs for your guests and an aisle down which you will walk.'

Libby was clutching Adam's arm, her excitement palpable, while Adam was smiling broadly. 'It'll be perfect,' he said, then turning to Ali, 'Don't you think so, Ali?'

Wondering how soon she could leave, Ali muttered something inaudible.

But Adam seemed to barely take notice. He was caught up in Bev's explanation of the arrangements.

'I think that's it,' Bev said at last. 'I want to congratulate you and to say how delighted I am you've chosen to use *Pandanus Weddings*. Let me know when you've decided on a date.'

'We will,' Libby said.

'I'm sorry, I need to go,' Ali said, seeing an opportunity to escape.

'Must you?' Libby asked.

But Adam seemed to understand. 'If you'd told me a few years ago I'd be planning a wedding, I'd have thought you were mad,' he said. 'But things can change. I met Libby.' He threw an affectionate glance at his partner, and his hand tightened in hers. 'Don't dismiss marriage too readily, Ali. It may not be for you, but you may change your mind in time.'

Too surprised to speak, Ali didn't reply. She hugged Adam and Libby, said goodbye to Bev and left, walking hurriedly to the car park. Once in her car she sat there staring out through the windscreen, Adam's words going round and round in her head. Was he right? Could she change her mind? Was what she felt for Neil enough to cause such a seismic shift of everything she'd held dear?

She was saved by the arrival of a text from the university, from the HR department. The position of Head of School was about to be advertised. Ali gave a sigh of relief. It was as if fate had intervened.

Thirty-four

It was two weeks since Barry's call, and Neil had sent off so many letters of application, he felt sure at least one would prove successful. The problem was, most were for positions interstate and far from his dad and Bronte. The fact his apartment was in Brisbane wasn't such an issue. He could easily rent it until... until the board came to their senses and reinstated him, as he was sure they would. But in the meantime, he had to find a position which would fill his time while he waited for the court case, which could take months.

He was walking along the beach – something he'd started doing each morning – when his phone rang. Expecting it to be Ali, since he'd spent the previous evening with his dad and Bronte, he answered with a smile, shocked to hear Pippa's voice.

'I'm on my way. I'll be there by twelve. Can we meet for lunch?'

'You'll be where?' Did Pippa think he was back in Brisbane?

'In Bellbird Bay. I presume you're still there, you and Bronte?'

So this is what it was about? Pippa was still angry with Bronte, so angry she was prepared to travel to Bellbird Bay to talk to her.

'We are, but there's no need...'

'There's every need. I can't believe you think it's okay for her to decide to stay there. I'll be at Harry's at twelve.' She ended the call, leaving Neil aghast.

His steps had slowed while Pippa was talking, and he now became aware of the large dog splashing in the shallow water by his feet.

'Milo!' a voice called.

Neil looked up from the now silent phone to see Libby running towards him, calling her dog. 'Hello, Milo,' he said, bending to pat the dog's head.

'Sorry,' Libby said breathlessly. 'He took it into his head to run off ahead. He doesn't usually. I'm sorry,' she repeated, gesturing to Neil's now soaked cargo pants.

'No worries,' Neil said. 'They'll dry. I hear congratulations are in order. You and Adam.'

'Thanks.' Libby beamed. 'Did Ali tell you?'

'No. It was Will. At the club.' Neil had wondered at the time why Ali had remained silent about her brother's proposed marriage, assuming she still held strong views about the institution, views he hoped he might be able to change one day – though not if they lived miles apart, as seemed likely.

'Right. Ali... Adam's worried she thinks we'll end up like their parents. And now she's become so involved with the women's centre and the refuge...' She shook her head.

Neil looked down at his feet, unwilling to badmouth Ali, but curious as to what Libby might say.

She didn't say any more on the subject. Instead, she said, 'We were about to go back. Do you have time to join us for coffee? Adam's due to take a break. He's been up since the crack of dawn editing his latest manuscript.'

'Thanks. It's kind of you.' Neil relished the opportunity to get to know Libby and Adam better. From his previous encounters with them, they seemed like a nice couple, people he'd like to have as friends. Though, he reminded himself, it was unlikely he'd be around Bellbird Bay long enough to make new friends.

When they reached Libby's gate, Milo pushing ahead of them, Neil could see two men seated on the deck, Adam and another with cropped grey hair. Both rose when Libby and he walked in.

'Hey, Neil. Good to see you. Iain was sketching on the boardwalk and dropped in,' he said to his wife.

'Hi Iain. I'm just going to dry Milo off and make some coffee. You'll have some?'

'Yes please. If it's not too much trouble. Good to meet you again, Neil.'

It took Neil a moment to remember meeting Iain and Bev on Nick's yacht. There had been a crowd of people and he'd been preoccupied with Ali. 'Good to meet you again, too – you, too, Adam.'

'Take a seat, Neil,' Adam said, as Libby disappeared inside followed by Milo. 'We were just discussing a recent corruption case that's been in the news.'

Neil's stomach lurched until he realised they weren't talking about the one he was marginally involved in. It seemed there had been a local scandal. He vaguely recalled Will Rankin mentioning something about it but hadn't been aware how it impinged on the garden centre and Bev Cooper's council approval to get *Pandanus Weddings* up and running. He listened with interest to how the corrupt hotelier had been brought to justice.

'What happened to his hotel?' he asked.

'It's up for sale,' Iain said. 'Evidently there's interest from one of the big hotel chains, but we're all hoping it stays independent. There's no telling what a large conglomerate would do to it. We don't want them in Bellbird Bay.'

Neil thought of the large chain interested in buying *Bay Books*. Bellbird Bay residents wouldn't be happy with that either. But his dad might have no option but to accept their offer.

Libby soon appeared with coffee and a plate of scones warm from the oven and spread with ginger jam. Milo was at her heels, ready to devour any stray morsels which might come his way.

The conversation changed to a discussion of grandparents' day at the local primary school which all three of the others intended to attend, and Neil let his mind wander. It was pleasant sitting here in the sun, the snuffling of the dog reminding him of his childhood. When he was growing up, they'd always had a dog, but Bingo had died many years ago, and Harry had never replaced him. When Bronte wanted a pet, Pippa had steered her in the direction of smaller animals – goldfish, guinea pigs – ones which didn't need so much care or to be taken for walks. It was only now, in the relaxed atmosphere of Adam and Libby's home, Neil realised he'd missed the companionship of a dog.

Seeming to sense Neil's thoughts, Milo padded over to lie at his feet with a sigh. Neil's hand automatically dropped to pet the furry creature who responded with a gentle grunt.

By the time Neil left, with an invitation to drop in anytime, he was in a better frame of mind. But the prospect of Pippa's visit hung over him like a dark cloud. He could imagine how Bronte would react to her mother's arrival and didn't look forward to the fireworks and war of words which would ensue. He was sure Pippa, used to getting her own way, wouldn't accept Bronte's decision. And Bronte, like her mother in many ways, would refuse to give in to Pippa's demands. Neil just wished he didn't have to be the one in the middle of the argument which was bound to follow.

*

It was almost midday when Neil arrived home. He just had time for a quick shower, to change into a pair of clean chinos and his blue linen shirt, and throw the salt-encrusted pants in the laundry, when there was a loud knocking at the door. Pippa had arrived and, true to form, was letting the whole street know.

With a sigh of annoyance, Neil went to the door.

'Where is she?' Pippa pushed past him into the house.

Shaking his head in disbelief, Neil followed more slowly. When he reached the kitchen, Pippa was standing in the middle of the room looking around.

'Where's Bronte?' she asked again. 'Didn't you tell her I was coming for lunch?'

'No, should I have?' Neil asked, amused at her assumption Bronte would be waiting to meet her. 'Bronte's at work. She'll be home around half-five, unless she goes out straight from work.'

'Work! Is that what you call it? Playing around is more like it. How could you allow her to become involved with… with…' Words seemed to fail her.

Taking advantage of the break in her stream of invective, Neil said, 'There was no need for you to make this trip, but now you're here, why don't we go out to lunch and discuss this in a civilised manner? There are several good cafés in town.'

Pippa stared at Neil as if seeing him for the first time. She opened her mouth as if to start berating him again, then took a deep breath. 'Okay,' she said. 'Lunch would be good.'

Pippa had mellowed somewhat by the time they were seated at a table on the deck of the surf club, Neil with a beer, and Pippa with a glass of white wine. 'This is nice,' she said grudgingly, gesturing to the beach where a game of beach volleyball was in progress. People were swimming in the ocean and children were playing in the shallows between the flags. 'I'd forgotten what Bellbird Bay was like.'

'Remember the times we came here when Bronte was small?' Neil asked, hoping the mention of their daughter wouldn't set off another diatribe.

'Those were good times,' Pippa said, taking a sip of wine, 'with your mum and dad. How is Harry? He must be getting on. He's still running the bookshop?'

'Yes. But his health isn't so good. He may not be able to manage for much longer.'

'I'm sorry.' Pippa did sound genuinely sad, but Neil knew it wouldn't be long before she remembered the purpose of her visit.

He was right. As soon as their meals had been served – local prawns with salad for Pippa and a steak sandwich for Neil – she began to air her annoyance with Bronte again. 'It's all your fault,' she declared, pointing at Neil with her fork. 'You should have stopped her. I've worked so hard to give her a good education, to provide her with a foundation which would stand her in good stead… and you manage to ruin it.' Her eyes flashed, reminding Neil of one of the reasons they'd split up.

'Pippa, Bronte is twenty. She's an adult, capable of making her own decisions.'

'Even if they're wrong? As parents, we should be guiding her in the right direction.'

'And that would be in the direction in which *you* want her to go?'

'I'm her mother. I know what's best for her.'

'And I'm her father.' Neil could see they were at an impasse.

He was wondering where to go next when a familiar voice said, 'Dad? Mum? What are you doing here?' Looking up, Neil saw Bronte, closely followed by Owen. They were accompanied by Will, and all three looked as disreputable as each other in shorts, *Bay Surf School* tee-shirts, hair tied back in untidy buns. They had obviously come straight from the beach. Neil stole a glance at Pippa's face. Her expression was priceless. For once she was speechless.

'Neil?' Will raised an eyebrow. 'Didn't expect to see you here.'

'Hi Will. This is Pippa, Bronte's mum. Pippa, Will and I were at school together. He's...'

'Is he the surfer who's...' She stared at where Bronte and Owen were still standing as if unsure what to do or where to go. 'Bronte!' she said, 'aren't you going to introduce me?' Her voice was icy.

'This is Owen, Mum,' Bronte said proudly, pulling him forward to meet her mother.

'Hi, Mrs Simpson. It's good to meet you. Bronte has told me about you.'

I'll bet, Neil thought. He could imagine exactly what Bronte had said about her mother. None of it good.

'Mind if we join you?' Will said easily. If he felt the tension in the atmosphere, he was choosing to ignore it.

'Please do.' Neil couldn't hide the relief in his voice. Though it might be difficult for the two young people, he was glad to have Will's support in what was going to prove to be a difficult lunch.

By the time they were all seated, had ordered, and the three newcomers were supplied with beers, Pippa's face was a picture.

'Dad didn't tell me you were coming,' Bronte said, sitting close to Owen for support.

'Your mum only rang this morning. You were at work. I didn't see any reason to interrupt.'

'I wasn't actually,' Bronte said. 'We were at the beach. Will was helping Owen train for the surf championships, and I was...' she grinned affectionately at Owen, '...cheering him on.' She nudged him.

Deciding to ignore Pippa's disapproval, Neil turned to Will. 'How do you rate his chances? Can he do it a fourth time?' He could sense Pippa fuming but didn't care.

Will patted Owen on the back. 'No reason why not... if he doesn't allow himself to become distracted.' He pretended to glare at the young pair.

'Da...ad.' Owen shrugged off his dad's hand.

Pippa didn't say any more during their meal. But when they'd all finished, and Bronte and Owen rose to leave, she put a hand on Bronte's arm. 'Can we get together later, Bronte? We need to talk.'

'Sorry, Mum. We'll be working late tonight. We spent the morning on the beach, so are behind at work. The website went up two days ago and we've been flooded with orders. I need to update the database and contact our distributer, then get onto some new designs for our tee-shirts and hoodies. You should have told me you were coming,' she said as a parting shot.

Neil had no doubt it would have made no difference, other than for Bronte to ensure she was nowhere near anywhere her mother might be.

'Well done, you two,' Will said, high-fiving Owen. 'You're going to be more successful than I've ever been.'

When the two young people had left, Will turned to Pippa, 'You should be proud of your daughter,' he said. 'With her skills in business, IT and design, she's managed to expand Owen's business. They're getting orders from all over the world. They're a power team.'

Pippa didn't reply. Neil could see she was trying to process what Will was saying, wondering if she could accept the assessment of someone who looked like a beach bum, but spoke like a businessman.

'I'll leave you to it. I have a class in five minutes.' Will walked off, leaving Neil with Pippa.

'She's happy, you know,' Neil said, wondering how Pippa could have missed the happy glow on Bronte's face which only faded slightly when she saw her mother.

'So it seems, but it won't last. She'll come to her senses sooner or later and expect me to pick up the pieces. You don't realise what you've done, helping her ruin her life like this in this godforsaken little town.'

Neil remained silent. Had Pippa forgotten her earlier praise of Bellbird Bay?

'Well, it seems I've wasted my time coming here, and cutting short my holiday. Geoff's still in Bali,' she said peevishly.

Geoff must be the younger man Bronte had said her mother was seeing. But it appeared the personal trainer had done nothing to mellow Pippa.

'Maybe you should go back and join him?'

'Possibly I will. Thanks for lunch. It seems you've reverted to type now you're back home, colluding with your old school friends,' she sneered. 'The school board was right to suspend you.' With that parting insult, she rose and stormed off, leaving Neil gazing after her in surprise. She might be mad about Bronte's decision, but there was no need for her to suggest Neil had anything to be ashamed of.

Thirty-five

Ali was procrastinating. She knew she should complete her application for Head of School – it had been her dream for so long – but something was holding her back. Although she had seen notification of the vacancy as fate taking a hand, it was now two weeks since she'd received the email and she still hadn't done anything about it.

But today she would, she decided, as she sat on the balcony drinking her early morning lemon and ginger tea. She'd almost given up making her own coffee, as the brew offered by the many cafés in town were so much better... and there was always the chance of running into Neil. Although she might try to tell herself she didn't care, she knew in her heart that she did, reminding her of Ruby's admonition to follow her heart – something she had no intention of doing. But, in the meantime, she intended to enjoy his company when she could.

She went inside and was soon busy at her laptop, updating her CV and providing the detailed document outlining her vision for the school in the next decade. It wasn't an easy task and several times she almost gave up. But she persevered and three hours and several cups of coffee later, she was finished.

Now she needed a cup of proper coffee. Ali changed into a strappy summer dress and set off in the direction of the esplanade. Although she'd seen Neil only the previous evening, she wanted to see him again and he'd mentioned he might be helping in the bookshop today.

As she took a seat outside *The Bay Café*, Ali glanced across at the bookshop, hoping Neil would appear. She supposed she could go in, ask if he would join her, but didn't want to appear too forward. He might think she was more interested in him than she was willing to admit, even to herself. And it only took the memory of the women at the refuge to remind her why marriage was a bad idea, why she intended to focus on her career.

But, as she sipped her coffee, enjoying the underlying hazelnut flavour, her eyes kept returning to the door of the bookshop, watching people entering and leaving, none of whom were Neil. It was a surprise, therefore, when she heard his voice at her shoulder.

'What are you doing here?'

'Drinking coffee.' Ali had trouble keeping her voice steady. 'Not working in the bookshop today?'

'Had to run an errand for Dad. I need to pop into the shop, then I can join you... unless you were about to leave?'

'No, I was about to order another coffee,' Ali lied.

'Good. Be with you in a bit.'

Ali's second coffee had already arrived when Neil returned. He ordered, then took a seat. 'Good morning?' he asked with a smile.

'Busy. I finally got round to completing the application for Head of School and sent it off. Now it's a matter of waiting.'

'How long are they likely to take?'

'I'm not sure. I suspect Hugo Martin and I will be the only internal applicants, but there's no telling how many external ones there'll be.'

'Hugo Martin, isn't he the guy...?'

'Who assaulted one of my students. He is.'

'And they'd consider him for the position?'

'He got off with a warning, so no stain on his character. It would be a disaster if he was appointed, not only for the students, but for the reputation of the university and the future of the school.' For a moment, Ali imagined what it might be like if it did happen. One thing was sure. She wouldn't be able to work under his leadership. 'What's happening with your applications?' she asked.

Neil grimaced. 'No luck so far. But I'm sure something will turn up. It always does. Some poor sod will have an accident or decide they can't hack it any longer and yours truly will get a call.'

'Your old position...?'

'No chance. But they have set a date for the court case, so it may not be a complete disaster in that quarter if all goes well.'

'You'd prefer that?'

'Of course. It would be difficult going back into the classroom after being in charge, though the thought of having less responsibility does have its attractions.'

'And you would go anywhere?' Even Perth, she wondered, though what might that do to her carefully constructed barriers?

'Anywhere that'll have me. Beggars can't be choosers. I may still be on salary at the moment, but it's not clear how long it will last, and I can't live off Dad for ever.'

'Of course not.' Ali had an inkling of how he felt. Although she wasn't accepting Adam and Libby's hospitality while in Bellbird Bay, she sometimes felt beholden to them. It wasn't a comfortable feeling for someone who was used to being independent. At least her volunteer work at the women's centre gave her some degree of satisfaction, and she was becoming good friends with Maxine. She was learning so much from her about the workings of the centre. It was much more complex than she'd first imagined and helped so many people.

As if reading her mind, Neil asked, 'And what you're doing at the women's centre...will that help you when you go back to the university?'

'It certainly will. I'm much more aware of the issues facing women in situations of domestic violence. I can now talk knowledgably about them, rather than relying on cold statistics. And I can draw on my experiences working with Maxine to demonstrate the different ways in which women can help women overcome the challenges many face.' It wasn't till she finished speaking, Ali realised just how much she had gained from volunteering at the centre. She'd be sorry to leave it... and Maxine, and she intended to keep in touch with the older woman when she returned to Perth – or to whatever university she might end up in. It was strange to think she might have to move universities, perhaps even states, but it's what happened when you chose to follow a career path. There was no guarantee the promotion you sought – even deserved – would fall into your lap in the university of your choice.

'No more word from your ex?' Ali asked, changing the subject. She knew Neil had been annoyed when his ex-wife had arrived in town two weeks earlier, but he hadn't mentioned her since.

'No, thank goodness. Bronte says she's gone back to Bali... to her personal trainer. I did tell you she stayed in town overnight, and Bronte did meet her for breakfast?' He shook his head. 'I don't know what they talked about, but Bronte seems to think her mother has accepted her decision to stay in Bellbird Bay. I suspect the opposite and that Pippa's just waiting for Bronte to get tired of it... and Owen. Although I don't think there's much chance of that happening in this lifetime.'

'They're close... your daughter and Owen?'

'Like this.' He held up his hand with two fingers crossed. 'Like Pippa and I were at one time, but Bronte's not like her mother. With her, I think it'll last.'

Ali suddenly felt uncomfortable with the way the conversation was going, wishing she hadn't asked about Bronte and Owen. It was too close to her and Neil's relationship. By what she assumed was a common agreement, neither of them had discussed the possibility of there being any future to it. How could there be? Neither had any idea where they'd be in a few months' time. But Ali lived in constant terror Neil would want to talk about a future together... a future she could never agree to.

To her relief, Neil didn't pursue the conversation. 'What else do you have on today?' he asked.

'I promised to drop in to the women's refuge this afternoon to give them a hand in the garden,' she said. She had started doing that a couple of times a week. As Eleanor said, it was therapeutic, and she found the women talked more freely as they worked together in the vegetable patch.

'Okay. I should get back to Dad now. See you tonight?' Neil asked, a twinkle in his eye.

'I'll be home.' Ali smiled at the thought of another night together. She might be opposed to their relationship having a future, but Neil was an attractive man, one she found sexy and charming and who was excellent company. She had to admit she'd be sorry when their liaison came to an end... but come to an end it must.

Thirty-six

Neil had almost given up hope of receiving a response from his job applications when two emails arrived, one after the other. The first expressed regret that they weren't able to offer him anything but promised to keep his CV on file in the event anything should become available.

He grimaced.

The second was more promising. It indicated a position might be available the following term and invited Neil for an interview. It was a teaching position, but the school was in an outer suburb of Brisbane, so he'd be able to stay in his apartment. He was on his way to the kitchen to tell his dad when he heard an almighty crash, followed by a guttural cry.

His heart in his mouth, Neil rushed into the kitchen to see Harry lying on the floor, obviously in pain, but trying to get up. There was a gash on his head where he must have struck it on one of the drawer handles.

'Don't move, Dad,' he said, reaching for his phone. 'I'll call an ambulance.'

'No!' Harry said weakly. 'Just give me a minute.'

But Neil could see the older man needed medical care. This is what he'd been afraid of after the last time. The doctor had warned him about the danger of repeat falls along with the onset of other symptoms. He slid a cushion under his dad's head, taking care not to disturb the injury, and prepared to wait for the ambulance to arrive, all thought of the job interview forgotten.

*

Neil had been waiting in the hospital for what seemed like hours. The ambulance had arrived quickly, and he'd followed in his car with a sense of *déjà vu* This time things looked more serious. Harry had been quickly whisked off to x-ray and for various other tests, while Neil had been left to cool his heels. He'd gone to the hospital café, drunk coffee, and now he was pacing the floor in the corridor outside the room where Harry was still being examined.

'Mr Simpson?'

Neil turned rapidly, almost bumping into the young man in blue scrubs, a stethoscope hanging out of the top pocket. 'Yes. How is he?'

'Take a seat.'

Looking around, Neil saw a row of blue plastic seats he hadn't noticed before. He sat down next to the doctor.

'I understand Harry – your father – has been diagnosed with stage three of Parkinson's.'

Neil nodded.

'And he has taken a fall before?'

Neil nodded again, wanting desperately to hear something new.

'It seems this time he's sustained more serious injuries. Do you know how it happened?'

'I wasn't with him at the time. Dad was in the kitchen. I found him lying on the floor between the fridge and the kitchen cabinets. The fridge door was open. I can only assume he was taking something out or putting something in when he lost his balance.'

'Ah, yes. Parkinson's affects the balance.' He cleared his throat. 'Your dad has sustained a fracture to his elbow and shoulder and received a nasty blow to the head which may or may not be serious. We're checking for concussion. We'd like to keep him here for a few days to monitor him, then we can make a decision how to proceed.'

'But...' Neil couldn't hide his distress, '...he will be all right? Sorry, I know that may have sounded strange. I'm aware my dad's sick, but he's been managing. The illness didn't seem to be progressing. I suppose I hoped...' He dragged a hand through his already dishevelled hair.

'Why don't you go home and get some rest? There's nothing you can do here. Your dad will be caught up with a series of tests for most of the day, but you can pop in to see him this evening during visiting hours.'

'This evening. Right.' In a dream, Neil made his way out of the hospital and found his way home. Once there, he couldn't settle. He called Bronte to tell her what happened and refused her offer to come home. There was nothing she could do here. It would be best if she kept busy. He should do something to keep himself busy, too. The bookshop! Neil couldn't believe he'd forgotten about it. It would be the first thing Harry asked when he saw him.

Hurrying back to the car, he drove the few blocks to the esplanade to find several people standing outside the still closed shop. 'Sorry,' he said, 'family emergency. We're open now.'

There was a steady stream of customers all day, each forcing Neil to explain his dad had been taken ill and would be back soon. He mentally crossed his fingers as he said this, hoping it to be the case. But what if it wasn't? He knew the day would come when Harry wouldn't be able to return. What would they do then? He thought again of the offer from *Wham Bam Books* and flinched. There had to be a better solution.

Neil closed up and dashed home for a quick bite to eat before returning to the hospital. This time, he was accompanied by Bronte who insisted on seeing her grandfather.

'He will be all right, won't he?' she asked in a tremulous voice when they reached the door of the ward where Harry had been taken.

'I hope so, honey. But your grandad's an old man, and he's sick. We'll see what the doctor has to say.'

'He has to be,' she said, clinging to Neil's arm as they caught sight of Harry lying very still.

'Dad?' Neil moved towards the bed, Bronte following more cautiously.

Harry's eyes opened. 'I'm not done for yet,' he said with a weak smile.

Now they were closer, Neil could see Harry's arm – fortunately his left one – was strapped to his body, there was a plaster on one side of his head, and he was hooked up to all the usual bits of medical equipment.

'You took a bad fall this time, Dad. Do you remember what happened?'

'Of course I do. I was taking the milk out of the fridge. I turned to close the door and… I must have slipped. The kitchen floor is pretty hard.'

Neil remembered seeing the carton of milk on the kitchen bench. He'd automatically returned it to the fridge without thinking. 'The doctor said you've broken a couple of bones, and looks like your head took a beating, too. They want to keep you in for a couple of days to check on you.'

'Doctors! More tests? I seem to have spent all day being pricked and prodded and asked questions. I just want to go home.'

'And we want you home, Grandad,' Bronte said, 'but you need to do what the doctor says. We want you better.'

'I'll never be completely better, Bronte,' Harry said sadly. 'This Parkinson's thing has got me beat, but… What about the bookshop?' he asked Neil, as if suddenly remembering.

'Don't worry about the shop, Dad. I opened up today, and I can do it until you're back on your feet.'

'I can help, too, Grandad. Like I did before Christmas. Owen's okay with it. He understands.'

'You're a good girl.' Harry seemed to relax against his pillows at the news his bookshop was in safe hands.

Neil bit his lip. How could he tell his dad about his interview? And how could he attend the interview while his dad was still incapacitated?

After a few minutes, Neil could tell Harry was wilting, so he and Bronte said their goodbyes and left, promising to return next day.

'What do you think, Dad?' Bronte asked on the drive home. 'Grandad doesn't look good. This is the second time he's had a fall, and this one looks as if it was worse than when he collapsed in the shop. What if it happens again, when there's no one around to help?'

'I don't know, sweetie.' It was worrying Neil, too. They couldn't be with Harry all the time… and, with this illness, there was the danger he'd suffer more falls. They'd been warned it could happen. But Harry was so independent. He wouldn't take kindly to being monitored 24/7.

*

'I'm sorry about your dad.'

After a quick shower and change, Neil had dropped round to see Ali and tell her what had happened.

'Thanks.' Neil took a gulp from the glass of cold beer Ali had poured as soon as he arrived.

'Do you know how long he'll be in hospital?'

'The doctor said a few days, but I doubt he'll be ready to go back to work, though…' Neil shook his head, '…I don't look forward to being the one to tell him.'

'When's your interview?'

'Next Monday. I'll have to cancel.'

'Don't do that.' Ali put a hand on Neil's arm. 'Maybe… if your dad's still recovering… I could help out. You said Bronte will be in the shop. How about I observe for a day, then be her assistant?'

'You'd do that?'

'Why not? Isn't that what friends are for?'

Neil kissed Ali on the forehead. 'It would be a big help. I don't hold out much hope, but I'd hate to miss out on the opportunity – if there is one.'

'It's settled, then. I'll come in on the weekend to observe and help out if I can, and I'll be Bronte's offsider on Monday while you attend your interview. If your dad's home by then…'

'He'll want to be there, too. I don't know what we're going to do, Ali. Can I risk him being on his own in the shop… or at home? What if he falls again when he's by himself?' Neil thought of dreadful tales he'd heard of old people lying in their house for days – or even weeks – before anyone knew something was wrong.

'Have you thought of a personal alarm? Mum had one towards the end. She hated the idea, but it put my mind at rest when I was at the university, and she was home alone.'

'Hey, that's an idea. Maybe I can check it out with the doctor… and with Dad.' Neil could imagine his dad's reaction… probably much like Ali's mother's. But it was a good solution and would ease his worry… and his guilt when he had to leave Bellbird Bay again. He thought of Bronte's assurance that she'd still be here. But he couldn't leave a twenty-year-old with the responsibility of her grandad's safety.

'I wish there was more I could do to help.' Ali stroked Neil's brow.

'It's enough you're here.' And it was… for now. But later, when they were curled up together in bed, their bodies slick with sweat, he wished they could be together for ever.

Thirty-seven

Sunday had been fun. It was the first time Ali had worked in a shop since she had a summer job in their local newsagency when she was sixteen. She'd been too embarrassed to tell Neil about it as she knew that eight weeks selling newspapers was hardly comparable to working in his family bookshop. But, to her surprise, there weren't too many differences, and by the end of the afternoon Neil was convinced she and Bronte would be able to cope.

Harry was a different story. He'd been discharged from hospital on Thursday and, after staying home for two days, had insisted on coming to the bookshop on Sunday. He had accepted Neil's dictum that he wasn't allowed to do any work, so had sat in a chair at the side of the counter ostensibly chatting to customers. But Ali had felt his eyes on her all day.

Today was Neil's interview in Brisbane, and she knew he'd left Bellbird Bay early in order to stop in at his apartment to change, before heading to his early afternoon appointment. He hadn't said much about it, but Ali knew he was banking on this one working out for him. It would enable him to be only a few hours away should anything happen to his dad.

Bronte and Harry were already at the bookshop when she arrived, Bronte setting up behind the counter and Harry in his chair, in the same position as the day before. Both greeted her with a friendly smile, and Ali thought she detected some relief in Bronte's. *Had Harry been giving her a hard time?*

This was answered when, as Ali joined her behind the counter, Bronte whispered, 'Grandad says he's well enough to cope.'

'Okay there, Harry?' Ali asked, fixing him with her eyes, much the way she fixed her eyes on students asking for an extension on an assignment. It didn't work on Harry as well as it did on her students.

Harry muttered something inaudible which Ali chose to ignore, saying, 'Why don't I get us all a coffee? *The Bay Café* is open.'

Fortunately, there were fewer customers than Ali had anticipated – Harry said Mondays were usually slack. 'It's when I do my paperwork,' he said glumly, staring down at his immobilised arm. 'Maybe…'

'Not today, Harry. I'm sure Neil will take care of it when he's back,' Ali said, hoping it was the case. But Harry continued to grumble as the day progressed. Although Ali knew it was partly caused by his illness, and his inability to be in charge of his shop, she still found it wearing and had to work to keep her temper.

She was glad when it was time to close up, even gladder when Neil appeared in the doorway as they were about to leave.

'Dad!' was Bronte's heartfelt greeting, while Ali just wanted to throw her arms around him.

'Let's get you home, Dad,' Neil said and, looking at the old man, Ali could see he appeared tired.

'Thanks, son. These two did pretty well today,' he said to Ali's surprise. 'How did your day go?'

Neil grimaced. 'Not so well,' he said. 'I doubt I'll be hearing from them again.'

Ali felt her heart ache for him. Job interviews were hard, and she knew how much Neil had hoped this one would work out for him. Now he'd have to keep putting in applications. She would, too, though, fingers crossed, if she got the Head of School position, she could stay there till she retired. Retired! She tried not to think of what Sally said about being old and alone. She enjoyed her own company. That wasn't going to change.

'Join us for dinner?'

Neil's question broke through Ali's thoughts. Dinner at his dad's? It was something she always avoided – a family dinner. Neil was waiting for a reply. Harry and Bronte were looking at her. It would be rude to refuse. 'Thanks,' she said, 'I'd like that,' and to her surprise, she knew she would.

*

Ali was feeling buoyant as she prepared to go to the women's centre next morning. She was glad she'd agreed to dinner at Neil's home the previous evening, despite her initial reluctance. The evening had gone well. Bronte heated up a lasagna which they'd bought in a local bakery, and Neil opened a bottle of wine. Once home again, Harry perked up and entertained them with tales of the early days of the bookshop, interspersed with Neil's memories of spending time there as a child. Apart from the black contraption holding his arm to his body, it was difficult to believe there was anything wrong with Harry. It was only when he began to become confused with his memories that Ali noticed Neil and Bronte share concerned glances.

After dinner, once Bronte had left to meet Owen, and Harry had gone to bed, Ali and Neil snuggled up together on the sofa in front of the large television screen with another glass of wine and watched a rerun of one of her favourite episodes of *Vera*. It was all so domesticated, like being married, and for a brief moment, Ali thought how nice it would be to be able to do this every night. Then she remembered, not every night would be like this. She remembered her mother, the women at the refuge. They, too, had been lulled into similar thoughts – and look what happened to them. But it had been nice, and she'd been sad when it was time to leave, Neil murmuring, 'I wish I could come with you,' as he kissed her goodnight.

Ali smiled at the memory as she pulled on the loose blue pants and white shirt which had become almost her uniform for the centre. It was a comfortable outfit and suitable for whatever the day might bring. This morning, she and Maxine were planning to relocate the centre library from the small room it currently inhabited to a much larger one which would enable users to have more privacy – and would allow them to extend the collection to include a large number of donations which were currently being stored in boxes.

Maxine looked paler than usual when Ali arrived at the centre, but waved away Ali's concern, keen to get started on their task. They were in the process of packing the existing collection into boxes ready to be moved, when Maxine stopped, put a hand to her chest, said, 'I need to…' and collapsed in a heap on the floor.

Reminded of Harry's collapse in the bookshop, Ali yelled for help, taking out her phone to call for an ambulance, before bending down to see what she could do to help Maxine, who was lying horribly still.

Almost immediately, two women came running into the room, one of whom was Joy, who Ali had met on her first visit to the centre. 'Let me,' she said, moving closer to Maxine, 'I used to be a nurse.' A moment later, she raised her head, her eyes filled with tears. 'It's too late. A heart attack. She... she knew her heart would give out, but... What will we do without her?' She started to cry in gulping sobs, her hand covering her mouth.

Ali gazed at her in shock. 'You mean?' Was Maxine dead? She couldn't believe it. 'Are you sure? Shouldn't we wait till...?' She heard the wail of the ambulance siren with a sense of relief. There would be paramedics. They'd be able to help. Joy must be mistaken.

Suddenly the room seemed to be filled with people as two paramedics appeared and forced Joy and Ali out of the way. They leant over Maxine for what seemed like for ever. Then one stood up. 'I'm sorry,' he said.

Ali felt the tears course down her cheeks. How could this vibrant woman who, only a few minutes earlier, had been chatting to Ali about her future plans for the centre while piling books into boxes, be dead? She and Joy hugged each other while the paramedics made calls to report on Maxine's death. There was a flurry of movement; they were urged to leave the room. Then it was over. Maxine's body was removed.

The whole building was shrouded in silence. It was as if the very walls knew what had happened, and everyone was moving around on tiptoe and speaking in whispers as if by doing so they could change the course of events. There didn't seem to be much point in continuing with her task, so Ali allowed herself to be led away and found herself seated in the centre kitchen clutching a cup of hot, sweet tea with little idea of how she got there.

There was nothing more Ali could do there, so she made her way home. But once there, she couldn't settle and found herself walking up the boardwalk past Adam and Libby's house to knock on Grace's door, hoping she'd be there.

From Grace's face when she opened the door, Ali knew she'd already heard the news. 'You poor dear,' Grace said. 'You were with

Maxine when…' She drew Ali into a warm hug and, for the first time since she'd seen Maxine collapse, Ali felt comforted.

Grace didn't ask any questions, merely motioned Ali to take a seat and brewed a pot of tea. The two drank their tea in silence for several minutes before Grace asked, 'Do you want to talk about it?'

Ali thought for a moment, then nodded. 'It happened so suddenly,' she said. 'One moment we were chatting, laughing together, the next she was lying there… and she was dead, Grace. I still can't believe it. Maxine was so full of life, so full of plans, she seemed invulnerable, as if she'd live for ever.'

'None of us do that,' Grace said gently.

'Sorry. You've known her longer than I have. It must have been a shock for you, too.'

'Probably not so much. I knew she'd had heart problems in the past, but Maxine wasn't one to let anything stand in her way. She'd have wanted to go the way she did… in her beloved centre. It's just such a pity you were there to witness her passing.'

The pair sat in silence for several moments remembering the woman who had done so much for her fellow women. Then Grace rallied. 'She wouldn't want us to grieve like this,' she said. 'Maxine believed life was meant to be lived and wouldn't want us to be sad for her. She'd prefer us to continue her work at the centre.'

Ali nodded, too overcome to speak.

Thirty-eight

Harry was making progress. His elbow had almost healed, and his shoulder was forming new bone. 'I've had enough of sitting around making polite conversation,' he said one morning at breakfast. 'I'm fit enough to get back to work.'

'Oh, Dad, I don't think so.' Neil was stacking the dishwasher. 'Give it another few weeks.'

'Another few weeks and I'll be a raving lunatic,' Harry said. 'Lucky it's my left arm. I can cope with this one.' He waved his right arm in the air. 'And when you're off at one of your interviews, Bronte will be there to make sure I don't fall again, won't you, sweetheart?'

'Of course, Grandad.'

But Neil could see from her expression, she was itching to get back to working with Owen again, sure his business couldn't cope without her. He knew she often worked into the night in her bedroom, maintaining the database and placing orders. It wasn't fair to keep her at the bookshop.

But he didn't want to leave his dad there on his own and he did have a couple of interviews lined up, one on the Gold Coast and one in Sydney. He remembered Ali's suggestion of a personal alarm. Maybe, once his dad was able to cope again, he'd agree to having one. It would put Neil's mind at rest. Harry had a follow up appointment with his doctor later in the week. He'd enquire about one then and bring it up with his dad.

Neil hadn't seen as much of Ali as he'd have liked since Maxine's

189

death. It had been such a shock to her. Libby had taken Ali off to stay with her and Adam for a few days and she'd asked him to be patient. He understood her need to grieve for the woman she'd come to like and admire and wondered if she'd continue to volunteer at the centre now Maxine was gone.

Meantime, he'd continued to send off job applications and attend interviews, becoming more and more disillusioned as one interview panel after another told him they'd let him know if anything turned up.

The one light at the end of the tunnel was the fact the court case looked like going ahead soon. If all went well, maybe he wouldn't need to worry about finding something else. Maybe he'd have his old position back. But things didn't look good in that direction. The word from Barry was that enrollments were down, and he had accepted a teaching load in addition to his role as acting principal. It didn't augur well for the future. The school might not survive this catastrophe.

Even if it did, Neil had the impression it would be a very different place from the one he'd left. Would he really want to return to a slimmer version of the prestigious establishment he'd led for the past ten years? Or would it be better to have a fresh start? He hadn't forgotten the subversive thoughts he'd entertained during that call from Pippa, when he'd wondered if he was on the wrong track. But he didn't know anything other than teaching, and he loved working with young people. Maybe he just needed to change his attitude, or find a position in one of those alternative schools he'd read about back in university. He remembered visiting one once, on an excursion. It was called The School Without Walls. It did have walls, of course, but provided students with much greater freedom than traditional schools. But he couldn't imagine himself in a place like that, either.

'Dad?'

'Sorry, sweetheart.' Neil forced himself back to the present. Both Bronte and Harry were ready to leave for the bookshop. He needed to focus on the here and now. Today, he was manning the bookshop for his dad with Bronte assisting. Tomorrow was another day.

Thirty-nine

The few days after Maxine's death – and her funeral – passed in a blur for Ali. She was vaguely conscious of the large gathering – mainly women – who attended the service and the reception at the women's centre afterwards, conscious only of her own regret that she hadn't had the opportunity to know more of the woman she'd come to admire.

However, a week later, an email from the university changed her mood from one of sadness to one of exhilaration. It was to invite her to an interview for the position of Head of School to be held in a week's time. It meant she'd have to go back to Perth for a few days at least. The trip was too onerous to make it in one day. She quickly replied with her agreement to attend and sent another email to Sally asking if she could stay with her during her visit, her mother's house still being rented out. Then she sat down and stared out the window at the view she'd come to love, a bubble of excitement fizzing up inside her. This was her chance to prove she was the right person for the job, to show all those who'd scorned her, who'd belittled her devotion to women's studies, that she was a worthy candidate for Head of School. She would have the chance to make Maxine proud of her.

Ali hugged the news to herself all day. She didn't tell Adam and Libby, not even Neil when they had dinner then came back to her apartment. She was still hugging it to herself next morning as she lay in Neil's arms. 'I had some good news yesterday,' she said, pushing herself away so she could see his face. 'I have an interview for the Head of School position.'

Ali sensed Neil's withdrawal. 'The one you've been waiting for?' he asked. 'Well done. When is it?'

'Next week.'

'So you'll be going back to Perth?'

'For a few days. I'll stay with Sal. It'll be a good chance to catch up. I'll be back by the weekend.'

'Right.' Neil sounded okay, but the mood was broken.

'Tea?' Ali slipped out of bed and made her way to the kitchen. By the time the kettle was boiling, Neil had followed her and was dropping two slices of bread into the toaster. The day had begun.

*

Ali planned to go to the women's centre that day. It would be the first time she'd been since she saw Maxine die there and she knew it would be difficult to forget the sight of her motionless body. But Maxine had trusted her, and she owed it to her to continue the work she'd started.

To Ali's surprise, she was greeted with what seemed like relief by Joy and a couple of the other women. 'We didn't know if you'd be back,' Joy said, 'and we didn't know how to contact you. There's to be a big meeting today.' She nodded to the closed door of what Ali knew to be the boardroom. She'd never been inside, having no need to do so. While she was aware there was a board of community members which handled funding and made executive decisions, everything else had been in Maxine's hands. She supposed they'd be replacing her. The centre would need a director. Life went on. But no one could replace Maxine in Ali's mind.

She was in the library, continuing with the packing up of books, trying to avoid looking at the spot on the floor where she'd last seen Maxine, and to stem the sobs which threatened to overwhelm her, when a woman she didn't recognise appeared in the doorway. She was short and dumpy, her white hair neatly trimmed, and was dressed in a pair of grey tailored pants and a white blouse. In her sixties, she gave the impression she was accustomed to organising everyone around.

'Can I help you?' Ali asked, embarrassed to be found with her eyes wet with tears.

'Ali Wells?'

'Yes.'

'I'm Dorothy Turner... Dot,' said the woman, as if Ali should know who she was.

'Yes?'

'I'm the secretary of the board of the women's centre. We've been meeting to discuss the dilemma we face with Maxine's untimely demise.'

Ali flinched, but she couldn't see how this would affect her... unless they didn't want her to continue with what she was doing.

Dot went on, 'Maxine apprised us of the assistance you were providing, of your background, of your indubitable experience in the field.'

Ali was still puzzled. She wished the woman would get on with what she had to say.

'I have been asked to invite you to apply for the position of director of the centre.'

'Oh!' Ali almost dropped the books she was holding This was the last thing she'd expected. 'But... I... I have a position... a university position... in Western Australia... in Perth,' she stammered, knowing it might not be exactly accurate.

'But surely you'd consider our offer? The renumeration would be substantial.' She waited, clearly expecting Ali to jump at the opportunity.

When Ali didn't respond, the woman appeared perplexed. She didn't appear to be accustomed to being ignored.

'I'm sorry, Dot, but I don't think...'

'Would you at least consider it?' The woman smiled and held out a folder Ali hadn't noticed she was holding. 'Here is the information pack we've put together. It includes the position description, information about the centre and the renumeration package. You'll find it's generous. Take your time to go through it. We'll expect your application. We want to move on this quickly.' She nodded and walked away, closing the door behind her and leaving Ali staring at the folder in her hand.

*

Ali needed coffee. After Dot's appearance, she'd found it difficult to concentrate, so had decided to take a complete break, knowing if she stayed at the centre she was bound to be asked what Dot had wanted of her.

She was driving aimlessly, trying to come to grips with the idea the board might consider her suitable to take Maxine's place – though no one could do that – when she realised she was passing the garden centre. Remembering the delicious coffee and the ambiance of the café there, she swung into the car park and made her way through the plumbago hedge into *The Pandanus Café*.

Once there, she was greeted like an old friend by Cleo and, ordering a cappuccino and a slice of decadent sounding raspberry crumble she sat back and relaxed, letting the atmosphere of the café calm her shattered nerves. How could the board even imagine she'd be interested in the position? How could she contemplate staying in Bellbird Bay? Her life was in Perth. Her career was in universities.

Her coffee and cake arrived. She took a sip of the coffee, enjoying the caffeine hit, and opened her bag where she'd shoved the folder Dot had handed her. She took it out.

'Hello, Ali. How lovely to see you. Are you expecting anyone, or may I join you?'

Looking up, Ali saw Grace Winter smiling down at her.

'No, I'm on my own. Please do.' She hastily shoved the folder back into her bag. She'd decide what to do with it later.

Grace took a seat, ordered a pot of lemon and ginger tea, then sat back and peered at Ali. 'Is everything all right, Ali? I know Maxine's death hit you hard. Have you been back to the women's centre? I'm sure Maxine would want you to continue.'

'I have. This morning, and… Oh, Grace, the strangest thing happened. This officious little woman who said she's the secretary to the board appeared and asked me to apply for Maxine's position. Can you imagine? How could I?'

Grace chuckled. 'That officious little woman is my sister.'

'Oh, hell. I'm sorry, I didn't know.'

'How could you? I agree, by the way, but she has a good heart, and she works hard for the centre. It was her who introduced me to Maxine. And I think you'd be perfect for the position. What's the problem?'

'I couldn't. Maxine was a one-off. I could never hope to replace her. All my work has been at the theoretical level. I've learnt so much from volunteering there, but...'

'Don't dismiss the idea too quickly. I know it would be very different to what you're accustomed to but think of the good you could do.'

'Mmm.' Ali took a sip of coffee and forked up a piece of cake. 'What brings you here today?'

'I had a meeting with Bev earlier. And, after this, I intend to buy a few new plants for the garden. So, you intend to return to university teaching?' she asked, seeming unwilling to let the subject go.

'That's the plan. I actually have an interview for the position of Head of School next week, so...' she spread her hands.

'I can't persuade you to consider the centre position?'

Ali shook her head. 'Not you, too?' she asked, conscious of the folder lying in her bag.

When she arrived home, it was to find Neil waiting for her. They went for lunch, then to the beach. It wasn't till next morning that she thought of it again.

'What's that?' Neil asked, when she took the folder from her bag.

'Nothing.' Ali was about to drop it into the wastepaper basket.

'Doesn't look like nothing.' Neil took it from her unresisting hands. He opened it, scanned the top page then looked at Ali. 'Director at the women's centre? You don't want to apply?'

Ali shrugged. 'It's not my thing. When I was there yesterday, this woman appeared and suggested I apply. But I have the university interview next week.'

'What harm would it do? If they've asked you to apply, you'll score an interview. It would be good experience, if nothing else. That's how I'm looking at things.'

'Sorry.' Ali put a hand on Neil's shoulder. She knew he'd been for so many interviews which went nowhere. Maybe he was right. Her CV was already updated. She could compose a quick letter of application, no need to sweat over something she didn't want. What harm could it do?

Forty

'Come on, Dad.' Neil watched as Harry slowly made his way to the door. They were due at his follow-up medical appointment in less than half an hour, and this morning it had taken his dad longer than usual to get ready, shrugging off all of Neil's offers to help. Bronte had already gone to open the bookshop. Neil and Harry would join her later, despite Harry's protests he could manage on his own.

At the hospital, they were immediately ushered into an interview room, where, to his annoyance, Harry was asked a series of questions, before being taken off to have his arm x-rayed. While he was gone, Neil went down to the hospital cafeteria for a coffee and called Ali.

'Any news?' he asked. He knew she'd sent off her application for the position at the centre and that they didn't want to waste time.

'I had a call from that Dot woman. They want to interview me tomorrow.' She sounded annoyed.

'That's good, isn't it?'

'Why?'

'As I told you. Look on it as practice for the one at the university next week.'

'I suppose. How's your dad?' she asked, an indication she didn't want to talk about her interview.

'Being x-rayed. The doc seems pleased with his progress.' He bit his lip.

'That's good, isn't it?' She echoed his words.

'I guess so. The problem is, he'll now want to take over in the bookshop again. Bronte will be pleased, but...'

'You're worried about him?' Ali could read his mind.

'I'm worried something will happen when he's there on his own.'

'Have you suggested a personal alarm?'

'Not yet.' It was a reminder to Neil to ask the doctor about it. 'I should go. He'll be back from his x-ray. See you tonight?' Ali had agreed to come to dinner again, and Neil was looking forward to another cosy evening with her. Even though they wouldn't be able to spend the night together, he enjoyed cosying up with her on the sofa like an old married couple – though he and Pippa had never done that much.

Harry was being wheeled back from x-ray when Neil returned. He had a smile on his face, indicating to Neil that the news was good.

'The shoulder is healing well,' the doctor said when they were all back in the interview room. 'The new bone is forming just as we hoped. We'll schedule a few appointments with our physiotherapist who'll give Harry some exercises to get his shoulder and arm working again as it should.'

Harry's eyes lit up, but Neil was still concerned. His fears were realised when the doctor continued, 'This latest fall is a worry. Along with the other tests we took, it shows further deterioration in your condition.' He turned to Neil. 'You should be prepared to expect further falls and perhaps other signs. It's fortunate there was no concussion this time.'

'Do you think it would be wise for Dad to have a personal alarm?' Neil asked.

'An excellent idea. It would keep him safe, and put your mind at rest.'

'Thanks. Hear that, Dad?'

'What next? You'll be packing me off to a nursing home?' Harry grumbled, but he didn't argue when the doctor explained how a personal alarm could detect when a fall had occurred and summon help. 'You wear it round your neck like a pendant,' he explained to Harry who, by this time, appeared to have reluctantly accepted the idea.

'As long as I can get back to my bookshop without your interference,' he said to Neil grimly.

*

Harry had been very quiet for some time. Irritated by what he referred to as Neil's fussing when they returned from the hospital, he'd said he was going to catch up on paperwork and disappeared into his study.

Pleased his dad had agreed to have a personal alarm, Neil had decided to let him be for a time, but it had been over an hour, and he was beginning to worry. He made a pot of tea and, carrying a cup brewed exactly how his dad liked it, he knocked gently on the study door.

'Tea, Dad?' he asked, pushing his way in.

Harry was staring at the computer with a puzzled expression. He turned at the sound of Neil's voice. 'I can't figure it out,' he said. 'Something's wrong. The figures…'

'Let me see.' Neil laid the cup down and peered over his dad's shoulder. What should have been a neatly organised database seemed to have become a mass of unrelated figures. His dad was right. Something was very wrong.

'I was just… I don't know what I did. The screen all blurred. I hit some keys, and…'

'Have your tea and I'll see if I can work out what's happened.'

'Thanks, son.' Harry seemed bewildered.

When Harry had moved from the desk, Neil took his place, and with a few clicks managed to restore the screen. 'That's it, Dad. Back to normal.' He swung round to see Harry slumped in his chair, his eyes dull.

'But *I'm* not, am I? It's not only my balance that's gone. I'm losing my mind, too.'

'No, Dad. It was a simple mistake.' But Neil knew it was more than that. It was a further sign of the deterioration they'd been told to expect. But this had come on so suddenly. He hugged his dad. 'It'll be fine, Dad. Bronte or I can do the books. There's no need to…'

'There's every need,' Harry shouted. 'It's my job. I've always done it.' Then his voice dropped. 'If I can't do that, then I might as well give up.' The old man began to weep, bringing tears to Neil's eyes, too.

*

The two men were still feeling emotional when Bronte arrived home, only to get changed and leave again. Remembering Ali was coming to dinner, Neil considered calling her to cancel, but decided not to. Her presence might help. But he couldn't face cooking. 'How about we have takeaway tonight, Dad?' he asked. 'What do you fancy?'

'Isn't Ali coming tonight?' Harry asked, seeming more like himself. It was as if the incident in the study had never happened, but it had, and Neil knew it could and would happen again.

'She is. What do you think? Chinese? Thai? Indian?'

'They do a good curry at the Indian on the opposite end of the esplanade,' Harry said.

'Right, Indian it is.'

'There's a menu in the kitchen drawer. I often order when I'm on my own.'

Neil rifled in the drawer to discover menus from a variety of takeaway joints. His dad must order them a lot. He had never thought about how Harry managed, all alone since Neil's mother died. He'd been too wrapped up in his own life. He'd take more interest now, he vowed. Wherever his new position might be, he'd keep in touch more regularly, visit more often and... the memory of *Wham Bam Books* reared its ugly head again. How long could Harry hold on to the bookshop?

Ali and the takeaway arrived at the same time and, in the general kerfuffle at the door, it was easy to pretend everything was normal, but Neil could detect a question in Ali's eyes. Maybe he wasn't managing to hide his worry as well as he thought.

Forty-one

It felt strange to Ali to dress once again in her smart navy pantsuit, tailored white shirt and court shoes.

'Looking good,' Sally said, when she walked into the kitchen. 'You'll slay them.'

Ali wasn't so sure. She was still exhausted from the flight delays which had added hours to her trip, and the late night catching up with Sally hadn't helped. 'I'll do my best,' she said.

But when just over an hour later, she entered the room where the interview was to be held, she wondered if her best would be enough. Seated around the table were a collection of heavyweights from the university. She recognised most of them, including Richard, her former boss and the present incumbent of the position. Then there was the token woman, a member of council. Ali knew her opinion wouldn't hold much sway. She took a deep breath and sat down in the seat indicated by the committee chair.

It was as she expected – a series of tough questions followed by the opportunity to state why she felt she was suitable for the role. Glad when it was over, she gave a sigh of relief when she walked out of the room, only to see Hugo Martin waiting. He smirked when he saw her and nodded an acknowledgement, before he was called in for his interview.

*

'How was it?' Sally was waiting for her in their favourite seafood restaurant, a bottle of white wine chilling on the table.

'Don't ask!'

'I am asking.'

'It was exactly as I expected. A group of middle-aged super-conservative men with one token woman who barely spoke. And bloody Hugo was being interviewed immediately after me. I think I did pretty well on my statement of intent though. I saw a few nods. But who knows what they're looking for. A clone of Richard? I'll never be that. Maybe they're not ready for a woman Head of School.'

'Don't put yourself down. You could beat them all, hands down. As for bloody Hugo...'

'Don't get me started on him. He thinks he's invincible.'

'Well, let's forget about them and have lunch. They have fresh oysters and grilled barramundi on the menu. Let's splash out. My treat.'

'Thanks, Sal. Sounds good.'

They were halfway through their meal and making a dent in the wine when Sally asked, 'This position with the women's centre. You're not interested in it?'

'Not really. I only went for the interview to please them. And, as Neil said, it was good practice for today. Can you imagine me running a women's centre and rape crisis centre plus a women's refuge?'

'Quite easily. I think you'd be brilliant at it. And you'd be making a difference to the women there. It's more than you could do held back by the restrictions the university would place on you.'

'Have you been talking to Grace Winter?'

'Who's she?'

'Someone I know in Bellbird Bay. She was the one who got me involved with the centre in the first place. She was a friend of Maxine's.' Ali was silent for a moment, remembering the woman who she admired so much. 'Now *she* made a difference. You wouldn't believe what she managed to accomplish. They were about to celebrate the anniversary when...' Ali felt her eyes moisten. She brushed away the incipient tears. 'Damn! I thought I was all cried out.'

'There's nothing wrong with tears. It shows you cared.'

'As I said, she was an amazing woman. I could never take her place.'

'But someone will have to... and wouldn't it be better if...'

'That's enough, Sal. Sounds as if you don't want me to come back to Perth. Tell me what you've been up to since you got back. I did most of the talking last night.' She peered at her friend who had gone red. 'You haven't, have you? You've met someone, someone special?' Ali remembered Sally's comments when she visited Bellbird Bay. But it had only been a couple of months ago. Surely she hadn't had time to…?

'You'd like him, Ali.'

Ali stared at her friend in disbelief. 'When? How?'

'You'll never believe how it happened. It was at my niece's wedding – one of these ginormous Italian family events, the type I try to avoid. But in my family… Anyway, I went to the wedding under sufferance. I love Annabelle to bits. Don't know why she agreed to the whole white wedding catastrophe, why she and her fellow couldn't do it quietly and save the money. And…' she paused for effect, '…the groom's father turned out to be this hot guy.'

'Never!'

'Truly! The funny thing is, Mum has been trying to set me up with him for ages – Italian, widower, successful businessman – and I always managed to avoid him. To think of all the time I wasted…' She gazed into space.

Sally had got it bad.

'So, you think this is it? You're going to give up all your strongly held views for this man you met… when?'

'Three weeks ago. Three wonderful weeks. Mum's planning the wedding already.' She laughed. 'Only joking, but it's not out of the question.'

'Well!' Ali took a gulp of wine, unable to believe what she was hearing.

'What about you? What's happening with your love life?'

'Nothing's changed. I plan to come back here, and Neil is applying for positions all over Australia. He's probably at an interview somewhere right now.'

'Don't leave it too long, Ali. We're not getting any younger.'

Ali gave her friend a searching look. Was this Sally talking, sounding like Libby or Adam? 'Can it, Sal. I have no intention of following you up the aisle, if that's where you're headed. But I'll be there to pick up the pieces when it falls apart.'

'I take back what I said about you and the women's centre,' Sally said. 'You always were anti marriage. I know, I know,' she said, raising her hands defensively. 'I was, too. But all this involvement with women who've been abused… it's affected you, reinforced what you saw in your mother, made you forget there *are* some happy marriages out there, made you lose hope.'

Hope? Was it hope Ali saw in Libby and Adam's eyes, what she felt when she was in Neil's arms? A wave of longing swept over her, making her shiver although it was a warm day. 'Enough!' she said, taking another gulp of wine.

But next day, on the flight back to Queensland, Ali thought about Sally's words, and the way her friend glowed with happiness when she talked about the new man in her life. Would it be so bad to give way, to allow herself to feel that way? Immediately the image of Neil appeared in her mind, Neil as she'd last seen him, his eyes crinkling with laughter, his hair falling over one eye. She remembered how good it felt to have his arms around her and began to wonder if Sally was right.

Forty-two

Neil wasn't attending interviews while Ali was in Perth. The court case had been brought forward and he'd been called as a witness. Around the same time as she was sitting in the interview for Head of School, he was driving to Brisbane preparing to be grilled on his involvement in, or knowledge of, the misuse of funds by the former chairman of the board of *Beckwith Boys' College*.

The morning proceeded much as Neil had expected. It was his first experience in a court of law, and he very much hoped it would be his last. When the judge thanked him and he was free to leave the witness stand, he gave a sigh of relief and moved to sit in the back of the courtroom to hear the rest of the trial.

There was a cheer from the gallery when the former board chair was found guilty and remanded to be sentenced at a later time. Neil glanced up to see the gallery filled with parents he recognised, plus several of the staff.

Outside the court, Neil caught up with his old friend. 'Glad that's over,' he said. 'Feel like a beer?'

'Good idea.' Barry clapped him on the shoulder. 'You did well in there, Neil. Must have been difficult. I know you and Jake were close.'

Neil looked at his friend in surprise. 'Not very. It was part of my role to work with him as chairman of the board. You must know that, now you're acting principal.'

'Yeah, but... It didn't look good, did it?'

Neil gazed at his friend in amazement, the first inkling it might be difficult for him to return to his old position making itself felt. 'Come on, Barry, you don't believe I knew anything, do you?'

'No... not really. Anyway, you're free and he's banged up, so let's get that beer.'

They made their way to the nearest pub and no more was said about the corruption or the former chairman of the board. But for Neil, it was there in the background, like a cloud which wouldn't go away, and he knew something had shifted in his relationship with his old friend.

It was no surprise to Neil when, later that day, he received a call from the current board chairman inviting him for a meeting at the college the following morning.

*

'You okay, Dad?' Bronte asked next morning at breakfast.

Neil hadn't said much about what happened in court, merely that he was glad it was over and that he had a meeting at the college.

'They're going to reinstate you, aren't they?' she asked. 'That's what the meeting's about?'

'I guess I'm going to find out, honey.' Neil wasn't convinced there would be a favourable outcome. Barry's manner the previous day had worried him. He hadn't acted like a man who was about to lose the position he'd been acting in for the past months, more like someone who didn't want to pass on the bad news.

'Of course they are, son.' Harry seemed a lot brighter today, the pendant which was the personal alarm hanging round his neck. It was the condition Neil had insisted on before he'd agree to Harry being in the bookshop on his own.

'Maybe, Dad. We'll see.'

Both Bronte and his dad had already left when Neil got into the car to take the two-hour drive to his old workplace. It was strange to drive through the college gates after such a long time, to park beside his old parking spot – the one which now held Barry's car – and to walk in through the door he'd entered every morning for the past ten years until...

The meeting was to be held in his old office, Barry, now a teaching principal, being busy teaching a Year Ten class. When Neil knocked on the familiar door, he had a premonition he wasn't going to like what he was about to hear.

'Come in.' The voice of the new chairman, a man Neil had never got on well with, summoned him. Taking a deep breath and straightening his shoulders, he entered, the familiar scent of the room a reminder of what he'd lost.

'Take a seat,' Len Hawkins said after shaking hands. He seated himself behind Neil's old desk.

After the usual pleasantries, during which Neil found it difficult to concentrate, wishing he'd get to the point, Len said, 'You have to realise we are in a difficult position. We need to take account of the wishes of the parent body. It's important for the future, for the very survival of the college that we attract more students and…' he hesitated, putting a finger to his pursed lips, '…there is a sentiment among the parents that it would harm our future prospects to have a principal who, however innocent, is tainted by association with the former board chairman.'

Neil flinched. Although he'd been expecting something like this, he resented being classed alongside someone who was a convicted criminal. He wanted to protest his innocence, claim he was duped like everyone else, but knew it would make no difference. They'd decided he was surplus to requirements. Barry would be the new principal and Neil would be cast aside like a bag of dirty laundry.

'Thanks.' Neil rose and walked out, ignoring the outstretched hand. A bell rang as he strode along the corridor, which was soon teeming with students, some of whom paused to say, 'Hello, sir,' as they passed, before running on to their next destination, immediately forgetting him. To them, he was already yesterday's man.

Outside, it was a lovely day, the sun sparkling on the Brisbane River as Neil drove across the Go Between Bridge. Named after the popular Australian indie rock band *The Go-Betweens*, the bridge, opened in 2010, spanned the river from North to South. After his experience at the college, Neil wasn't ready to go home. Instead, he decided to park at South Bank Parklands, a favourite spot when Bronte was a child and he and Pippa would bring her to the manmade beach on fine weekends, then to a favourite café for lunch. That café was long gone, but there were still lots of eateries.

Neil parked in the underground car park and made his way up into the sunshine, his mood lightening somewhat when he reached the walkway through the bougainvillea- covered arbour. Finding a licenced café, he ordered a beer along with a pie and chips and sat down to consider his future.

Forty-three

Ali wondered how Neil was getting on. Although she'd told Sally he would probably be in an interview, she knew better. But she'd heard nothing since the brief text to say the court case had been brought forward, he was called as a witness, and to wish her luck in her interview. That had been two days ago.

She was surprised there had been no word, not even an enquiry about her interview. Now she was back in Bellbird Bay, she'd peeked into the bookshop to see Harry there alone. There was no sign of either Neil or Bronte. She stifled the urge to pop in, to ask Harry about Neil and walked quickly past to buy croissants in the bakery before heading up the boardwalk to see Adam and Libby.

'How did it go?' Adam asked, when they were seated on the deck with croissants and coffee. 'And how did it feel to be back in Perth?'

Ali looked at him with a smile. They may have been apart for years, but her brother still understood her better than anyone.

'It was strange to be back,' she said. 'Everything was the same, but... maybe it was me who was different. Anyway, I think the interview went well. I should find out soon. They said they'd be making a decision "in the near future" whatever that means.'

'I'm sure you'll get the position if it's meant to be,' Libby said.

Ali gave her a searching look. What did she mean? Did she know something Ali didn't?

Adam clearly thought the same. 'What do you mean, Libby? You sound like Ruby Sullivan.'

'Sorry, I didn't intend to sound weird,' Libby said. 'I just have a feeling Ali will do what's right for her.'

'Of course I will,' Ali said, still puzzled by Libby's words.

The comment was forgotten when Ali's phone buzzed. Despite feeling rude, she slipped it out of her pocket and glanced at the screen, a wide grin splitting her face when she saw Neil's number.

'Take it,' Adam said, seeing her expression. 'Neil?'

Ali nodded, surprised how delighted she was to hear from him and trying to subdue the frisson of excitement. She pressed to accept the call as she walked out the gate on to the boardwalk.

'Can you talk?'

'I can now. I'm at Adam's, but I came out onto the boardwalk.' Ali leant against the barrier, her back to the ocean, the roar of the waves in her ears almost drowning out Neil's voice. 'How was the court?'

'The court proceedings went okay. As expected, Jake was found guilty and remanded for sentencing. It was what came afterwards,' Neil said bitterly. 'I was called in to a meeting at the college with the new board chairman. I'm out.' He gave a sigh. 'So, it's back to the drawing board. At least I have a few irons in the fire, but they're all interstate.'

'Oh, Neil. I'm sorry. What will you do? Your dad?'

'I'm not sure. But what about you? How was your interview? And how was Perth?'

Ali detected a grim note in his voice leading her to believe he didn't want to hear good news, so she tried to downplay her response, but wasn't able to hide her impression it had gone well. 'But Hugo was being interviewed too, and they may prefer a man in the position,' she finished, knowing it was highly likely she might be considered to be a loose cannon who would rock the boat.

'Dinner tonight?'

'I'd like that.' After a few more minutes, and with a smile on her face, Ali ended the call and walked back to the deck.

'Your coffee will be cold. I'll make you another cup,' Adam said, busying himself with the coffee machine.

'Neil?' Libby asked.

Ali nodded.

'He's a good man. You won't find better,' Libby said.

'I'm not looking for a man.' It annoyed Ali how everyone – even Sally these days – seemed to think a man was the answer to everything. 'Anyway, his future is as much up in the air as mine… probably more so. He won't be going back to his old school.'

But Libby didn't seem to hear. 'You're not being fair to him,' she continued. 'If you don't intend your relationship to have a future, you should tell him. Men have feelings too, you know.' She gazed lovingly at Adam who, seemingly ignoring the conversation was still busy making coffee.

'He knows. He's not interested in anything with a future either,' Ali said hotly. But even as she spoke, she wondered if it was true. Neil and she had never discussed the future, so she'd assumed he was of the same opinion as she was. But sometimes, she'd caught an expression in his eyes that might suggest otherwise. What if she was wrong? What if their relationship did mean more to him? She ignored the little voice telling her it meant a lot to her too. Maybe tonight was the time to talk about it, to agree that everything between them would be over when she returned to Perth, and he found another position.

*

But the opportunity to have that conversation didn't arise.

Neil picked Ali up and they went to have dinner at *The Firenze*, an Italian restaurant on the esplanade, one Ali hadn't been to before. There, over the cannelloni and gnocchi, washed down with chianti, Neil poured out his worries.

'I don't know how Dad's going to cope,' he said, taking a long drink of wine, then refilling his glass. 'It looks like I won't be living nearby, and Bronte's making noises about moving into the share house with Owen and his friends. It's only natural she'd want to be with other young people. And *Wham Bam Books* keep upping their offer, but they won't wait for ever for a response.

Ali put her hand on Neil's. 'I'm sure you'll end up doing what's best for everyone,' she said, feeling a bit like Libby with her platitudes. 'It wouldn't be the end of the world to sell the bookshop, would it?'

'Probably not.' Neil drew his hand away and pushed it through his hair. 'But it would be the end of Dad's world… and the end of an era for Bellbird Bay. But the old man won't be able to cope for much longer, and we need to have something sorted before I leave again. I'm not sure how long he'll be able to manage at home, either, but I haven't raised that with him yet.'

'Where would he go?'

'I've been making enquiries. There's a villa available at *Bay Village Lifestyle Resort*. He could be independent there, be part of a community, and there is the option of more levels of care when it becomes necessary. But…' he sighed, '…I can't see him agreeing to it.'

'I'm sorry.' Ali was glad it hadn't come to that with her mother. She'd been able to die in her own home, in her own bed.

'Sorry to dump all this on you,' Neil said, clasping Ali's hand. 'Let's order dessert and talk about something more cheerful.'

They ordered a dish of three flavours of crème brûlée to share and began discussing forthcoming Easter celebrations for which Bellbird Bay was famous.

It wasn't till they were lying in bed, bodies entwined after making love, that Ali remembered what she'd intended to discuss.

Forty-four

Neil had a few days free before his next round of interviews. He met with the representative from *Wham Bam Books* to discuss their latest offer, promising to give them an answer soon.

He also approached the idea of a move to *Bay Village Lifestyle Resort* with his dad. Harry's response was much as he'd expected.

'This is my home, Neil. It's where your mother and I moved when you were born. She died here, and I intend to breathe my last here, too. You're not going to get me into one of those homes for old folks.'

'It's not...' Neil started to say, but he could see Harry's mind was closed. *Bay Village Lifestyle Resort* was an over 50's village, populated by people of Harry's age and younger. His dad could be happy there among like-minded people, and Neil could pursue his career secure in the knowledge Harry would be able to get further care as and when he required it. 'Okay, Dad, have it your own way,' he ended up saying. But he knew they'd have to have this conversation again and again until Harry finally agreed.

He was optimistic about his next few interviews. Unlike those he'd already attended, three principal's positions had come up in prestigious schools interstate and all sounded interesting and interested in what he had to offer. It would mean selling his apartment in Brisbane, but he'd discovered he wasn't as attached to it as he'd imagined, and now Bronte was based in Bellbird Bay there was no possibility of her wanting to spend time there.

He just needed to persuade Harry to agree to sell the bookshop and move house, neither of which was going to be easy. Ali had behaved strangely the last time he'd seen her too, but he put it down to her being concerned about the result of her interview – or interviews.

Deciding to go to the surf club for lunch, it was a relief to walk into the now familiar building and see Will Rankin and Martin Cooper standing at the bar. Their company would be a welcome relief and would distract him from his own concerns.

'Hey, Neil,' Will greeted him, as he ordered a beer, Nate's presence as the barman reminding Neil of Bronte's ultimatum at breakfast.

'I'm moving out, Dad,' she said. 'I don't care what you say. The guys have a free room, and if I don't take it, they'll get someone else.'

'Hey.' Neil picked up his beer and took a long draught. Gosh, it tasted good. He wiped his mouth with the back of his hand.

'That bad, mate?' Will asked with a chuckle. 'Join the club.'

'Don't listen to him,' Martin said. 'He's only been moaning about the fact that Owen's likely to take out the championship for the fourth time making him a greater hero than his dad.'

'Not at all,' Will argued. 'I'm proud of the boy. He's trained hard for this. He deserves it.'

Neil laughed, their friendly bickering putting his own problems into perspective. Everyone thought they had the monopoly on trouble, but it was all relative.

He ended up joining the two men for lunch and thoroughly enjoyed their company and learning more about what had been happening in Bellbird Bay in the years he'd been gone. By the time he returned home, and when Harry and Bronte came home for dinner, he found his mood had changed. He still didn't have a solution to what was worrying him, but he'd decided it was pointless to flog a dead horse, to use one of his dad's favourite sayings.

This time, when Bronte raised the subject of moving out, instead of raising objections, he asked her more about the share house, to discover she had thought it through carefully.

'I can still pop in on Grandad,' she said. 'It's only a couple of blocks away, and Owen and Nate can help if there's anything Grandad or I can't manage.'

Harry threw her a grateful look when she said this, and though Neil knew it wasn't the ideal solution, he said nothing. Time enough to discuss it again later. It was pleasant, sitting around the table with his dad and his daughter. He'd missed Bronte when she was living with her mother, only seeing her briefly on the rare occasions she deigned to drop in. It had been wonderful to get to know her better this summer – and to spend time with his dad again. Neil wondered what would have happened to Harry if he hadn't been there when he collapsed, or again when he had his second fall. He guessed that was one plus of the whole mess at the college – he'd been there for his dad.

'I had lunch with Will Rankin and Martin Cooper,' he said, in a break in the conversation.

'Good lads,' Harry said. 'They've had the sense to know where their roots are, though it took Martin a good few years to come to that realisation.' He peered at Neil.

'You know I can't find work here, Dad,' Neil said. 'I've never taught in state schools and there isn't a private college in Bellbird Bay.' He sensed the thinly veiled criticism in his dad's words.

'I know, I know. And I'm proud of you, son. Your mum was, too.'

Neil didn't know why, but his dad's praise made him feel as if he needed to defend himself. He was saved by Bronte saying, 'I'll go and tell the guys I'm moving in. I want to get some of my stuff from Mum's. Owen said he'd help on the weekend. We can take his ute down to Brisbane.'

'Right.' Neil's gut clenched at the thought of how Pippa was going to react. She'd been incensed enough when Bronte started working with Owen, started seeing him outside work. Now she intended to move in with him, albeit with two others and in a room of her own – Neil wondered how long that would last – Pippa would hit the roof. He was glad he wouldn't be there to see it, but she'd no doubt blame him all the same.

Forty-five

The two offers arrived on the same day. Ali stared first at the letter with the embossed university crest offering her the position of Head of the School of Business and Women's Studies, at a salary that made her gasp aloud. Then she looked at the single page offering her the Director's position at Bellbird Bay Women's Centre. She wanted to laugh as she compared the two.

The university position was what she'd always wanted, an opportunity to make her mark, to give women's studies the profile it deserved, to… yes, to show all those male lecturers she had more to offer than a pretty face. In addition, it would provide security, a substantial pension when she came to retire, the chance to buy the penthouse apartment on the river she coveted.

Then she considered what the other position could offer. It would provide her with the opportunity to actually make a difference, to become part of a community in which she was already feeling at home, to be able to give something positive to those women she had only written and lectured about till now, to spend more time with her family.

There was really no choice.

Regretfully, Ali penned her rejection of the university position, knowing it would automatically go to her nemesis, Hugo Martin. She sighed thinking of her poor students, but knew she was making the right decision. At least she would no longer be subjected to the thinly veiled taunts and jokes she'd had to suffer for the last ten years.

With a smile, she took up her pen to reply to the board of the women's centre, to state how delighted she was to accept their generous offer. It was modest compared to the salary of a university Head of School, but she'd be rich in so many other ways... and it would be so much more rewarding to be carrying on the process which Maxine had set in motion, a fitting memorial to that amazing woman. Ali was glad to have known her, even for a short time.

Once she'd done it, she sat back with a smile on her face and a sense of profound relief. Her only regret was she'd be so far from Sally... and Neil, a small voice in the back of her mind reminded her. She had no idea where Neil would end up. He'd been sending off applications all over Australia since *Beckwith Boys' College* chose not to re-employ him as principal.

That was one thing Sally had been wrong about. When they said goodbye at the airport, her friend had grinned and said, 'I have a good feeling about your Neil. He's one of the good guys. You should get over your misgivings about marriage and hang on to him.'

Ali had snorted and vowed to forget Sally's words, much the same way she'd ignored Libby and forgotten those spoken by Ruby Sullivan. But now, Ruby's words came back to her – something about a crossroads and the direction not being what she might expect. A shiver ran up her spine as she realised how accurate the old woman had been.

She still hadn't what she thought of as *that conversation* with Neil. There hadn't seemed much point when she didn't know if she was going back to Perth, and he was likely to be living in another state. Now she knew she was staying in Bellbird Bay, there was even less reason. She knew Neil planned to sell the bookshop and persuade his dad into some sort of retirement village.

Now she'd made her decision, she needed to tell people, and the first to hear must be Adam and Libby. She stuck stamps on the two letters, shrugged her bag over her shoulder and set off along the esplanade and up the boardwalk, only stopping to drop the letters into a mailbox.

'You're looking very pleased with yourself. Good news from the university?' Adam greeted her with a smile and a hug.

'Yes. I do have something to tell you. Libby around?' She didn't want to have to share her news twice.

'She's somewhere. Libby!' he called, 'Ali's here. She has news.'

'Coming!' Libby's voice sounded from the other end of the house, followed by the woman herself.

'Coffee?' Adam asked. 'Or is bubbly called for?'

'Isn't it a bit early for bubbly?' Ali asked.

'Never too early, but let's have coffee for now,' Libby said, 'and there's still some of the hot cross buns we got at the bakery.'

'Hot cross buns already?' Ali asked.

'It'll soon be Easter,' Libby replied, opening the fridge and taking out the half empty packet.

'Now,' Adam said, when they were seated on the deck, Milo, excited by the scent of warm hot cross buns, padding around them before settling at Libby's feet with a sigh. 'Tell all.'

'Well,' Ali said, determined to make the most of both pieces of news, 'I received two pieces of mail today.' She looked across at Adam and Libby who were waiting with bated breath, then changed her mind about drawing out what she had to say. 'I received offers from both the university and the women's centre.' She saw their expressions change from delight to bewilderment.

Libby was the first to speak. 'From both?'

'So, you'll be going back to Perth,' Adam said. 'I'm pleased for you. I know it's what you wanted, and you deserve it. But it's a pity. We were just getting used to having you around, to getting to know you again.' His face mirrored his disappointment.

But Libby's eyes held a different expression. 'What have you decided?' she asked.

Ali took a deep breath then, with a smile said, 'I've accepted the position as director at the women's centre.'

There was a moment's silence, then Adam said, 'Blow coffee. This calls for bubbly.' He headed into the house.

'I'm so glad,' Libby said quietly. 'I knew you'd do the right thing, the right thing for you, the right thing for Bellbird Bay... and the right thing for us. It'll be lovely to have you living here permanently.'

'Thanks.'

Adam reappeared flourishing a bottle of Yellowglen and three glasses, and with lots of laughs, they toasted Ali's new job while Milo wandered around wondering at the strange behaviour of his humans.

After they had discussed how Ali would need to return to Perth to pack up, decide whether to sell the house there, and where she would live in Bellbird Bay, Libby said, 'Dot will be pleased, too.'

'Dot?' Ali remembered the small officious woman who'd invited her to apply, and who'd been on the interview panel, the woman who was Grace's sister. 'You know Dot, too?'

Libby chuckled. 'We're in a book club together. Actually, I think Dot believes it's *her* book club. But she's a kindly soul and her heart's in the right place.'

'Mmm.' Ali remembered Grace saying the same thing. Perhaps she'd misjudged the woman and should give her another chance. Then it occurred to her. There would be lots of opportunities to do that once she took up her new position.

'When will you start?' Adam asked.

'I don't know. Soon, I expect, though I'd like to go back to sort things out in Perth first.' She frowned. 'Maxine will be a hard act to follow. I can never be another Maxine Henderson.'

'No,' Libby said, 'You'll be Ali Wells, and make your own mark.'

'Mmm,' Ali said again. She knew one of the first things she'd do was to ensure there was some sort of memorial to Maxine in the centre, something which let everyone who went there know what a wonderful woman and example she'd been. Then, as Libby said, she'd set about making her own mark. She already had some ideas. It was amazing, once she'd made the decision to accept the position, how right it felt.

'You'll stay to dinner?' Libby asked. 'Or maybe we should go out to celebrate?'

'No. Thanks, but there's something else I need to do.' It was only four o'clock and, with a bit of luck, she'd catch Neil at home. They had made a tentative arrangement to meet later that evening, but she couldn't wait to share her news with him. She hoped he'd be pleased for her, though she did feel slightly guilty at having had two offers of employment when he was yet to receive one.

*

Ali was still brimming with excitement when she rang the doorbell at Harry's house.

'Ali, what are you doing here? Didn't we arrange to meet later?' Neil stared at her in surprise.

'I couldn't wait. I had to tell you. Guess what I received in the mail today?'

'You got the position? Congratulations. I'm pleased for you.'

Ali could tell he meant it, even though her success must emphasise his lack of it.

'I got two positions!'

'Two? You mean...? Oh, you applied for the one at the women's centre, too.'

'And I accepted it!'

'You accepted...?' Neil looked puzzled.

Ali realised, in her excitement, she'd confused him. 'I accepted the one at the women's centre. I'm staying in Bellbird Bay.'

'But the university position, the Head of School. It was what you wanted.'

'It was what I thought I wanted,' she corrected him. 'I didn't know what I really wanted until I held both offers. Then it became clear. I can do so much more at the centre than I ever could in a university.'

'Well, I guess we should celebrate.' Neil pulled her into a warm hug and kissed her soundly on the lips.

While enjoying his arms around her, Ali felt uncomfortable, knowing Neil's dad and daughter could walk in anytime. 'Not here,' she said, pulling away and giving him a peck on the cheek. 'Later.' She intended to enjoy his company for as long as she could, to store up the memories before he headed off to the position he'd inevitably find interstate.

Forty-six

Neil was sitting in a hard chair, waiting to be called in for one more interview. He'd done this so many times by now, every school was beginning to look the same. They even smelt the same – the smell of boys' sweat and floor wax. A bell rang and there was the sound of doors opening and feet running somewhere above him. Today it was Tasmania, yesterday Melbourne, last week… He'd lost count of the towns and schools he'd travelled to in a vain attempt to find work. Why was he doing it? Why was he putting himself through what was turning out to be a pointless exercise? His story was going before him. No one wanted to employ a has-been, tainted by the corruption of his school board. And it looked as if Barry was going to be confirmed as principal at his old school. Good luck to him. He'd do well.

What was he doing here? All of a sudden it struck him, like a bolt from the blue. All the people he loved were in Bellbird Bay – his dad, Bronte and Ali. Now Ali had accepted the position at the women's centre, she was on track to become a valued member of the Bellbird Bay community.

Neil thought back to the night over a week ago now, when, on her return from Perth where she'd gone to sort out her affairs, they'd gone to the surf club to celebrate her new appointment. Somehow the word had got around, and their meal had been interrupted by her being congratulated by first, Grace and Ted, then Ailsa and Martin, then a small woman Neil had never met, but whom Ali called Dot. Later, when they were alone, she'd said she'd felt like a celebrity and it made her feel uncomfortable, and she hoped she could be one tenth of the sort of person her predecessor had been. She had emphasised her intention to make the centre her prime focus, to be as devoted to it as Maxine had been, to make a difference to women for whom life had become insufferable. Although she didn't say it in as many words, it was clear to Neil, there would be no room in her life for any permanent relationship. At the time, he'd thought it just as well he was going to be relocating.

Neil had hugged her and wished things could be different.

Why was he traipsing around Australia in search of work, work he didn't even want? Meanwhile *Wham Bam Books* was edging closer to taking over *Bay Books*, the shop his dad had owned all Neil's life, the shop where he'd spent some of his happiest times, which held his happiest childhood memories.

Instead, he could stay in Bellbird Bay, take over the bookshop, be there for his dad, allow Harry to remain in his own home, spend his final years in the shop he loved with Neil beside him, be there for Bronte. He might even be able to persuade Ali marriage to him wasn't such a bad idea.

He rose.

A door opened.

'Mr Simpson, they're ready for you now,' the obsequious young man he'd met when he arrived was staring at him.

'I'm sorry. I have to go.' Grabbing his briefcase, Neil almost ran out. If he hurried, he could perhaps make an earlier flight. He could be home for dinner – home in Bellbird Bay. He'd be in time to stop the sale of *Bay Books* from going through.

*

It was late when Neil drove his car into the garage to park next to his dad's old Holden Commodore. The car was almost as old as Bronte and had served Harry well. The lights were still on in the house, so someone was awake. Aware of the lateness of the hour, Neil slid his key gently into the lock and pushed the door open.

'Dad!' Bronte's voice greeted him. 'We didn't expect you back till tomorrow. Did something happen?'

'Son,' Harry called from where he was seated in his favourite armchair, in the pool of light from the old standard lamp which had been there as long as Neil could remember. He looked so small and frail sitting there. Neil knew he'd made the right decision. This was home.

Suddenly exhausted from his momentous decision and the long trip, Neil collapsed into a chair. 'Give me a minute,' he said.

'Can I get you something, Dad? Tea, coffee, something stronger?' Bronte asked.

'Coffee would be good.' He wanted to tell them his decision but needed something to pick him up first.

'So,' Bronte said, handing him a mug of coffee. 'Did you get the job?'

'No.' Neil took a sip of coffee, feeling his energy returning as the caffeine entered his system. 'I walked out on the interview. Well actually, I never went in.' Seeing the looks of surprise on both faces, he continued, 'I decided I was mad applying for all those positions, putting myself through hell to help another generation of boys into a future they may not even want.' Neil remembered his thoughts when he talked with Pippa. It felt good to be done with all that.

'But you're a teacher, Neil. It's what you do, why you spent all those years at university. Your mother was so proud of your achievements,' Harry said.

'I know, Dad.' For a moment, Neil experienced a twinge of regret. He knew his mum would never understand his decision. But he sensed his dad would.

'What will you do, Dad?' Bronte asked.

'I'm going to stay here. With your agreement, Dad,' he glanced at Harry who was leaning forward in his chair, 'I'll take over the management of the bookshop. You'll still be able to be there – for as long as you want. And it means you can continue to live here, too. No more talk of *Bay Village Lifestyle Resort.*' He saw his dad grin in the first time for a while and felt guilty for what he'd put the old man through.

'What about the *Wham Bam Books* people?' Harry asked. 'They came in again while you were gone, seemed to think it was a done deal.'

'Nothing's been signed yet, Dad. I guess they'll be disappointed.'

'This calls for a celebration,' Bronte said. 'Do we have any bubbly?'

'It's too late, and it's been a long day. I just want to crash,' Neil said.

But there was one thing he wanted to do first. Once he was in his bedroom, he'd call Ali.

Forty-seven

Ali couldn't believe her ears when Neil called to tell her his news. The last thing she'd expected was that he'd decide to stay in Bellbird Bay and take on the bookshop, that he'd leave teaching. But she could hear the excitement in his voice as he outlined his plans and knew his decision hadn't been made lightly.

Three weeks had passed since then. She'd gone back to Perth for a week over Easter to finalise things there before starting in her new position. After packing and putting the house on the market, Ali said goodbye to the friends she'd made over the years, promising to come back to visit. Then there had been the tearful farewell to Sally.

'You'll come back for my wedding?' Sally asked.

'Has he…?' Ali thought of the tall, grey-haired, Italian man who had charmed her friend, making her change her opinion of marriage.

'Not yet, but he will,' her friend gurgled with delight. 'Who'd have thought it at this time last year? Mum's thrilled.'

Since coming back to Bellbird Bay, Ali had been seeing Neil regularly. Now they were both to be located here permanently, it was more difficult to convince herself there was nothing serious about their relationship. She could no longer pretend it was a holiday affair, and if not that, what was it? So far, she'd chosen not to examine things too closely but to "go with the flow" as her brother would say. But she sensed Neil hoped for more from their relationship, though they had still never discussed it.

Last night had been a turning point for Ali. After Neil left, and she'd gone to bed, she'd tossed and turned for ages. She thought about Sally with her newfound love, Adam and Libby moving into marriage with the confidence things would turn out well, and she began to wonder at her own bullish determination that marriage wasn't for her.

Visions from the past rose up behind her eyes. She could hear her dad's voice yelling obscenities, her mother screaming, the thud of her mother's body against the door. Tears streamed down her cheeks at the memory of what her mother had suffered at the hands of the man who vowed to love her. She'd always believed that was what love did to you – promised the world then turned into abuse and violence.

Then, as if in a dream. she heard Adam's voice. 'Love… marriage… commitment… doesn't have to be like our parents' life, Ali. Look at Libby and me, Grace and Ted, Bev and Iain.'

It was only when she was falling into a doze as dawn was breaking, that it struck her. She sat up in bed staring into the darkness with the realisation she might have been wrong. All this time, when she'd vowed to avoid anything that smacked of a permanent relationship, to avoid letting her heart rule her head, she'd fallen in love with Neil.

She hugged the knowledge to herself, knowing it would have pleased her mother who had never tried to turn her against marriage. In fact, she remembered her mother telling her before she died that she hoped Ali would find the happy ever after she'd known only briefly. At the time, Ali had put it down to the ravings of a sick woman, but now she wondered if her mother had indeed been hoping Ali would find the sort of love which had eluded her.

Today, she and Neil were going on a picnic. After the events of the past few weeks, it would be good to spend some time relaxing. It had been a few weeks since the surf lifesaving fundraiser, but, last night, Neil had reminded her of the item he'd won at the silent auction. It was time, he said, to claim his picnic hamper from *The Greedy Gecko*. He was being very secretive, saying he would be picking her up and taking her to a surprise location.

*

It was a glorious April day. Ali dressed casually in a pair of jeans and a tee-shirt she'd bought in the market in Perth over Easter. She stuffed a shirt in her bag in case it became cooler and wondered where they were going. Then she sat out on her balcony to wait for Neil to arrive.

It was amazing, she thought, how everything had fallen into place. Once the Perth house was listed for sale, there was a rush of buyers and it sold within days. She'd been able to extend the lease on her apartment here, saving her the bother of finding somewhere else to live. Her furniture was in storage for the time being.

Her new work at the centre was proving to be all she had imagined. She'd been warmly welcomed by the women, most of whom she'd already met, and quickly fallen into a routine, determined to do her best. It was as if she could feel Maxine looking down on her, encouraging her.

She was still thinking of Maxine when Neil drove up. Grabbing her bag, Ali hurried down to meet him, surprised when he got out of the car and gave her a hug, then said, 'I want this to be a surprise,' and fitted a soft sleep mask over her eyes, before helping her carefully into the car.

'Dad's looking after the bookshop. He's having a good day,' he said, in response to her unasked question.

Ali knew that, some days, Harry needed Neil to be there. She was glad this wasn't one of those days. Their day out had been predicated on Harry's ability to cope on his own. She gave a sigh of relief, her anticipation building as she wondered anew what Neil had in mind, and where he was taking her.

Without saying anything more, Neil started the car. He turned on the radio making conversation difficult. Ali sensed they were driving out of town, as she tried to work out their possible destination. Just as she was about to ask, they drew to a halt.

'Wait there,' Neil said.

Ali felt a bubble of excitement building up inside. It was like playing a children's game. She wanted to giggle.

Then, Neil gently drew her out of the car. As she stood up, the scent of the sea filled her nostrils. They were close to a beach. She felt his hands carefully remove the mask, saw his smiling face, then he took her by the shoulders and turned her around to face the most glorious stretch of white beach she'd ever seen.

'Dolphin Beach,' Neil said proudly, as if it belonged to him, as well it might. There was no one else in sight.

'Wow! I didn't know about this. It's amazing.'

'Isn't it? It was one of my favourite spots as a teenager. I haven't been back since, but it hasn't changed.'

Ali stood staring at the wide expanse of pristine sand in the bay protected by two hornlike promontories and the soft waves lapping on the beach, while Neil fetched a blanket and the picnic basket from the car. The only sound was the call of the seabirds and the rush of the waves as they met the shore.

When she turned around, it was to see Neil carrying the wicker picnic basket, out of which poked the neck of a wine bottle. 'Did the wine come with the basket?' she asked.

'I have to admit I did add it, but all the rest comes from *The Greedy Gecko*. The basket should come in handy later, too.'

They made their way down the slope to the beach. Once there, Neil placed the blanket and the basket in a shaded spot, then held out his hand.

Slipping off her sandals, Ali took his hand and allowed herself to be led down to the edge of the ocean. The water was cool on her bare feet as they wandered along in the shallows, hand-in-hand.

'Penny for them?' Neil said, when they had been walking in silence for several moments.

Ali stopped, dropped her head back and gazed up into the clear, blue sky. 'This place is magic,' she said. 'I wish I could stay here for ever. Thank you for bringing me here.' Everyone and everything else seemed to fade away. It was as if they were the only two people left in the world.

Neil pulled her to him, his lips meeting hers.

Ali melted into his embrace. This was where she wanted to be. She didn't want today to end.

Slowly they drew apart. Neil gazed into Ali's eyes, his arms still holding her tenderly. 'I love you, Ali Wells. Will you marry me?'

Ali froze. The colour drained from her face, the sound of the waves loud in her ears.

'What's wrong, Ali? I ask you to marry me and you look as if you've seen a ghost.'

Ali shook her head to dispel the images of the night before. Ghosts... that's all they were Neil was in the here and now. He loved her. She loved him. She really did. It was time she admitted it, to herself and to him. What was stopping her?

'Sorry, Neil. My mind was wandering. I do love you. I love you so much. It's taken me a long time to admit what I think others saw before I did. You're a good man, kind, gentle. I know you'd never hurt me. Yes, I'll marry you.' As she spoke, it was as if a huge weight was lifted from her shoulders, as if she'd escaped from the bonds of the past which were holding her back, preventing her from finding the happiness she deserved.

Ali had barely finished speaking when she felt herself being lifted up in the air and twirled around and around, before being set down again and kissed... and kissed.

When she was able to think again, Ali remembered Ruby's words, and knew the old woman had been right. It was time to follow her heart.

The End

If you've enjoyed Ali and Neil's story, a way you can say thank you to me is to leave a review on Amazon and/or Goodreads. A few words will suffice, no need for a lengthy review. It will mean a lot to me and help other readers find my books.

The next book in the series, *Second Chances in Bellbird Bay*, features Greta Roberts who has appeared as a supporting character in the earlier Bellbird Bay books and is the owner of the fashion boutique, *Birds of a* Feather. It's book seven in this series but, like all my other books, it can be read and enjoyed as a standalone novel.

Following her divorce, *Greta Roberts* has found solace running *Birds of a Feather*, an upmarket boutique in the seaside town of *Bellbird Bay*. But when a ghost from her past reappears, Greta's peaceful, single life is sent into a spin.

Leo Carlson has built an empire of hotels and resorts but has never forgotten the perfect summer he spent in *Bellbird Bay* in his teens. When the opportunity to purchase a hotel there arises, he finds it difficult to pass it up.

Meeting again, Greta and Leo are quick to discover they are different people from the young couple who kissed on the beach and vowed to love each other for ever. Beset with challenges which threaten to keep them apart, can Bellbird Bay work its magic and provide these two with a second chance at love?

A heartwarming tale of family, friends, and how a second chance at love can happen when you least expect it.

You can order it here https://mybook.to/seondchances

From the Author

Dear Reader,

First, I'd like to thank you for choosing to read *Escape to Bellbird Bay*. I hope you've enjoyed this trip to Bellbird Bay as much as I've enjoyed writing it.

I'm really enjoying writing about my fictional town in the part of Queensland where I live and populating it with characters who I hope you will come to love. It's the sixth book in this series, but like the others, can be read as a standalone.

If you'd like to stay up to date with my new releases and special offers you can sign up to my reader's group.

You can sign up here

https://mailchi.mp/f5cbde96a5e6/maggiechristensensreadersgroup

I'll never share your email address, and you can unsubscribe at any time. You can also contact me via Facebook, Twitter or by email. I love hearing from my readers and will always reply.

Thanks again.

Acknowledgements

As always, this book could not have been written without the help and advice of a number of people.

Firstly, my husband Jim for listening to my plotlines without complaint, for his patience and insights as I discuss my characters and storyline with him, for his patience and help with difficult passages and advice on my male dialogue, and for being there when I need him.

John Hudspith, editor extraordinaire for his ideas, suggestions, encouragement and attention to detail, and for helping me make this book better.

Jane Dixon-Smith for her patience and for working her magic on my beautiful cover and interior.

My thanks also to early readers of this book – Helen, Maggie and Louise for their helpful comments and advice, and to Pat for ensuring the Bellbird women's centre was a true representation of such places. Also, to Annie of *Annie's books at Peregian* and Graeme of *The Bookshop at Caloundra* for their ongoing support.

And to all of my readers. Your support and comments make it all worthwhile.

About the Author

After a career in education, Maggie Christensen began writing contemporary women's fiction portraying mature women facing life-changing situations, and historical fiction set in her native Scotland. Her travels inspire her writing, be it her trips to visit family in Scotland, in Oregon, USA or her home on Queensland's beautiful Sunshine Coast. Maggie writes of mature heroines coming to terms with changes in their lives and the heroes worthy of them. Maggie has been called *the queen of mature age fiction* and her writing has been described by one reviewer as *like a nice warm cup of tea. It is warm, nourishing, comforting and embracing.*

From the small town in Scotland where she grew up, Maggie was lured to Australia by the call to 'Come and teach in the sun'. Once there, she worked as a primary school teacher, university lecturer and in educational management. Now living with her husband of over thirty years on Queensland's Sunshine Coast, she loves walking on the deserted beach in the early mornings and having coffee by the river on weekends. Her days are spent surrounded by books, either reading or writing them – her idea of heaven!

Maggie can be found on Facebook, Twitter, Goodreads, Instagram, Bookbub or on her website.
https://www.facebook.com/maggiechristensenauthor
https://twitter.com/MaggieChriste33
https://www.goodreads.com/author/show/8120020.Maggie_Christensen
https://www.instagram.com/maggiechriste33/
https://www.bookbub.com/profile/maggie-christensen
https://maggiechristensenauthor.com/